The Colour of a Dog Running Away

Richard Gwyn was born in Wales. Poet, editor and translator, his website can be found at www.richardgwyn.com.

The Colour of a Dog Running Away

Richard Gwyn

Parthian
The Old Surgery
Napier Street
Cardigan
SA43 1ED

www.parthianbooks.co.uk

First published in 2005
Reprinted 2006
© Richard Gwyn 2005
All Rights Reserved

ISBN 1-902638-72-7

Editor: Gwen Davies

Cover design by Marc Jennings
Inner design by type@lloydrobson.com
Printed and bound by Gomer Press, Llandysul, Ceredigion

Published with the financial support of the Welsh
Books Council

British Library Cataloguing in Publication Data
A cataloguing record for this book is available from the
British Library

Rose

Contents

Prologue

The sun has just gone down over the western plain. I stood watching it from a rock beyond the tower, smelling the woodsmoke from my chimney, then returned inside and piled more olive logs onto the fire. The dog is curled in the shadows at my feet.

Last winter I invested in a laptop computer and this fine oak table. An extravagance, but well worth it.

These little things, they make such a difference.

The seasons have passed by, unhurriedly. Spring was torrential, summer hot and dry. My almond tree produced its first full harvest of fruit. It is now October, and the autumn rains have just begun.

And the wind.

This wind, the mountain wind, infiltrates every corner like a spinning incubus, growing inside each perception, every mundane act, taking them over utterly. Eventually you become aware only of the immediate and hallucinatory impact of whatever stands before you: the silent apparition of the dog waiting expectantly in the doorway; a dead sheep lying beside a roadside elm. The wind sucks out everything from you, leaving you exhausted and chastened. People have been known to commit murder on account of the mountain wind, or else go slowly insane over several seasons.

The tower is built on the crest of a hill, a sheer and isolated outcrop in a landscape of wooded hills. Nothing distracted its architect from the principle of the straight line. In the distance, if the light allows, you can see the jagged peaks of high mountains, granite-grey in summer, snow-capped from November through till June. There are three storeys, connected by a spiral stone stairway. A final staircase connects the third floor with the flat, turreted roof. I rarely stray beyond the ground floor, for it provides me with everything I need: an open fire, a window, a place to write and cook and sleep.

Much of the year it is a cold place to live, but the cold doesn't bother me. I wrap up warm. Sometimes I sit in this chair and look out through the window over the valley, and the white road which twists and threads between the tree-covered slopes. In the walls of the tower's upper storeys are slits through which defenders might once have fired arrows at their enemies. However, I doubt whether anyone ever tried to take this tower. There is nothing to defend, and there never was. It was built, I was told, in the thirteenth century, with the single purpose of confining the last surviving heir of an unwanted lineage. He was incarcerated here, on the third floor. That is why there are two rooms on the third floor: one for the prisoner, the other for his gaoler.

4

Below the tower the land falls away through gullies and ravines and dramatic cliffs to the plateau, a thousand metres or more below. These are the flatlands, which stretch westward beyond the nearest town, and south, towards the city. The landscape which the prisoner looked out on has probably not changed much since the days when he was locked up here, with only his guard for company. I am the guardian now, but there is nobody to guard, just as there is nothing for me to protect from my enemies.

My job is to look after the grounds, and there is a plot of land where I grow vegetables. Nobody comes up here except the owner, who claims to be a baron and lives in the city, and his visits are rare. He never stays for long. He walks about the grounds for a while, or climbs to the top of the tower to inspect the lightning conductor, and he gives me money.

Sometimes I don't see the Baron for a month or more and then I have to visit his office in the city, a hundred kilometres away. I set out early since it's a morning's walk to the nearest town and its railway station. The train journey takes about an hour and a half. In the city I collect money from his secretary in a brown envelope with nothing written on it. This is not because the Baron does not know my name: it is simply a convention we have arrived at, like any other.

In the daytime I spend hours walking in the nearby beech woods, with Filos, a tawny mountain sheepdog. Filos is my sole companion here. We rise early and look for mushrooms, then just walk for the pleasure of it. At present the paths are waterlogged and muddy after the autumn rain. Evenings I stay in and cook a simple meal: beans, potatoes, bread. Then, beside the fire, I sit and write my story. Last October I gave myself a year to do this. One cycle of seasons. I've tried to remember the story as it happened, rather than in a way I would have liked it to have happened, or have even convinced myself that it did happen. But I can never be entirely sure. A story is only ever the version that presents itself at any particular moment. And it is subject to change, since our lives are composed of countless such moments, leading from a vaguely remembered past, through a sequence of events towards some equally ill-defined concluding moment. But they are all we have, these moments. They constitute the fabric of memory. We go over them again and again, with countless revisions and substitutions, until we arrive at a version that suits us, and we call it our story. Even then the story is not truly ours, since it refers to the people we once were, or believed we were; or more usually, the people we aspired to become.

I'm grateful for the little tasks I have to carry out, the daily routine I am expected to pursue. Like checking the meteorological instruments, which are kept in a squat, white beehive behind the tower. The Baron has not told me why he requires such a service to be carried out, and I have never asked him. It has occurred to me to ask, but I have desisted. My suspicion is that it either reflects an aspect of his character that demands attention to the minutiae of things, or else he requests it simply in order to justify paying me a caretaker's wage.

This morning, while closing the door of the weather station, I noticed a hare grazing in the meadow at twenty metres' distance. Filos and the hare also spotted each other at precisely the same moment. Man, dog and hare were freeze-framed for an instant, then Filos darted away, taking great bounds to clear the scrub of brambles, and the hare took flight. It was a buck, hind legs pounding the grass, his thickening winter coat making him appear a giant among hares. His scut bobbed frantically, as he plunged into autumnal undergrowth. Filos pursued, the colour of a dog running away.

In the language here this idiom refers to something of an indeterminate or vague and shadowy appearance, perhaps suggesting a fugitive reality. It seems to fit, somehow. Both the episode with Filos, and with the story I am writing.

I wanted to write of the events that took place one summer in the last decade of the twentieth century, which now seem like sequences from a movie that is already ended, but whose returning images will give no peace. When you leave the cinema, you stand in the foyer, with all the other people emerging, and you are touched by a sense of grief and loss for a life not lived, a path not chosen. Something has brushed against your mortality, perhaps an incident in the film, or a phrase spoken; or more generally, the intractable sense of longing evoked by a particular character. This is the way any story might begin: an elusive nostalgia for something distant but intimately known, that for a moment flashes before you, and then is gone.

La Torre de Vilaferran

Part One

We can never know what to want, because, living only
one life, we can neither compare it with our previous
lives nor perfect it in our lives to come.
Milan Kundera

1. A postcard

One evening in May as I was walking home, I witnessed a mugging, and did nothing to prevent it. I could see what was going to happen. It was in the Gothic quarter of the city, just off the Ramblas. Ornate lamps lined the street, reminders of a more grandiose era, and narrow lanes led off into labyrinths unvisited by daylight. As I passed the entrance to one such lane, I noticed a pale young man standing there, reptile eyes scanning the human traffic. I slowed my pace.

I had gone barely ten strides when I heard a woman's voice, shouting a single word in shrill English. The man had pounced, and was trying to wrest the shoulder bag from an ash-blonde, sunburned woman who wore a short pink dress. The bag's strap had become twisted around the woman's arm. The thief kept pulling, the woman stumbled, and as she fell into the road, the bag slipped free. The thief ran back across the street and up the alley, clutching his prize tight against his chest.

This all happened in an instant. I couldn't move.

The woman stayed in the gutter for a few seconds, the pink dress up around her hips. Lying there, half on the sidewalk, half in the road, she looked sad and vulnerable. She was heavily built and her legs were red. Clumsily, she got to her feet, shouting, 'Stop the bastard!'

She was looking straight at me.

Fortunately, there was a helpful citizen nearby, quite close to the alleyway. He was youngish, dressed in a lightweight blue suit. He turned and gave chase, disappearing into the darkness, before returning a few seconds later, his arms spread in the Latin gesture of hopeless endeavour. He commiserated briefly with the woman, who understood nothing he said, then shrugged and went on his way.

The woman dusted off her dress with a few angry brushes of the hand. She looked as though she were about to cry. I still hadn't moved. Several other people, who had stopped briefly at the time of the theft in the hope of some excitement, had begun to move on. I was wondering, among other things, what might have been in the bag.

'You could have stopped him. Bastard!' She spewed out the first vowel of that word, as though gagging on a lump of gristle.

It was clear that she was addressing me, but I was unwilling to look up and face her, to respond to this accusation. She was probably right. Had I been able to move, I was the person best placed to detain the thief. I was bigger than he was. I could have tackled him as he sped into the alleyway. Alternatively, I could have tripped him, sent him flying, then strode up and placed my boot on his neck, spat insults in his ear, pummelled him with feet and fists. I could have humiliated and thrashed him, and come away a hero, to be blessed with the gratitude of the sunburnt tourist, the applause of passers-by. The pink woman would have invited me to dinner in her hotel, confiding in me the squalid details of an unhappy marriage, an unsatisfactory job, her decision to strike out on her own, her now-thriving little business in the south-east of England, her trips to what she would call 'the Continent'. As the evening wore on, the prospect of some drunken sex would have arisen, or worse, become reality. The calm of my life would have been shattered. And for what? A few American Express cheques, a passport, a ticket, a hotel key, a powder puff, a lipstick. Suntan lotion of an overoptimistic factor. Besides, the junkie needed the money more than she did. You just had to look into his eyes.

I stared at the woman in front of me, and to my relief was unable to summon a trace of compassion. My feet came to life and I continued on my way. I did not look back. I continued up Carrer Ferran, past the City Hall with its ornamental pots of greenery and its air of abandoned colonial glory. Over the cobblestones and past the solitary policeman, and a huddle of beggars. Across Via Laietana and the noisy traffic.

Choosing a familiar bar near Santa Caterina Square, I sat down at the counter, next to the espresso machine. I ordered a beer and a brandy; sank the beer, and nursed the brandy. A pimp was arguing with one of his girls further down the bar. They left soon after I came in. The place was quiet. I was shaken up by my experience on Ferran. And yet I saw such things almost daily. Why, this time, had it affected me? Because the woman looked at me and spoke, in English. 'Bastard,' she had said, three times. The final one was definitely for me. I hadn't lifted a finger to help.

I told the barman, Enrique, about the mugging. I glorified my own inaction and exaggerated the awfulness of the victim. Enrique laughed, unamused, and in retaliation told me about a knifing that had taken place in the bar the month before. I had heard the story twice already, and I wasn't listening. I drained the brandy and left.

My apartment was on Santa Caterina Square. It was the atico, the top floor, up eight flights of steep steps. The place was small, and draughty in winter. The best thing about it was the rooftop veranda. Sitting on the veranda I was slightly higher than most of the neighbouring rooftops. I could sit and watch the lights of Tibidabo, a spectral funfair in the night sky. Or I could look down on the dirty glass roof of the old Santa Caterina market, sprawling beneath me like an empty railway station. Mostly though, I could lie back on my hammock and look at the stars, while listening to the sounds of the city below.

When I opened the door of the flat there was a picture postcard lying in the hallway. It showed a reproduction of a painting by Joan Miró. I turned the card over. Neatly written, in green ink, was what appeared to be a date and a time: 20 May – 11.00. There was no explanatory message, no indication of who had written the card. The printed details told me that the reproduction was entitled *Dona en la Nit* in Catalan, or *Woman in the Night*. The painting could be found at the Miró Foundation. May 20 was the next day.

Mail delivered to my flat never came upstairs. It stayed down in the letter box by the front door for me to collect. Whoever slid this under my door had let themselves into the building, or else was a resident. Quickly discounting all the occupants as possible authors, I decided to call on Manu, my Andalusian neighbour, to see if he could supply a clue. Manu lived on the third floor with his wife and teenage daughter. He kept rabbits on the flat roof, behind my kitchen. In the evenings he would sit on the roof near the rabbit hutches and drink white Córdoba wine. I sometimes joined him on the rooftop patio. Our friendship manifested itself in this undemonstrative evening ritual. We enjoyed each other's company. From our vantage point on the roof we sustained a laconic commentary on the neighbourhood and world affairs. If Manu was lonely he would knock at my door, or tap on my kitchen window (which looked out onto our shared rooftop with the rabbit hutches, a table and some chairs) and ask me out for a glass or two. He worked as a warehouseman at the docks.

Manu came to the door, eating. We greeted each other.

'Oy, Manu, did I have a visitor this evening?'

He wiped his mouth with a dirty napkin.

'*Coño*, how would I know?'

'I've been out. Someone's put a card under my door.'

'I haven't heard anyone. Wait.'

He shouted to his wife and daughter. They both called back in the negative.

Manu was wearing a white vest, and had a round belly. He smelled of wine.

'Come in. Have a drink. Something to eat.'

'Thanks, no.'

'As you wish. Hey, don't worry.'

'What?'

'Maybe they'll come back.'

'Who?'

'Whoever called. Your visitor.'

'Possibly.'

'You seem preoccupied.'

'I can't understand it. What I can't understand pre-occupies me.'

Manu thought about this, visibly.

'You know what preoccupies me? My rabbits. Rabbits should screw. Those rabbits don't do any screwing.'

This was contrary to the truth. Manu's rabbits fornicated and reproduced at a formidable rate.

'Perhaps your bunnies are consumed by higher thoughts. The life of the spirit. Barcelona Football Club. The local elections. Or they have a different sexual orientation.'

'You think this hadn't occurred to me also?'

'Of course. See you tomorrow.'

'Until then.'

I went back upstairs and looked at the card again, unable to think of where to begin. An unsigned note with no message, only an instruction, or an invitation, or both. I walked onto the rooftop veranda, with the card in my hand, and smoked a cigarette, the red tiles still warm under my bare feet. Lights were on all over the city. A warm breeze blew in from the sea, carrying the smell of salt and the promise of summer. I stood there a long time, leaning on the parapet, listening to the night sounds start up: taxis, dogs, a couple screaming at each other through the open shutters across the way. I decided to take a shower and have an early night.

At five o'clock the next morning the sound of trucks woke me, as they began unloading at the market. This happened most days, and it suited me: I liked rising early. The bedroom adjoined the veranda, and I slept with the window wide open. The fresh fruit and vegetables were piled steeply in boxes on the cobblestones below, along with flowers and other indoor plants that were sold at the market. The air smelled good on a morning in May.

I was thirty-three years old. I suffered occasional liver pains and vague yearnings for domesticity, a steady income, children greeting me on my return home. The yearnings often came along with the pains. Three years before, after a bout of prolonged drinking and vindictive liver pains, I had gone to see an acupuncturist in Maragall, a district in the north of the city. The acupuncturist was a young woman called Fina Mendes. She attended to her craft enthusiastically while I suffered multiple impalations with a grinning masochism. My liver pains got better and I started seeing Fina in a non-professional capacity. She followed a macrobiotic diet and smoked Winston cigarettes. She encouraged me to eat quantities of brown rice and fresh green vegetables. She had jet black hair, surprising blue eyes, and drove a sporty Volkswagen Golf at dangerous speeds. She had graduated in biochemistry at the Autónoma University, enjoyed loud rock music, and believed in an impending invasion by extraterrestials. We became lovers and I moved into her apartment.

Most weekends we didn't work, and made breakneck trips into the Pyrenees, taking just a couple of blankets, plenty of fruit and nuts, a pan for making tea. Parking the car on an unmarked dirt-track, we climbed to a suitable vantage point and I would make a fire, cook some herb tea. Fina would sit and scan the sky for likely spacecraft movements. She could do this for hours at a time, without losing faith. Sometimes she lay on her back, with her head on my belly. I looked at the sky too, wondering at the vastness of the constellations.

'Look,' she said, one night, after we had been lying there for an hour and a half, 'there's one.'

'That's an aeroplane,' I said, without really looking. 'It's probably going to land at Girona.'

'Aeroplanes don't flash like that. It's a different colour light. A different sort of flash. Besides, this one's not moving.'

The light in question was a silvery blue, and it was impossible to tell how high the craft was flying. It was either stationary, or else moving very slowly.

'It's hovering.' Fina said.

I had no idea what the blue light was, but I was never going to agree to it being a UFO. I reached over for one of Fina's cigarettes, lit it, and stared at the tiny light. The sky was definitely nearer, up there in the mountains, and the great celestial curtain appeared fuller than usual, millions of stars exploding through seams of blackness.

'Why here, Fina? Why do you think they come here, particularly?'

'The Pyrenees have the highest rate of UFO sightings in Europe. Especially the triangle between Montserrat, the Cap de Creus peninsular and Andorra. There are indications of some kind of cosmic receptivity. The number of stone circles in the area. Important religious centres in the Middle Ages. These things all point to special energy levels.'

Sometimes she sounded like a New Age tour guide.

'But what are they doing?'

'They're waiting, I suppose.'

'What for?'

'Until we need them, of course.'

'So they're kind of inter-galactic social workers?'

Fina generally ignored remarks of this kind.

'There will come a stage when humans push things too far. War, plague, devastation. Destruction of the environment. At that point, something extraordinary will take place.'

'How long before that happens, do you reckon?'

'Oh, five or six years.'

I sat up to add some wood to the fire. Fina's theories fascinated me, but I did not share her beliefs in flying saucers. She had even voiced the opinion, early in our relationship, that I was an extraterrestial, but that I didn't realise it. This had been on a previous nocturnal excursion, and thankfully she hadn't returned to that theme, perhaps sensing my hostility to the idea. Now she sat up as well, agitated; leaned over and pulled spiky seed pods off my sweater, tossing them away as though I were infested with giant lice. I continued to poke the fire with a long stick.

'You think I'm deluded.'

'No, it's not that,' I replied, quickly. 'But how can you be so definite about something so, well, so unproven.'

'It's just a feeling that ultimately, we're protected by a force out there.'

'Like a faith in God.'

'No, not like a faith in God. Just an inner certainty.'

'Fina. You've been trained as a scientist. In other circumstances you believe in rational explanations, testable theories, all that stuff. But, without a jot of evidence, you insist on this idea of alien invasion. You're too many contradictions.'

At times I needed to provoke her, because her belief in UFOs irritated me. It seemed to be a caving in to groundless silliness, whereas her study of acupuncture and her faith in herbs and essential oils and shiatsu were at least founded in some kind of organic evidence and proven practice.

But it was not her contradictions that caused a rift between us. Rather, there was a growing sense that we wanted different things from each other. Within a year of moving in with her, I allowed my job to become more demanding, and began to work late in the evenings. Often I would come home at eleven o'clock and Fina was already in bed, pretending to be asleep. She started to become unreasonably demanding. When she wasn't pretending to ignore me she instigated sustained and energetic sex. I didn't object to this, far from it; it was the increasingly stressful periods in between that got to me first, and then the disparity between these two aspects of our relationship: the silence and the sex. There was no middle ground, no fertile patch that might provide a place for getting to know each other well. Perhaps we shared less in common than we had wanted to believe at the outset.

One night I got drunk and crashed my car on the city ring road in the company of a one-armed Colombian poet and a transvestite Flamenco singer. I couldn't remember anything about the accident, and spent a week in hospital. To make things worse, there was another car involved, and a big insurance claim in consequence. I was in danger of losing my licence, but couldn't recall being breathalysed or spending time in a police cell. On leaving the hospital, things became difficult with Fina. We started throwing things at each other, and dragging up past grievances: always a bad sign. I went to stay with Carlos, the Colombian poet, who lived in the Gothic quarter, and by the end of the week I had found the apartment on Santa Caterina.

Now Fina and I hadn't seen each other for two years. Thinking about her both aroused and disturbed me. I pulled on shorts and padded to the kitchen, brewed some coffee, and went to sit on the veranda. The sun was appearing above the distant cranes of the docks. It was going to be a warm day. Without making a conscious decision, I knew I would be going to the Miró Foundation that morning, and that at eleven o'clock I would be standing by the painting *Woman in the Night*, wondering who or what I was supposed to be looking for.

I belonged to a health club off Maragall, a remnant from my clean-living days there. I decided to go for a work-out, to occupy a couple of hours before turning up at the Miró Foundation. The metro station was busy, but most people were travelling in the opposite direction, on their way to work. At the gym I warmed up with a stint on the treadmill, moving in ghostly synchrony with the office workers around me, each of us enclosed in a private project of dutiful self-improvement. I had to be careful not to overdo things, having been absent from the gym for two weeks. Nevertheless, I turned to the weights and pumped iron, flexing arms and sinews in a succession of increasingly painful movements. Finally I went for a sauna and a long swim. Most of the clientele were gone by now and I had the pool and the sauna to myself. I enjoyed the calm of the hot-room. It was a quiet haven after my exertions, and sweet with the smell of eucalyptus and new pine. I tried some breathing exercises. My mind was as empty as it ever got and I watched the rivulets of sweat as they coursed down my chest and stomach.

The door opened and, to my surprise, one of my oldest friends came in. Eugenia Fabre was a Catalan sculptor and painter who lived in the Gràcia district of the city. We had known each other since before I moved to Spain, having met in Athens some fifteen years earlier. There was an ascetic strain to Eugenia: she was a person accustomed to carrying out arduous and self-imposed tasks. She was dark, restrained, and serious, although possessing the quietly subversive humour of a subtle trickster. Her face carried a mark of animal kinship: if she had not been born a human, she would have been a fox.

'Eugenia. I didn't know you were a member.'

She kissed me lightly on both cheeks.

'A friend gave me an invitation. So here I am. And what are you up to?'

'I'm pursuing an invitation as well, after a fashion,' I said, and told her about my postcard.

'That's very mysterious. You know of course that Miró did more than one painting with this title?'

'No, I didn't.'

'Yes. Also, *Woman with Birds*; *Woman in the Night with Birds*; *Woman Surrounded by a Flight of Birds*. And so on.'

'*Bird in the Night Surrounded by a Flight of Women*?'

'I think not.'

'But, it's odd. You see, first the postcard shouldn't have been there at all; and second, it seemed to arrive at a significant moment.'

22

'Why significant?'

'It was just after I saw someone getting mugged. I could have helped, but I froze. As though it was happening on a television screen. I was more interested in watching than in doing anything.'

She took a while responding.

'It sounds bad. But actually it's normal. It's in the air. We live inside bubbles. Everything outside is treated like a malignancy, or an unwanted incursion. Drop around to my apartment. You make me feel sane.'

'Is that a compliment? I suspect not. But thanks, anyway. I will.'

'It's been too long. Lethargy. Inertia. You need to take a trip. Walk in some mountains.'

'Right, Eugenia.'

A second, younger woman with short blonde hair entered the sauna and took a seat very close to Eugenia. She glanced at me suspiciously until Eugenia made a hurried introduction. I didn't catch the woman's name. My mind was elsewhere. It was becoming too hot for comfort in the sauna so I took my leave, enjoyed a long cool shower, and dressed, my limbs saturated with a luxurious sense of weightlessness.

There was a small café next door. I bought a Spanish newspaper and had breakfast: an omelette and bread washed down with a *San Miguel*. By the time I had read the paper it was past ten o'clock. I left the café and caught the metro.

When I got onto the train, an incident was in progress. Four teenage gypsies were terrorising a red-eyed drunk at my end of the carriage. The drunk slurred back at them: *¡Déjame en paz!* – 'Leave me in peace!' They didn't. They seemed to be goading him, trying to get him to reveal something to them. The vagrant shuffled towards the door at Drassanes station and I noticed that he was carrying a little dog under his coat. The *gitanos* jostled him. As he prepared to step out, a jet of piss issued from the puppy, squirting the nearest boy and soaking his shirt in the stream. The kid stepped back with a shout of disgust, and then lunged forward at the drunk, precisely as the doors closed. There was a glint of metal, and just as quickly, the knife was withdrawn. For an instant I was taken in by the dramatic quality of the performance, and expected to see the victim crumple to the platform floor. But it was simply playacting on the boy's part. As the train pulled away the drunk turned angrily, talking to himself and re-arranging his coat around the little dog. Inside the carriage one of the gypsies re-enacted the scene with the knife, taking on the role of the vagrant, who in this version tottered cinematically in the aisle, falling in a slow pirouette. The one with the wet shirt didn't smile. The others laughed, and then wandered down the carriage, looking for further entertainment.

2. Woman in the Night

I got off the metro at Poble Sec. The Miró Foundation is on Montjuíc, quite a walk from the station. A long stone stairway leads up the hill, then you follow the road a little way, and there it is, perched on the edge, overlooking the city. An understated, concrete building. I bought a ticket and went in. The exhibition space was bright and cheerful, a place that exuded sunshine, like its creator's work. It was five minutes to eleven. There was a tightness in the pit of my stomach. Partly because of the picture's title I had convinced myself that the postcard foretold an erotic encounter of some kind. Perhaps its very anonymity, and its appearance during a long bout of sexual abstinence impelled me to expect that, and yet there were many other possible outcomes to my visit.

I identified the correct painting, *Woman in the Night*, from the postcard. She hung in one of the upper rooms, but there was nobody standing near her. A few people milled around, mostly tourists, many of them Japanese. One young woman stood apart from all the other visitors. She didn't appear to belong to any group, and had an air of knowing precisely what she was doing. She was dressed in black jeans and a brightly-patterned silk shirt, and moved with the proprietorial elegance of Barcelona women. I realised I was staring at her, and without thinking about it, had begun to follow her as she moved to the next room. I was conscious, too, that if my postcard indicated an appointment of some sort, then my appointee might well be watching me, even as I watched this girl in the silk shirt. Whoever they were, I didn't want to be observed, observing. I attempted to be nonchalant, pretended to inspect a painting, then glanced around the room before leaving. But I didn't want to lose sight of the girl. I followed her into the large central gallery. She was taking her time. She didn't need to try and look knowledgeable: it was apparent that she knew the art works by the way she approached them with a relaxed familiarity. She in turn was easy to watch. There was a poise about her, a lack of self-consciousness.

I looked at my watch. It was eleven o'clock. My palms were sweating. It felt as though something crucial were happening, or about to happen, but that it would pass me by if I did not recognise the clues. This was a test I could not afford to fail. But I could not focus on what I was supposed to do next. I thought maybe I should be next to the painting, waiting, but also felt compelled to follow this girl as she moved from room to room.

I was confused. I never followed women in public places. I was convinced she was a part of the set-up, whatever it might be. But she didn't seem to be going anywhere in a hurry so I left her standing next to a huge embroidery and walked quickly back to the room that displayed *Woman in the Night*.

It was two minutes past eleven. I stood in front of the painting, but didn't see it. Instead, I had a sensation of indistinct but thorough desperation. There was a white leather sofa in the room. I sat down and looked around. A middle-aged English couple hovered nearby. I ruled them out. Likewise a gaggle of blonde Nordics, clutching sketch pads. Then a dark and intense-looking woman of fortyish came in, looked around carefully, and eased herself on the sofa next to me, offering a thin smile as she did so.

I was certainly not going to make the first move. I was thinking wildly now. Why had this woman sat down next to me? Why did she smile? Could it be that I knew her, but had forgotten her, or was she simply making an insignificant gesture? Perhaps some unknown person held a grudge against me: perhaps I had been misidentified to some local mafioso during one of my nights out with local lowlife, and this woman was a decoy, or bait, intended to lead me to a dockland execution.

Over the next ten minutes, several people passed through the room. My neighbour had begun to read a book, Kierkegaard's *The Sickness unto Death*, in Spanish. I considered this to be a bad sign. I still had not discounted her. But nobody appeared to be looking for me. I wondered whether my appointee had been and gone, because I had not been on the spot at precisely eleven o'clock. Perhaps they had left behind some kind of clue, a further message. I got up and approached the painting, looking at the floor for scraps of paper. Nothing. I ran my fingers down the side of the frame.

I even knelt and inspected the join between the floor and wall. Returning to the painting, I thought I spotted something, a different configuration of light at the edge of the frame, on the bottom right corner. It could have been a slip of paper. I touched it, hunched over, trying to work a fingernail under the frame.

There was a tap on my shoulder.

'You can't do that.'

The security guard placed himself squarely between me and the painting. I began to mutter excuses, using English in order to convey maximum incompetence, and feeling myself blush as I did so. I could sense the eyes of people turned on us. I heard myself say, ludicrously, that I had lost something, that I thought it had fallen down the back of the painting.

The guard stared at me, as if deciding whether I was unsafe or merely an imbecile. The woman who had been reading Kierkegaard was looking up from her book with undisguised interest.

Slowly, mouthing inanities, I backed out of the room. The attendant had one hand on his walkie-talkie. He didn't take his eyes off me. Once I had left, I returned to the space where the embroideries hung. The girl in black jeans wasn't there. I walked back the way I had come, making a circuit of the galleries. The room with *Woman in the Night* was empty. I didn't see the attendant, or the girl. I went to the entrance foyer, and searched for her in the souvenir shop. She had gone. I wanted a cigarette, and remembered that there was a roof garden. I climbed the stairs and out into the warm sunshine.

I didn't realise she was there at first. The terrace appeared to be deserted. I lit a cigarette and surveyed the view. The city stretched out below – an expanse of tower blocks, whitewashed houses and terracotta roofs, enclosed by hills and the sea. When I turned, she was standing by the railing, at the edge of the roof. She wore dark glasses, and was looking towards the harbour. I went straight over to her. I had no idea what I was going to say.

She flinched as I spoke, 'I thought you had gone.'

Silence. She turned to look at me.

'Do I know you?'

I ignored this.

'I thought you'd gone. I was looking for you.'

Her face was impassive. I wanted to detect a hint of curiosity, but there was none.

'For me?'

'Yes, I thought...'

She interrupted, 'Do you know me?'

The question had been somehow inverted, turning it into a request for information. She wasn't angry. She meant it quite literally.

'No. But I noticed you earlier and I thought perhaps we had an appointment.'

She paused, assessing me. 'You've been following me.'

She spoke Spanish with the trace of a Catalan accent.

'I thought you'd gone. I thought you were someone...'

'Someone else?'

'Yes. That is, I thought we were supposed to meet.'

'You and me?'

'Me and somebody. It might have been you.'

She laughed. Some kind of understanding broke through. 'You arranged to meet an unknown person in the Miró Foundation? And you thought I was she?'

'I didn't arrange to. They arranged it. But I don't know who they are.'

She laughed openly, quite unfazed. I managed to ease up a little.

'Let me explain. I received a message, to meet by a particular painting. There was no one there.'

This was not strictly true, of course.

'So you thought the person you were looking for was me. Incredible!'

'You could say that.'

'Are you saying that?'

'Look, I don't know the answer to your question because I don't know the reason for my being here, other than what I've told you. All I know is that somebody was expecting me to come here at eleven o'clock but I don't know who, and I came. I saw you, and thought, better to say I hoped, that you were that person. You obviously aren't, but what the hell, here we are anyway.'

She took off her dark glasses and looked at me. Her face had a rare, dangerous quality, and a kind of self-possession that left me feeling quite inadequate. Doubly inadequate now that my floundering speech had been met by this lengthening silence. I needed to extract a semblance of control from the situation. But she rescued me.

'I'm going for a drink. Would you like to join me? Tell me some more?'

Of course, I agreed to that.

We walked out of the Foundation and along the road. There was nothing promising nearby. I remembered a café in a little square with a fountain, near the bottom of the steps. It was quite a way, but my companion didn't complain, or question. Either she trusted me, or else possessed an exquisite indifference. I asked her about herself. She told me, among other things, that her name was Nuria, that she lived in the Poble Sec barrio and that she was twenty-seven years old.

We sat under a plane tree outside the café. I ordered two beers. When the drinks arrived I showed Nuria the postcard. She didn't demonstrate any particular reaction. She behaved as though it was of no real consequence to her why I had approached her, but she was far too refined and subtle to say as much. She didn't accuse me of lying, of contriving the whole thing, but then neither did she indicate that she believed me. She looked at the card, turned it over, and smiled. She was supremely non-commital.

'Perhaps it is some kind of joke,' she said, leaving me to ponder whether she was referring to the postcard's appearance under my door, or my use of it as an introductory gambit. I asked Nuria more about herself. Apart from her native Catalan and Spanish, she spoke French and English. She came from a small town near the French border, where she had grown up, and had a younger brother. She had studied art history and now worked as a researcher for a Catalan television company.

I told her a little of myself, of my father coming to Wales as a child refugee from the civil war in Spain and my own Welsh and Spanish upbringing in Carmarthenshire. Of travelling in Greece, Turkey and North Africa. How I'd come to Spain five years earlier and ended up working for a publisher, helping to compile an encyclopaedia, and freelancing as a translator and editor of literary texts. In other words, I gave her the briefest outline of a life, in return for hers, and as we sat there under the tree, I quickly re-invented the meaning of the postcard. To this new way of thinking, how it was planted under my door became less important, since because of it I had met Nuria. That I might have missed another appointment of consequence was rendered irrelevant by the meeting that had taken place instead. There was certainly little point in subjecting Nuria to a full-scale interrogation about her connection with the postcard. She had already laughed at me once, and politely tolerated my laborious explanation. A further inquiry would probably drive her away, and I didn't want that at all.

There was a familiarity about Nuria that would have been more disturbing had it been less pleasant. Her face, for a start, though I was certain we had not met before. Hers was not the kind of face you would easily forget. The hypnotic draw of those dark eyes and a smile that revealed small white teeth at unexpected moments – noticeably, I soon discovered, when I began to explain anything (my postcard story for the third time, perhaps) too earnestly. She was not, it occurred to me, laughing at the story, but at the strained sincerity of its telling, the rooted sense of an intrinsic connection between words and meanings, which most discourse takes for granted, but which for Nuria was apparently not so easily purchased. Her voice, when she did speak, curled around me like smoke from a brazier. There was a gratuitous sense of play about the way she used words. The effect was of a kind of chase: her words, sometimes hesitant, disappearing around corners halfway through a sentence to reappear as if surprised at themselves, or else dissolving into watery laughter.

'Do you like seafood?'

The question took me by surprise.

'Yes, very much.'

'Well, would you like to eat some?'

She emphasized the last two words and smiled: the mouth conveying a perfect innocence, but the eyes laughing. I didn't mind her laughing at me. On the contrary it felt reassuring.

'Sure. Shall we go to a restaurant?' I asked.

'Not now. I have things to do. I was thinking, well, later perhaps.'

What things? I wondered, but said instead, 'I'd love to. How about Barceloneta?'

'Barceloneta would be fine.'

She mentioned a restaurant I'd heard of, but never visited. We agreed on a time, nine o'clock that evening.

Then she got up, kissed me on both sides of the face, put on her dark glasses, and left. I watched her until she disappeared from view. She didn't turn around.

I found it hard to concentrate on anything for the rest of the afternoon. I wandered back towards the Ramblas, then up into the Gothic quarter. The shops were getting ready to close for the afternoon. I dropped in at my local grocery store, bought a chilled bottle of *cava*, some Serrano ham and olives, picking up a loaf from the bakery next door. Back in my apartment, I opened the olives, took one out, and sucked it between my teeth. I took off my shoes, slung my jacket over a chair and spat out the olive stone, aiming successfully for the waste-paper bin. Then I poured a full glass of *cava*, and prepared some lunch. I took a plate with ham and olives, half the loaf, and a big slice of melon from the fridge, and went out onto the veranda. I returned inside and fetched the wine.

The hammock on the veranda was tied to iron rings between the outer walls of the bedroom and the living space. It was the only shaded part at this time of day. I sat on the floor nearby and ate slowly, mulling over the events at the Miró museum. First, there was my pleasure in meeting Nuria. But the fact that I was flattered by her apparently warm feelings towards me did nothing to help any real understanding of the situation. As I sat on the veranda, I had to concede that the question of the postcard remained unresolved. I found it hard to believe that Nuria (who lived close to the Miró Foundation in Poble Sec), just happened to be visiting the museum at the time of my appointment there, and walked away with me as though we had known each other for years. There was something else too: her impassiveness or indifference, which I had chosen to interpret as cool sophistication. She gave the impression of knowing me, as though, rather than being endowed with a sublime sense of detachment, she had simply been briefed about me. If I was being paranoid, at least by going along to meet her this evening I had a chance to find out more. All this speculation left me vague and confused. Why didn't the author of the postcard contact me directly? I tried to think who I might have crossed in the three years I had been in Barcelona, or who might pull a trick like this on me, but drew a blank.

I had nearly finished the wine, and was feeling sleepy. The hot afternoon air was dusty and rancid. I watched a lizard scuttle along the veranda wall. A city lizard on a dizzy city parapet. It stopped and blinked at me, watching and not watching. Or if it waited, it was waiting for nothing. The lizard had been blinking in the sun, watching and not watching, waiting and not waiting, for the past twenty million years. My memory too, according to some beliefs, was lodged inside the skin of this lizard. The reptilian brain. I spoke to it in English, a brief experiment in the alchemy of naming: '*Lizard*,' I said. It did not move. '*Llangardaix*,' I said, trying Catalan, and stressing the luxuriant final syllable: lian-gar-*daysh*. Drowsily, I clambered into the hammock, trailing a leg. My foot grazed the warm tiles with the swinging motion of the hammock. Then, for no reason other than the sound it made I contrived another word: '*Languedoc*,' teasing the word apart in three descending whispers. The lizard ran back along the wall the way it had come, shot down the wall, and crossed half way over the red-tiled floor, before stopping still once again. It looked up, then made a little sprint across to my foot. '*Llangardaix*,' I whispered. Blessed be the creeping things, the slithering creatures of siesta hour. Blessed be the lizards of the blazing city sun, that crawl across the red tiles of a rooftop afternoon.

3. Je suis le plus beau du monde

The sun was quite low in the sky when I awoke, and realised that I had slept longer than I intended. Below, the streets were busy once again, but with the more restrained tempo of evening. Fruit in the market had matured in the course of the afternoon, and the air smelled dense and sweet. The couple in the top flat of the adjacent building, windows flung open, had begun a shrill exchange of insults in their southern Spanish. Curse followed condemnation, challenged by the blaring of a television, and the hoarse intervening yelps of an attendant crone:

Husband: Call this food? I've eaten better in the slammer.
Crone: *Aiee! Your words are honey.*
Wife: Go back there then. Or get your *puta* to feed you.

Husband:	I will. Like I did yesterday.
Crone:	*What man more brutish?*
Wife:	Swine. To think I ever let you touch me.
Husband:	Let you? Five times a night was not sufficient for you!
Crone:	*I will die of shame in this place.*
Wife:	Filthy liar. You were an octopus: a wandering eye on every tentacle.

(Obscure complaint of a teenage girl, shouting from an inner room.)

Wife:	If only we had had condoms, like the young today.
Husband:	Your damn church would not permit it.
Wife:	But at least your own atheist parents might have utilised them, to protect the rest of us from a vileness such as you.
Crone:	*May the Holy Mother have mercy!*
Husband:	Any man would leave this asylum.
Wife:	Go then, shameless one. Go to your syphilitic whore. But do not approach me ever again, for anything. Not to sew a button on your shirt. Nothing.
Husband:	Quiet, my sweet. Bring me coffee.
Wife:	You want coffee, my life?
Husband:	Yes!
Wife:	Well then: (with particular venom) fetch it yourself!

(Sound of something smashing, a child wailing.)

And the night was yet to begin.

Four floors down a posse of dogs trailed a lone bitch, around cars, in and out of doorways, circling lamp-posts. The male dogs sniffed one another and snarled, hackles raised, then busied away after the scent, tails erect. Always on the go.

I went inside and put some flamenco on the tape-deck – the singer El Chocolate – and a song of especially mournful intensity began to thrum and heave through the apartment:

No me quites la botella
Que quiero emborracharme....

I splashed water over my face and chest, and changed into a white shirt, blue jeans, and black linen jacket, slipping barefoot into soft leather shoes. The guitar runs echoed around the whitewashed room like a wounded bird, battering blindly against walls, and competing with the heartbreaking finality of the singer's croaking lyric, which implored the world to leave him to his bottle and solitary drunkenness. Closing the veranda door, I flicked the stereo switch, and went down onto Santa Caterina.

The evening, if anything, seemed warmer than the day. I was too early for my meeting with Nuria, but wanted to be outside, to be a part of whatever the streets had to offer. I walked down the narrow alleyways in the direction of the sea. There was an edge of muted excitement in the air. Barcelona often seemed like that: a city on the brink, infatuated with its own improbability. I loved these twisting alleys, the syncopated snatches of music drifting out from open windows, the long shadows, even the perpetual odour of an antique drainage system overlaid with sand, cement and cheap cigar smoke.

In a small square there was a café with chairs and tables outside. Nearby, a street performer had just arrived, and was preparing to eat fire, talking raucously through his pre-performance. He was barefoot, wearing loose pink pantaloons and a flimsy purple waistcoat. His exposed chest displayed the prominent tattoo of a dragon, in dark green and red. The fire-eater's face was smeared with black smudges, and his dirty blond hair tied back in a tangle. The eyes were bloodshot and he moved with a limp. I had nearly an hour before I was due in Barceloneta, so sat down at an empty table to watch. A waiter appeared and I ordered a whisky.

There were two cafés on the little square and about half of the seats outside the cafés were taken. Dwarf conifers in white boxes marked the division between the two businesses. The square, which was not open to traffic, was designed conveniently for a street performer, who could command the attention of both sets of clients.

The fire-eater swayed as he introduced himself, in a cocktail of languages: '*Buenas Tardes*, *Bonsoir*, Good Night. *En este jardín... Non... Pardon.*' He faltered, looking around as though he had forgotten his lines, or even any sense of where he was, before taking a swig of filthy-looking liquid from a plastic bottle. He at once regained some manner of control. '*Je suis le plus beau du monde,*' he announced, with finality. Then: 'I am ze man of foc,' punning on the Catalan word for fire. '*El Foc* Man,' he said, showing a shattered set of teeth, and clearly pleased with himself on account of the pun. The next utterance he bellowed with a stern theatricality: '*Profession*,' (pause) '*Vagabond.*'

This sounded familiar.

A couple of street kids, around twelve years old, watched him closely from the far side of the square. The café clientele weren't paying much attention. He cleared his throat and shouted hoarsely in an attempt to gain their attention: 'Laydees and Jennulmen, *Mesdames Messieurs, Señoras y Señores.*' A few people looked up.

I recognised him. I'd seen his act before, over four years earlier, in Granada. I remembered too how this inept fire-eater had prized himself on his psychic powers, and had given tarot readings. He claimed to be a Macedonian Greek, but his language was dominated by a variety of French. Yes, that was his pitch: 'Profession Vagabond'. The particular lingo, the ragged pony-tail and the dental bomb-site. The limp was a new development. But I remembered the watching faces of some locals in the audience when I had last seen him eat fire in Granada, as they turned by stages from bemusement, to incredulity, to disgust. His exhibition had been sordid, a mockery of circus, more an act of self-abuse. He had swallowed quantities of petrol during the act, something that clearly had not killed him, since he was still doing it. His tarot readings likewise made no concession to the client, or victim; they were carried out with bad grace in bars or on pavements, where he would aim to insult or terrify whoever opted for a consultation.

As the waiter passed by, I ordered another whisky, and settled back in my chair.

I didn't particularly want to be recognised by the fire-eater, but there seemed little likelihood of that, considering the brain damage he must have endured in the intervening years from all that petrol-quaffing. I watched his pyromaniac display, with mouthfuls of flammable liquid being swilled and spilled, and blasts of random flame issuing around his head. A few more people were watching now, some of them evidently riveted by the grotesque parody of the performance. At one point a woman approached the fire-eater and tried to argue with him, gesticulating at the bottle of petrol and shaking her head from side to side. He ignored her. He made no attempt at presenting himself as an artist: he was entirely in his element with this death-wish variety of street performance.

Yet I was strangely drawn to him. He produced a final volley of uninspired fire-breathing, and then, coughing and cursing, put down his fire-sticks, wiped his face with a dirty cloth, and approached the tables of the café with an outstretched woollen hat, collecting coins. He was moving quickly, dragging his bad leg, aware that one of the waiters might emerge from inside the café and shoo him away at any moment. He passed from table to table, hunched over, as though ducking unseen missiles.

He arrived at my table last of all, raised his head and squinted towards me. His face was a mess: deeply and prematurely lined, marked with some impressive scar tissue, his wrists polka-dotted with cigarette burns. He gave a broken-toothed grin, and then spoke in a formulaic variety of international hippy patois.

'Hey man, the show goes on.'

'Apparently so.'

He was holding out his hat. I dropped a coin into it. The fire-eater offered me a confidential wink, and said: '*Muchas gracias, amigo mio*. For you a special dispensation. *Ce soir*.' Spittled laughter erupted as a postscript to his thanks.

'Fuck off,' I said, without malice.

The fire-eater looked at me in confusion, then glanced quickly to either side.

'Hey,' he said. 'I *know* you, man. Watch out. They're everywhere. But you know about them already, yuh?'

'Who's that?'

'The orchestrators.' He slurred this, with a French enunciation.

'The castrators?'

'Ha ha ha! Very good. They are that, too. But they plan and scheme and play the tunes as well as doing the snip snip snip.' He cut the air with invisible scissors.

'You seem to know a lot about them.'

'I see far. I read the cards, report only what I find.'

'I know what you do. You predict catastrophe.'

He peered at me, as though seeing me for the first time.

'I know what *you* do,' he mimicked, 'too.'

'You do?'

'Yeah. You *watch* people. You lust,' he drew the word out, making it rhyme with 'burst', and rolled his eyes lasciviously, 'after what you cannot know, above all in the feminine form. You are a *voyeur*, and filthy son of a *putain*.'

'You know all this?'

'I remember the future, *tu sais*?'

'All too clearly.'

He looked around again, then seated himself nervously at my side.

'I read your cards.'

'Thanks but no thanks.'

'Of course.'

Undeterred, he produced a tattered tarot deck from the inside pocket of his waistcoat.

'Okay. No full reading. No time. *Te ayudo, nada más.* I simply offer my assistance to your present, *que est-ce qu'on peut dire... situation.*'

I remained impassive.

'Cut the deck,' he ordered.

'Not interested.'

The fire-eater sighed, as though dealing with a recalcitrant child.

'*Blah blah blah*,' he countered, releasing an elastic band from his pack of cards. 'Here,' he held out the deck towards me. 'Cut the cards.'

I folded my arms and stared at him.

He tutted and grimaced, attempted to impersonate someone staring fixedly into the middle distance, and then began to shuffle the cards.

'Come on. Not a full reading. A single card to indicate the er, the eventual *dénouement* of your current *situation*.'

'I have no *situation*,' I said, mimicking him in turn, 'to speak of.'

'You lie. *Menteur. Ta situation est très grave, mon frère.*'

I remained impassive, in spite of his absurdly assured suggestion. I was curious to know how he would resolve the impasse between us. He chose to interpret my silence as uncertainty.

'*Pues*, okay. I select for you a card.'

'In which case it will be your card, not mine.'

He did not respond, but continued shuffling the cards, and laid the deck on the table between us.

'You choose one card, which will be mine. I choose another, which will be yours. Our questions need not be stated. But we both know our own question *n'est-ce pas*? My variation on the yes no tarot reading, using only major arcana cards.'

I sighed, but was now only feigning indifference.

'All right. But I pick your card first.'

'*D'accord.*'

I pulled out a card, placing it in front of him. It was *The Moon*. It showed a face on a crescent moon looking down implacably between two towers. In the foreground a dog and a wolf were baying at the moon while a red lobster crawled unnoticed out of a pond behind them.

He looked troubled.

'That Card. *Merde.*'

He muttered beneath his breath for a while, as though reciting a secret mantra.

'So?'

'The worse for me. I want *The Star* and she send me this. Confusion. Delusion. Sickness. But why she send me this? The treacherous girl.' Then he added, in a sad clown's voice, 'I would not betray *her.*'

I shrugged. 'Who *she*? You been dipping your wick in illicit zones? Someone out to settle a score, payback?'

He remained quiet, concerned. '*C'est pas une affaire de rigolade*. Is not a matter for make fun. Something's wrong.'

'*Sans blague,*' I said. 'You're not bloody joking.'

'Now you,' he said, evidently keen to move on to my prognosis. 'I pick.'

He drew a card, and placed it in front of me. The card was reversed, or upside down. A priestly figure held a triple cross in one hand and raised the other in apparent benediction. At his feet sat two acolytes, a pair of crossed keys between them. The card was *The High Priest*.

'This means nothing to me,' I said. 'You'd better explain.'

'Huh. I better explain, yeah.'

He scratched at his hair vigorously.

'Card says you're a fucking *idiota*. *Un connard*. A er... *wanger*.' He broke off into self-congratulatory laughter. 'Arrogance and impotence. Weakness. Failure. Evasion. *Susceptibilité*. You think you know it all. But you don't. You coming to a big fall, my friend. You better watch your stepping.'

'I thought you might say that.'

'Oh yeah?' He grinned his grin. 'Then I think I make my first point already, no?'

Before I had a chance to respond to this, the waiter came out of the café to serve a nearby table. The fire-eater grabbed my new whisky, which I had barely touched, and drained it in one gulp, then limped rapidly away, head averted.

I remained at the table, and signalled the waiter for the bill. One of the two boys who had earlier been watching the spectacle was poking around in the fire-eater's bag when he returned to his spot. The other held a plastic dog's head mask in his hand and was stretching it over his face and leering at his companion. The fire-eater swore at them and they backed off, afraid of him, yet intrigued. Picking up the bottle of petrol, he offered it to the boy with the dog's head, lifting his outstretched thumb to his mouth in a drinking gesture with his free hand. Then he snatched the dog-mask from the boy and reached for a large pebble on the ground, making as if to throw it at them. The boys turned away and one of them paused to light a half-smoked cigarette, which he then passed to the other. From a distance, they stared back at the fire-eater and laughed.

I went inside to use the toilet, and by the time I returned outside to the patio the fire-eater had taken his fire-eating baggage and his dog-mask and left.

46

Taking my time, I set off on my way towards the sea. I had never considered myself to be especially superstitious but was bothered by this unexpected visitation. I had been spared too many encounters with individuals I'd rather forget about, but then the Gothic quarter was rich with phantoms, and according to a Spanish proverb, such sightings usually boded some kind of ill-fortune. I found myself almost believing that I had invoked the fire-eater, conjuring him back from an earlier life. And there was the irritating possibility – more, the likelihood, in spite of his mashed brain – that he had recognised me. Something else occurred to me as well. As he leaned across my table, I saw for the first time how his dragon tattoo was an essential fixture of his self-proclaimed identity. The fire-eater was a destructive force, an embodiment of chaos.

Something was in the air. I had been touched by a succession of seemingly unrelated events within less than twenty-four hours. The mugging, the Miró postcard, Nuria, the fire-eater – all of them now prompting in me the disconcerting possibility that the material world and the inner workings of the mind somehow operated in conjunction; that they brushed against each other and were indivisible, one taking up where the other left off.

Keep your eyes open, I told myself. It's that simple, isn't it? *You coming to a big fall... you better watch your stepping.*

The Mediterranean was straight ahead of me now, and I began to walk along the marina that follows the seaboard north. Yachts were lined along the quay. There was a large wooden sailing ship, of the kind used long ago. Its red sails were furled around the masthead;

slashes of uncompromising crimson against the rich varnished brown of the ship's timber, all of this framed against the blue of sea and sky. Why red sails? What forces were being explored when seafarers decided to use *red* sails? When they were wrapped close to the wood in that way they seemed to have such restrained energy, a concealed erotic intent. And when they billowed out in the full sea, the ship riding the waves like a great red rose in bloom, what a sight they must have been for any landlubber peasant who happened to be looking up from tying his beans, or weeding between his rows of cabbage. What sentiments of untold weirdness and forgotten longing lay in the vision of a crimson ship coursing through a wild blue sea?

4. In Barceloneta

I found the restaurant without much difficulty. Nine o'clock was early for dinner, especially on a Saturday night, so there was no problem securing a table for two. I chose to sit outside, looking towards the sea. There were a few evening promenaders. A cluster of gulls competed for scraps of bread, which were being distributed methodically by a silver-haired man in a pale green suit. He talked to the birds quietly as he fed them, chiding them when one or another became too eager or aggressive. The walk along the waterfront, and the pristine sea air, had me feeling buoyant, almost visionary. I ordered a beer and waited for Nuria.

She arrived shortly after nine, wearing a short white cotton dress and an embroidered grey cardigan. She seemed taller than I remembered from the morning. Her skin was rich olive, offset by the whiteness of her dress. She wore a plain silver necklace and her dark brown hair was combed straight back, and tied with a red cord. I stood to greet her and she kissed me lightly on both cheeks. A formality. She sat down.

'Were you followed?' she asked, in English.

'No. But I saw a dragon.'

'Here in Barcelona? Did it follow you from your misty wet Wales? Tell me about it. You can trust me.' She did all this deadpan.

'He was someone I knew from a few years ago. A vagabond.' I uttered the word with peculiar relish. 'He used to do tarot readings. One night in Granada I heard him predict a gruesome accident for an Italian girl called Pia. New-age, a bit daft. The next day she was knocked down by a nun on a moped. Broke a few bones. The dragon left town, but not before this Pia's boyfriend beat him up.'

'Beat up the dragon?'

'That's right. But what I remember most about that evening was the look on his face as the boyfriend punched and kicked him senseless. He was enjoying it.'

'*Un masoquista*?'

'Precisely. Part of his thrill, it seems, is to make these terrible prognoses, and then sit back and take the consequences. Of course, he breathes fire too. That's his big thing. This evening he was just breathing fire. And he remembered me too, I think.'

I decided not to tell her of my own abbreviated tarot session.

'How well did you know him?'

'Oh, hardly at all. I bumped into him on a few occasions though. Granada, Almeria, Cabo de Gata.'

'Cabo de Gata? Where the hippies hang out for winter. Were you one of them?'

'I would hardly call myself a hippy. I travelled for

a while, before living here.'

'I remember. You said. Why did you stop? No, hang on a second: why did you start?' Her laughter was infectious. Close-up, I noticed that her eyes were very dark, as near to black as I had ever seen. The whites were slightly bloodshot. I guessed she'd been smoking something other than tobacco.

'You want the long version or the short?'

'Hmm, let's see. Tell me the long version first. Then, if we've time, I'll hear the shorter one.'

She settled back and lit a cigarette.

'I studied music in London, but because of a trip I made to Greece when I was eighteen or so, I wanted to learn the bouzouki. I already played the guitar, but the bouzouki opens up another world. So I went back to Greece and found a teacher, travelling the islands with him in the summer. The winters picking oranges or olives, or working the press in an olive oil factory. Then later, I worked a season as a fisherman.'

'On a boat? A trailer?'

'Trawler. No. A smallish boat, using nets and sometimes dynamite.'

'Is that legal?'

'Definitely not. But it was only an occasional necessity. Then after three years or so I left, tired not so much of Greece, but what was happening to it. Travelled around France for nearly two years, working at odd jobs; planting trees in Savoie, the vendange in Roussillon, making Armagnac in the Gers. Then ended up in Spain. So you could say my travels have taken me in a westerly direction. Coming to Spain was a natural choice, since I spoke the language. Have done, though not very well, since I was a kid. I just took some time getting here.'

'Your Spanish is good,' said Nuria. 'But if you don't mind, I like speaking English with you. It gives me an opportunity not to speak Spanish, or Catalan for that matter.'

'Don't you like speaking Catalan?'

'Of course I do. It's my first language. But sometimes, especially with somebody new, I like to speak Castilian. Or English. In a way it's, uh, preferable for me. Not so, how would you say, laden? Comes with baggage for me, Catalan. And French I find a bit... *de trop*.' She trailed off into laughter, not offering any explanation, before continuing her interrogation.

'Why did you come here, not to the North? You must have relatives there. Asturias, Euskadi; where did you say your father was from?'

'I guess I do, though most of the old ones got killed or dispersed during the civil war. My father didn't keep in touch. He was that sort of man. He lived in the present, only read about the past. He had a great love of literature. And he encouraged me to read also.'

A waiter came and took our order. We ordered a *suquet*, a rich fish soup with potatoes, as the main course. We had servings of grilled octopus for starters, Gallego style, and a dry white wine. Nuria tasted the wine and stretched, looking around the restaurant terrace and then out towards the sea.

'Tell me about you,' I said.

'Oh there's not a lot to tell. School, study. A year in Paris, which I didn't enjoy, and two in London, which I did. Then back here. A small town in the Pyrenees. Rows at home. My father left my mother when I was a kid. Headaches. Migraines. For a while I was (her index fingers framed imaginary speech-marks) depressed. A brief desire that I might one day learn to fly an aeroplane. Other normal crazy stuff not worth mentioning. I went to a convent school over the border in France, although my mother never was particularly religious. After my trips to France and England, what happened?' She mused aloud, flicking the cigarette lighter on and off. 'I suppose, a lucky break. Some would call it lucky anyway, working in television. Except that I absolutely hate the bloody television. Never watch it. Funny, isn't it?'

She did being vague with a sort of unpredictability that made you wonder if it was her own life she was describing, or some stranger's. She chewed nonchalantly on a piece of bread. Her dark eyes scanned me restlessly, even while she spoke in these tones of affected detachment. Sometimes – who can know how often in a human life? – you have the feeling of walking out into a new and strange landscape, where the colours are shocking, and the light is not what it should be. Messages flash too quickly to be read, and unfamiliar birds crowd the overhead wires. The stories that you hold in stock do not correspond with any of this. They have no relevance, no place here. The rules are different. This is how I felt with Nuria. I didn't want to spoil things, to hear myself tell the story of my life as though it were the prelude to some inevitable romance. I didn't want to be 'interesting' for her, nor her to be for me. I simply wanted to enjoy the strangeness of our meeting up like this, without it having to signify anything.

The octopus came, and in spite of my earlier decision to probe her on the apparent coincidence of our separate visits to the Miró Foundation that morning, I did not bring up the subject of the postcard again. I had become more and more convinced that Nuria had no direct part to play in its delivery to my apartment. She, meanwhile, smoked, drew animal cartoons on the serviettes, and then, waiting for the main course, started talking about Wales, giving an account of a camping holiday in Snowdonia with an English boyfriend who climbed mountains, an affair which fizzled away after a few days of waiting in pubs for the rain to stop.

'I suffered a bad case of culture shock,' she explained. 'But so, I think, did he, the mountaineer. He was caught between me and my English, which was not so good at the time, on the one hand, and the local people, on the other.' She went on. 'I liked England. London, anyway. Apart from the weather, which was horrible. But I even enjoyed the rain for the first six months. You can sit at home by a fire and read novels and eat that weird chocolate. Varieties of weird chocolate. Drink muddy tea. I liked that sense of darkness and firelight and the rain pounding at the windows. It was for me – you might think this funny, but – well, exotic. But only for so long. Then I missed Spain and the Pyrenees and the sunshine and the fresh fruit. All fruit tasted the same in England. Like dry cotton wool.'

'I shared a house in Finsbury Park, with other Spanish and Latinos, and worked as a waitress in an Islington wine bar, off Upper Street; you know the kind of trendy place? Regulation black miniskirt and white shirt. Very chic. And I witnessed for the first time the drinking habits of the English. The way they descend from cold priggishness to semi-conscious *porquería* – uh, piggery. I learned to ward off the attentions of these drooling idiots, and began to wonder at a basic flaw in British manhood that rendered any kind of meaningful conversation quite beyond their repertoire without huge quantities of alcohol.'

'So, what did you like about London?'

'Oh, the sense of being where things were happening, like Barcelona, but more so. Barcelona has style and diversity, but London has breadth, scope, volume. I liked the sense of being in the middle of something so large, like a sprawling monster. I also liked taking walks on Hampstead Heath, and exploring alone, on foot, areas of London where I knew nobody, or nothing of the location. So I would take a tube to, say, Bethnal Green, and walk for two or three hours, until eventually I arrived at some place I had never heard of, find a bus stop or a tube station, and go home to Finsbury Park. I enjoyed the randomness of this kind of adventure. The anonymity.'

Parts of her monologue were in practically accentless English and sounded almost rehearsed. She was fluent, but sometimes seemed to be weighing up the effect of her words silently, her lips pursed, before uttering them. She carried on with her memories of London, talking in a matter-of-fact tone, while working her way through a serving of octopus. She looked up at me from time to time while chewing on the rubbery meat, or picking scraps from the wooden platter.

'It's funny,' she said, at one point. 'I had always dreamed of travelling alone in a desert. I remember having these nomadic dreams since early childhood. For instance, I would be in an empty landscape when a single feature would mark it out as definably mine: a woven bracelet in the sand, a cat stretched along the flowering branch of a solitary tree. An otherwise withered tree, with this one flowering branch, completely out of place in such a desert. But the desert was not always one of sand. On occasions it was a heath, or a marsh, under low-lying grey cloud.

Like in Britain. In a way, I suppose, I believed that in London, in places with names like Barking, Hoxton, Dalston, Stoke Newington, I had the same sense of walking through an impersonal landscape, the only unchanging feature being me, myself, walking, under grey skies. The knowledge of my two feet stepping out in front of me, directed towards no place special.'

The main dish of *suquet* was brought to the table in a simple china tureen, which the waiter set down between us. Big chunks of monkfish floated in a rich stock, strengthened with a picada of crushed hazelnuts laced with brandy. We applied ourselves to the meal in silence for a while. Then Nuria spoke again.

'This thing about your postcard. It's kind of weird,' (a favourite word of hers, it seemed) 'but I might as well tell you. When I first saw you in the gallery, looking at that painting, before you spoke to me – well, my first reaction was that I knew you. In fact I was about to greet you, but could not place where I knew you from. I've been searching my memory all day trying to figure out if I have met you before. This sense of recognising someone you happen to like the look of is supposed to be a common delusion, isn't it? But it isn't for me. It's very real, and very er, *particular*.' Here her enunciation conveyed the Spanish meaning of the word: personal, private. 'When you came up and spoke to me on the roof, I was almost, you know, relieved, as though at least one of us had the nerve to break through some ridiculous convention about who you do or do not speak with. I have never felt this certainty about a stranger before. I'm sure I shouldn't be telling you either – it's a very bad idea for, well, especially for women to disclose their intuitions at a first date.'

I grunted noncommittally. 'I don't know. Isn't that more to do with protecting ourselves against receiving wounds, of giving too much away?'

'Perhaps. Reserve certainly has its advantages. What I'm trying to say is that with you, the pretence at reserve seemed pointless, since I had this feeling that I was just picking up something I'd left off some time before. Does this sound ridiculous?'

I shrugged. 'I haven't thought about it. I suppose I singled you out as the person I was intended to meet because of all the people at the gallery you were the person I most wanted to meet.'

That bit at least was true.

Nuria looked at me steadily.

'Really? I find it hard to believe you haven't been thinking about this, this question of our having met before. It seems so strong to me.'

'I can't say I'd have expressed it quite like that. But yes, there was a familiarity about you. I think part of my trouble is that I don't really know what my first perceptions of people are any more. I'm sure I used to know. It's something that has just gone. But when I first meet someone now, my brain starts all the usual machinations, the acting out of roles. I lack that purity, that certainty of who I am, that says 'this is how you feel' – because fast on the trail of the first perception comes a second, and then a third, which all conspire to contradict each other. I don't know what I think half the time.'

'*Pobrecito*.' Poor thing. Half-mocking.

I realised immediately that I was giving her a dose of weary and vulnerable, a transparent but, for me, trusted seduction technique. I checked myself. It was obvious that Nuria did not require this kind of posturing on my part. A lot more was going on right now than I was capable of coming to grips with, and it was becoming obvious, too, that Nuria was smarter than me, certainly quicker at anticipating my reactions than I could hers, and more ready to express herself directly. Her eyes were like interrogatory antennae, seeking out clues, reading situations, not just those immediately in front of her, but always sweeping the peripheries to take in more; passers-by, conversations at a nearby table, the movements of the waiter. That single word, the Spanish diminutive *pobrecito*, seemed to *chide* me.

I felt duly reprimanded. She could, of course, have just let me continue, acting out the role of weary and vulnerable to my heart's content, but she had seen through it, recognised it for what it was (even in this moderated form) and decided to stifle it before it became established as a part of my ritual dance with her. She might even have felt insulted by me for adopting such a role, and she would have been justified if she had.

Just then a blast of music was carried on the wind, and hovered briefly around us, before being abruptly turned off – music for clarinet and orchestra by Mozart that seemed entirely out of place amid the frayed informality and bustle of Barceloneta on a Saturday night. It was an incongruous moment that cut in on the conversation, and on the pressure to perform which I had felt accumulating in me. The temptation to produce a role for Nuria dissipated rapidly with this translucent and uncomplicated music.

Nuria picked up on my changed expression.

'What is it?'

'Oh nothing. Just that you're probably right. I have a bad habit of laying things on a bit thick on a first date.'

'This isn't a first date,' she said coolly, contradicting herself. 'We're having dinner.' As though in response to the unexpected burst of Mozart, she changed the subject. 'What exactly did you study at university, or was it a conservatoire?'

'University. Composition and piano. I could never play piano very well, though. I just wanted to compose music that didn't sound like anybody else's. When I got there I realised that that was what everyone else wanted too. And that most likely we would all wind up writing theme tunes for television soaps, if we were lucky.'

'That wasn't enough to put you off, surely?'

'No. But I became distracted.' I was being evasive, not wishing to re-visit that period of my life. 'And then Greece and the bouzouki thing. In parts of Greece at the time there was a musical tradition that was still relatively uncorrupted. And I thought, if I'm going to compose music, I'll set about it in my own way, whether it pays or not. But that dream kind of slid away, and without the discipline of exercising it daily, of composing a certain amount of music as a matter of routine, I drifted into forgetting what it was I wanted. I ceased to aspire, I suppose. Became happy, if that's the word, which it isn't, to be a kind of pseudo-sophisticated delinquent. I never really found my feet.'

'Your putting yourself down in this way: is it a British Thing?'

'Or just another aspect of the chat-up technique? A Man Thing.'

'Okay then. A British Man Thing.'

'Perhaps. Except about the feet. I still haven't found them.'

I looked down, wondering whether I had meant what I had just said. This was often the case: not knowing whether I was saying things for effect or because I really believed them.

The waiter cleared the table and then returned with bowls of strawberries. The restaurant was full now, and people were milling casually around the streets looking for places which still had free tables. I watched the passing faces, and gave a start as I recognised the woman from the Miró Foundation that morning – the thin reader of Kierkegaard. She passed by without looking at us directly, but I could have sworn that she had caught my attention because she had been staring at us the moment that I looked up. The unmistakable sense of being observed. I touched Nuria's arm.

'That woman,' I said, indicating the figure as it passed along the promenade, 'she was in the Miró Foundation this morning. Sitting on a sofa by the *Woman in the Night*.'

Nuria followed my gaze.

'Coincidence?'

'Perhaps.'

In a city of two million, how often do you notice the same stranger twice in one day, in distant parts of town? I didn't pursue the topic with Nuria, but the possibility that we had been followed, were somehow under surveillance, struck me forcefully for the first time.

Nuria yawned and stretched again, lazily. I ordered coffee, and a brandy for myself, which Nuria declined. During the silence at the end of the meal, Nuria's complicity and grace were company enough.

It was she who eventually spoke. 'Well, are you going to show me where you live, or not?'

We paid the bill, and I followed Nuria out onto the street. There was a full moon rising above Tibidabo, and a breeze had begun to blow in from the sea.

As soon as I had closed the door of my apartment, Nuria turned to face me. She pushed me firmly back against the door and, encircling my neck in both her arms, pressed her body hard against me and we kissed. She felt tight and warm, a furnace of energy and resolve. With a dancer's ease, she lifted herself off the ground and into the cradle of my arms, the soft skin of her underthighs nestling on my upturned wrists, my hands supporting her buttocks. I stepped to one side and held her up against the white wall of the living-room and we kissed again, her tongue flickering over my lips, my teeth. She kissed my eyes and cheeks, and ran her hands through my hair. I lifted her closer and felt the compact weight of her body under my arms, smoothing her with the palms of my hands as she unbuttoned my shirt and fell to kissing my chest and nipples. She edged away from the wall and her hands continued downward, unbuttoning my jeans and urging me, with persistent tugs, to step out of them, and when I did so she slid to the ground, cupping me in her hands, squeezing and massaging. Kneeling, crouching, she pulled me down towards her, and I lifted her thin dress up over her head. She grabbed my shoulders and began kissing my mouth and face again, with a greater sense of urgency. As my hands learned the shape and pattern of her shoulders and back and breasts, her body seemed to shimmer with an unchecked exuberance. She shuddered and turned in response to the slightest movement of my fingers, which ran up and down her spine, into the little hollows of her collarbone, the recesses below her arms, the smoothness of her breasts and stomach. She pressed tighter against me and I breathed onto and into her skin, my tongue burrowing into the warm space between her thighs. Her hands tugged at my back, nails scraping me, drawing me upwards, pulling me closer, then enfolding and absorbing me inside of her; and now any sense of levity and play suddenly became replaced by something altogether darker, more desperate, needy. We moved, were joined together, in a universe I had barely approached before in the act of sex.

I saw her sprawled out in front of me in luminous points of light, as though shrouded in orange mist. I felt her body rise, her hips raised, trembling, and she was gasping in small white cries, as I too cried out, a hoarse bellow from the pit of my stomach; and then eased forward, into the soft fragrance of her breasts, her arms, her hair. Silently, we caressed each other, she running her fingers over my ears and neck, and I massaging her temples and gently stroking her eyelids as we lay still on the hard wooden floor.

After a while, I felt Nuria loosen herself from me and get up. I heard her moving in the bathroom. There was a blast of cool air from the open veranda, and I rummaged about the floor for my jeans. The living room was only partly illuminated by a lamp near the bookcase. I went through to the kitchen, filled a glass with cold white wine and lit a cigarette, grateful for a few moments' solitude to soak up the afterglow.

5. A freak show

Sunday morning. Early sun bursting through the blinds of my bedroom, and a bristling sea-wind. We had slept late, or rather, late for me. I looked over at Nuria, touched her face gently with my fingertips. Her lips brushed my hand, half-asleep. She turned over and settled again into the pillows. I got up and looked at her, lying face down and naked on the bed, her brown legs partly covered by a white sheet, which fell away over her thighs. I pulled the sheet over her body, went to the bathroom and showered. Standing a long while under the stream of warm water, I basked in blissful inebriation with memories of the night's foldings and unfoldings, broken by snatches of sleep. I washed with a coconut-scented soap and wrapped myself in a large blue towel, then dressed and returned to the bedroom. Nuria was still sleeping soundly. I decided to let her rest, and went down to the street to do some shopping.

Polyphony and a savage brightness on the street. I walked past the market and found a bar, ordered a coffee and a brandy, drinking the coffee first. I wanted to keep this feeling of dislocation with me, of being part of a fiction or a dream that had fallen about me like a purple cloak the night before. The brandy would help keep me there, I was sure. I could float for a while. But I knew I could not bear to float for long: the fly-boy hovering in some ethereal space kept banging his wings against the ribs of a steel cage. The drink was Fundador – heavy, dense and unsubtle. Fundamental. Hence, according to my private reasoning, its name. It was darker than many Spanish brandies, and with it, I hit the sea-bed fast. A large draught caused a minor explosion as the liquor hit the bloodstream. As if in direct response to the sexual alchemy of the night before, I was at once de-railed. I ignited a chain of projected details that would thwart any prospect of long-term happiness or even of a provisional contentment with Nuria. Like cinematic clips, my imagination provided scenes of seismic fights and fuck-ups. Of killing off this promise of abundance before it got too much to handle. All the familiar ecstatic strains surged upward, along with their constant counterpoint – despair and loneliness, dread and self-loathing. It was a pattern I knew well. I tried to shake it physically from me as I left the bar.

I bought the last two croissants from my local baker, and a newspaper and cigarettes from the corner kiosk. Unlocking the street door of my apartment building, I bounded upstairs, taking the steps three at a time, and passed a bewildered-looking Manu outside his door on the third floor. I called out a greeting, but was inside my own apartment before I caught a reply.

After busying myself in the kitchen, I returned to the bedroom, carrying a jug of coffee and the croissants. I arranged her breakfast on the bedside table. Nuria rose on her elbows, watching me sleepily. Sitting on the edge of the bed, I handed her a cup of coffee. She took a sip, then put the cup down. She took my face between the palms of her hands and planted a kiss on my lips.

'How are you this morning?' she asked quietly.

My moment of panic in the bar had passed.

'Sensational,' I replied.

I had agreed to go to a party held by some British and other expatriates, English teachers, self-proclaimed writers, artists and all-purpose time-wasters, in the Gothic quarter later that afternoon, a plan which my meeting with Nuria had caused me to forget. However, when I mentioned it, Nuria expressed an interest in coming along. For reasons bizarre to me, the expatriate British community within the city was a source of novelty and interest to her. For reasons equally unclear, I often went along to these functions, when invited, drawn like a dog to the smell of its own vomit.

The party was held in a large apartment among the maze of narrow streets that lie between the Plaça de Sant Just and Mercè. It was, of course, a full-blown calamity, in the manner of British expatriate calamities everywhere, with the partygoers, in the majority, too inflated with booze for much other than their usual brand of loud and vacuous chatter, inevitable complaints about the host country and its occupants (tempered by an affectation of protective indulgence) and a singular inability to regard themselves as anything other than a beneficial presence in an ungrateful world. Much of this last sentiment was seasoned with a painful and trendily anti-British remorse. They were, on the whole, peculiarly unaware that they were themselves, by their chosen profession as English teachers either actively perpetrating a variant of the same attitudes and assumptions of their forbears in the traditional colonial service, or else stooges, co-conspirators in the world takeover by Corporate America. Why not, I wondered, teach flower-arranging instead, or bunjee-jumping? But I too had taught English as a means of income, and was simply trying to assuage my sense of collusion for having done so.

One or two of the guests had the ill grace to wear sandals with white knee-socks, an aberration which I thought had been abolished along with Imperial Rule in India. They brayed like donkeys and swore loudly, lurched around the kitchen to be nearer the supply of alcohol, and became, by turns, affectionate, sentimental and belligerent with each other.

They had hired a street-dancer, technically a midget, to come and perform for their amusement. This dancing midget was named Antonio de la Palma, and the Brits pawed him, patronised him, plied him with drinks (which he didn't touch) and begged him repeatedly to dance some more. As a rule, Antonio de la Palma worked the streets for money. When there was a fiesta, he might make a little extra cash. Dancing at a private party was just another job for him. He needed to be sober to do his work. He appreciated an audience capable of regarding his work as a part of his cultural inheritance, rather than as a freak-show attraction. He was poor, but he had his dignity. This, of course, was something which the Brits, who had none, were entirely incapable of comprehending. They wanted to get drunk and fall about; they wanted to be entertained and they wanted a mascot. Antonio had been hired by Gordon, a crop-haired Mancunian – whose belligerent and misogynist exterior closeted a stricken gay in the full throes of denial – as a fortieth birthday present for Alastair, a tall, lumbering, public-school melancholic born into the Anglo-Scottish squirearchy. The birthday boy was delighted by his friend's generous and highly original gift. They stood together talking and laughing throughout the midget's performance, in love with the idea of exile but unable either to participate or to stand outside events.

I said nothing of this to Nuria, whose very presence coursed like a fresh breeze among all this degenerate dross. I felt secretly ashamed at bringing her. Perhaps, with my guilt and my zealous criticism of all around me, I was just like all these other people after all.

Antonio, meanwhile, danced and danced again, but once he had done enough, he bowed politely, collected his money (charging double the arranged price when he realised that he was performing for a bunch of drunken *guiris*, or foreigners) and left. Only at the door did he permit himself a scowling valediction which most of his audience would not, in any case, have understood.

Nuria and I sat and chatted with a young woman from Liverpool who went by the name of Susie Serendipity. Susie was a singer, and had recently formed a women's singing group by the name of *Serendepans*. They sang the whole range, from *a capella*, through jazz, to their own compositions, and were recording their first album. Blonde, energetic, attractive and articulate, she was the only other expatriate who was clearly embarrassed at the dubious patronage of Antonio de la Palma by the partygoers. I had known Susie for a couple of years, as she had, until recently, lived next door to two other acquaintances of mine: Igbar Zoff and Sean Hogg, who were sitting nearby, talking agitatedly over a bottle of single malt whisky. Igbar the human salad, so named for the variety of foodstuffs that could, on a normal day, be found adhering to different articles of his clothing. Claiming a White Russian ancestry from some lesser branch of Romanoff princelings, Igbar had been educated at the finest schools in England, Switzerland and the USA, and had been thrown out of all of them. He spoke with a pronounced and absurdly incongruous upper-class English accent, at odds with his astonishing dress-sense, which was made up of charity throwaways spattered randomly with globs of paint as well as the remnants of breakfast. Every meal was breakfast to Igbar, since he only ever ate when aroused from a deep sleep, usually brought about by his habitual inebriation. And yet Igbar possessed an idiosyncratic charm, which singled him out from others at the party. When caught at the right time, in that window between the first drink and cognitive meltdown, he could be a fund of obscure and esoteric information as well as an unstoppable raconteur.

Sean Hogg, a Europhile New Yorker, acted straight man to Igbar's Fool. He was a thin man in his early thirties, with an oval face, refined good looks that gave prominence to cheeks and nose, and rather bulbous, dark, enquiring eyes. Sean played flamenco guitar and had studied for a prolonged spell in Jerez. He had also published some quirky and depressingly accurate poetry, almost entirely bereft of adjectives, and occasional essays on contemporary art that appeared in unmarketable international journals. Apart from Susie, they were the only partygoers present I had any time for, though I recognised among the others Dickie White, a small-time crook and professional conman, for whom I held a certain fondness, and who claimed to be writing a novel set in the Gothic quarter. No one had seen any evidence of such a book, which Dickie White declared to be a ten-year project. Nor, in fact, did he ever appear to write anything at all, passing most of his time arranging 'deals' with the local criminal fraternity, ingesting category A drugs, and spending occasional vacations in the Modelo prison. Perhaps that was where he did his writing.

None of these friends were employable as teachers of English as a foreign language, even if they had aspired to such work. It might have been said that where Zoff was concerned, all languages were foreign, hence his histrionic struggle with the aristocratic English that he affected. His father, once a renowned art-dealer and arm-wrestler, had lost the family fortune through a disastrous gambling habit. But Igbar had learned enough about art and artists (dangled from Marc Chagall's knee as a child, he claimed; 'breakfasting' with Picasso in Antibes) to have developed his own untutored style of demented and nightmarish expressionism, which at least provided him with the occasional windfall. A full-scale exhibition was rather beyond his powers of concentrated forethought, and this was where Sean Hogg's entrepreneurial skills came in handy. True, the New Yorker had helped organise only two Barcelona shows of his friend's work in the past seven years, but when they occurred, they caused minor stirrings in the normally cynical and superior world of the Catalan artistic *cognoscenti*, and along with a show in London, and another in Bern, had pro- vided the pair with the occasional excuse to get thrown out of a better class of restaurant than they were used to. For as long as I had known them, Sean Hogg had been working on the New York Show that was finally going to bring about his friend's big break.

On seeing me, Igbar ambled over and slumped on the sofa between Susie Serendipity and myself. Nuria watched him in fascination. I expressed surprise at seeing him here.

'Not your kind of thing is it, Igbar?'

'Gate-crashed, Lucas old bean.'

Sean, also moving over to our company, elaborated.

'He can sniff out a bottle of single malt from half a mile.'

'Alastair's personal stash. Didn't hide it well enough. But I didn't come for the drink, far less the freak show. I simply felt deprived of the company of beautiful women. Living, as I do, with a hog.' Here he stared admiringly at Nuria, and then, as if in courtesy, glanced over at Susie, who rolled her eyes and sighed. As the less committed half of a longstanding gay item, Igbar insisted on maintaining an arch lecherousness in the company of women.

I introduced Nuria to Igbar and Sean, and added, to Igbar, 'Susie the serendipitous, you already know.'

'Charmed, I'm sure,' said Igbar, to nobody.

'There are many ways of putting fur on a cat,' said Sean Hogg, sitting cross-legged on the floor now, rolling a joint.

'Or a pelt on a pussy,' mused Igbar Zoff aloud.

Nuria blinked in simulated astonishment. 'What is it you do, Igbar. Is that your real name? Igbar? I mean, what is your, er, *function*?'

I could not tell whether Nuria was simply taunting him, or automatically accommodating to the strain of free association in Igbar's talk that either bemused or infuriated any audience that did not know him well, and many who did.

'My *function*?'

'Yes. I mean other than possessing such an improbable name. Presumably somebody has brought your *function* into question before now?'

Igbar Zoff considered this. He eyed Nuria lasciviously and smacked his lips, then wiped the remnants of something that had once been food from his drooping moustaches.

'Your request is most aptly countered by means of an anecdote, or allegory. Many years ago, probably before you were born, but who knows – you may have aged particularly well – perhaps on the very day that your own *function* was brought into question, as you emerged, no doubt as serene and beautiful as you now are from your mother's loins...'

'Christ,' moaned Sean Hogg, spilling tobacco from his half-rolled spliff. 'You are *such* an *ass*hole, Igbar.'

Igbar glared at his friend, before continuing.

'Many years ago I disembarked from a bus in a remote and impoverished village in central India. It must have been before the hippies did for India what the Russians did for Afghanistan, but that's beside the point. Well, not entirely beside the point.' He took a slug of his pilfered drink and fumbled in his pockets, finding a pack of the cheapest non-filter cigarettes that Spain provided. He lit one laboriously with a match, apparently having difficulty in judging the distance of the cigarette from his mouth. Blowing out a rank-smelling lungful of smoke, he added, 'Actually, it's probably all beside the point, just like the question,

71

but anyhow,' he continued, certain of his audience's attention, 'as I got off the bus in this middle of nowhere, humping an old rucksack; you know, I travelled light: a few sketch pads, pencils, pastels, a blanket.'

'No change of clothes,' said Sean.

'Dressed in the way one dressed in 1969: red or orange Turkish baggy pants, sandals, some kind of lurid floral shirt, shades. Beads, I'm horrified to say. Draped in beads like a sultan's bloody concubine. In the village square, just as I hoisted my rucksack onto my shoulders, I caught sight of this old man: long white hair and beard to match. Dressed in just a loincloth, you see, and, yes, beads. Well it took a moment, you realise. He'd never seen the likes of me before. This place, as I say, was way off the beaten track. He'd never seen the likes of me, and as for me, I'd never seen anything like him. A fucking fakir. There at the bus-stop in the middle of the middle of nowhere.'

Sean Hogg, meanwhile, had finished rolling his joint, and was lighting up.

'Well he looked at me, this fakir chappy, he looked at me long and straight, and I took off my shades and looked at him. We stood there for a long time in the square with all these people milling around, chickens, goats, stray dogs. And then he started laughing. He laughed so much I thought he was going to have a seizure. He laughed at me, and then I started too. I laughed until it hurt. And when I next looked up he'd gone. Vanished in the crowd.'

'So, yes,' he turned to Nuria again, wily now. 'Someone, at least, has called my function into question before today.'

Igbar shook his head when proffered the spliff by Sean, who passed it on to Susie.

'And you,' he asked, showing off his yellow teeth to Nuria, as he imitated her manner of questioning. 'What is *your*, er, *function*? Other than looking radiant, of course.'

'Me? I hang out on rooftops and eat raw fish. Cast spells. Fly on a broomstick. Embroider smoke. And rescue men in art galleries.'

'Meaning *him*, I take it. Llewellyn Lucas Morgan Whatsit.'

'Is that your name?' Nuria looked at me as though I had withheld some vital piece of information from her.

I shrugged. 'If he says so, it might be true.'

'Ha!' Igbar Zoff spluttered revoltingly, as though I had conceded him some minor triumph. 'She doesn't even know your bloody name!'

'Nor, it appears, do you,' I replied.

'Aw, shit, guys, a name's a name,' said Sean the peacemaker. 'What of it?'

'Well, buddy, you would say that, would you not? Old. Hogg.'

Igbar made it sound like a rare brand of Bourbon.

'Perhaps,' said Susie, 'perhaps your name is something you grow into. Though obviously not in my case, since mine's invented. Or earned. But your actual given name, and family name, maybe that is something that gradually folds you into it. You become the thing you're called.'

'Oh dear,' murmured Sean Hogg. 'That does for me.'

'Hash talk, old boy. Gal doesn't know what she's on about. Chin up. What's your real name, Susie? Robson, Dobson, Hobson?'

'Lawson.'

'Sorry, of course. Should have been Hobson,' asserted Igbar, merrily. 'Hobson's choice. Would have upheld your little theory.'

'Patronising git,' said Susie Serendipity.

'By which I mean,' continued Igbar, in pompous stride now, 'it would have explained your change of name. Hobson, offering no choice, to Serendipity, by which choices are made fortuitously and at random.'

'Ah, I get it,' said Nuria, catching onto this rapid exchange. '*Serendipismo.*'

'Precisely,' confirmed Igbar Zoff the Sage. 'How nice. Ser. End. Ee. Piz. Mo. The faculty of making valuable and fortunate discoveries by accident.'

'Where does this word come from?' asked Nuria, with what appeared to be genuine interest.

Igbar liked nothing more than to show off obscure articles of learning.

'A series of folktales from Sri Lanka, once called Ceylon, and before that Serendip. The story goes that there were three Princes of Serendip who went out into the world dressed as commoners in order to discover the ways of things, and they discovered, of course, that the world outside their palace walls was full of misery and hardship. There are many stories about these princes, probably added to by others from Persian sources. What they hold in common is that in the most dire and, er, forlorn circumstances, quite wonderful things sometimes turn up unexpectedly.'

We waited for Igbar as he refilled his glass, and lit up another *Tres Caravelas*, again singeing his facial hair in the process.

'One story concerns the princes and a merchant, whom they discovered weeping and cursing by the banks of a flooded river. He was dressed in fine clothes, and attended by servants, but nothing they could say or do seemed to placate him. The princes asked why he carried on in such a fashion, cursing the river and the gods, and he wailed that he had suffered a disaster of such great magnitude that he could barely bring himself to speak of it. Eventually they coaxed the story from him. It seemed that the merchant, who had been born and raised in this same place, had set out years before to seek his fortune, as is the case in folk tales of this ilk. He had encountered great success, travelling the world and making of himself a very wealthy man indeed. Now, he had returned to the place of his childhood in order to build a palace on the banks of the river he had played in as a boy. And for the first time in living memory the river had flooded its banks, carrying off his treasure chests, the fine works of art and tiles he had brought for adorning his mansion, leaving him with practically nothing.

'The Princes were not in the least alarmed. On the contrary, they told the merchant: "You have been granted a most wonderful blessing. If you find out the purpose behind your misfortune you will achieve even greater fortune than you had before." And with that – hardly the kind of message one wants to hear in times of such distress – they went on their way, leaving the merchant puzzling over their words.

'Some years later they were returning through the same country, when the Princes were met by a messenger, who told them that they must follow him to his master's palace, to enjoy the hospitality that he offered to passing travellers such as themselves. He led them to a mansion built high on a cliff that overlooked the river valley, and there they were greeted by the merchant, who, the last time they met, had been so miserable, and now was clearly enjoying a life of unparalleled prosperity. He invited them to dine with him, and then he told them his story.

'The last time they'd met, he said, had caused him to think a great deal. He had chosen the place by the river to build his house, he said, because, as a boy, he had spent such a happy time playing in the waters. But as the merchant looked around the valley he noticed a cliff, and realised that from there he would enjoy the most wonderful view, and decided to set up a temporary home, just a humble hovel, with his meagre remaining wealth, before discharging his servants and settling into the life of a hermit. But as his servants prepared the ground for his modest new home they came across a field full of precious stones and gems. The merchant was now even richer than before, and he built his palace and invited guests from all the places he had travelled in, to share his hospitality. He also invited travellers to rest there, and some were wealthy like himself, and brought him treasures for his palace, and others were poor and brought him only company and friendship. So, in time he grew to understand the nature of the gift he had been given by the river, which was that hospitality and friendship were worth more than all the finest jewels and treasures in the world.'

Here Igbar concluded his peculiarly mannered telling of the story, stubbing out his cigarette on a nearby plate. A young American, who had been talking with Susie when Nuria and I joined the party, leaned over the back of the sofa and commented, in the ensuing silence, 'Though I guess sharing hospitality and stuff is limited to those wealthy people with the good luck to have money in the first place.'

76

I tried to work this convoluted utterance out, then answered, 'On the contrary. It's usually the poorest people who are the most hospitable.'

Sean Hogg nodded his head in agreement.

'But that's not the point, you baboons,' wailed Zoff. 'The point is that out of any situation, whether apparently disastrous or not, can spring unforeseeable benefits.'

'Precisely,' said Susie suddenly, revealing that she too had researched her adopted name. 'I have another one. It tells of love, treachery and abandonment.'

'Bravo. That's the stuff,' Igbar gargled from the far end of his glass.

'The Emperor Beramo, I think that was the name, retained the three princes for a long time, convinced that they had extraordinary powers of divination. One day, after returning from one of their adventures, the princes discovered that the Emperor had been overtaken by catastrophe.'

'Catastrophe, catastrophe,' mumbled Hogg, in the manner of a Greek Chorus.

Susie cast him a warning glance.

'It transpired that during their absence, Beramo had fallen in love with a slave girl, who went by the name of Diliramma. One day this Diliramma did something to question her lordship's honour, and in public too, the uppity wench, and he, Beramo, had her tied up and dumped in a nearby forest. There are always forests in these stories, of course, and women always seem to find their way into them. Anyhow, be that as it may, the following day, Beramo, gutted with remorse, sent out a search party for his beloved slave girl but no trace of her was found. Not hide nor hair,' she added, pre-empting another inane choral interjection from either Zoff or Hogg.

77

'The Emperor Beramo, after the fashion of such men, became sick with guilt and sorrow. Inconsolable. The princes, needless to say, hatched a plan. They told the Emperor to build seven palaces in distinct parts of his realm, and to spend a week in each palace. The seven best storytellers from the seven greatest cities of the kingdom would be invited to tell the most compelling story that they knew.

'Obviously, what with the construction of the seven palaces and all that *that* involved, it was a while before the Emperor was ready to start his circuit of the country. The storytellers who came to him provided wonderful tales, and for the first six weeks Beramo listened with a growing interest: even his health began to improve. The therapy of storytelling started to do its work.

'The seventh story that he heard told of a ruler who spurns his lover and casts her out into the forest to live among the ferns and the wild beasts. She is found by a merchant, who takes good care of her, but all the while she is still in love with the man who cast her out. On questioning, the storyteller reveals that he in fact knows Diliramma, and that she is still loyal to Beramo in spite of his cruelty.

'The Emperor sends for Diliramma, they are reunited, and presumably, live happily ever after.'

'I should add,' said Susie, hurriedly, 'that I consider this story quite absurd, and, in fact, nothing to do with serendipity at all, more with the scheming of the wretched princes of Serendip.'

'That's the spirit,' said Igbar. 'But question the storyteller, not the story. If all stories are equally true, it's their telling and their interpretation that lends them any significance. We make of them what we will, like a reading of the I Ching, or the Tarot pack. The stories of the Princes of Serendip only reinforce our intuitions about the haphazard workings of the universe.'

The young American leaned further over the sofa's back, took a long drag of the circulating joint and said, 'Like, er, you never know what's around the corner, huh?'

Igbar Zoff snorted, and then answered wearily, 'Yes, old fruit; something like that.'

By ten o'clock, Nuria and I left the party, the clattering music, the increasingly befuddled guests. It was a warm evening. We returned to my apartment and my bed, the world outside diminishing into irrelevance, a mere abstraction compared to the immediate demands of sight and touch and sound between us.

The next day was Monday, and Nuria left early, in order to get changed for work at her own place. She stank, she said happily, like an old goat.

6. Like a detective story

In the two weeks that followed, Nuria and I spent every free moment with each other. We ate together, slept together, phoned each other when she was at work, and lived for the evenings and the nights. Sometimes we met at lunchtime in a small square near the Ramblas, where there was the gesture of some greenery, and a circular path on which were situated three or four benches. Although the square was relatively quiet, it contained the usual traffic of hustlers, bums and winos. At lunchtime however, some of these (those who were awake, and could still take solids) dispersed to eat at a nearby soup kitchen. Their places were sometimes taken by office workers and the occasional tourist, though the latter never stayed around for long once they realised that the low hedges and rockeries of the little park concealed the prostrate forms of slumbering streetlife: a pair of legs protruding from under an otherwise innocent-looking bush, or a hand outstretched, demanding the rental of the bench.

But one bench, our bench, was always miraculously unoccupied, over five or six visits. On the one occasion that a couple had been sitting there when we came into the square, they had upped and left by the time we reached it. This confirmed our shared belief that the bench had a negative effect on other people, and preferred us to sit on it.

One lunchtime I was already on the bench, having spent some time there reading over proofs in the morning sun with a bottle of cold beer. Nuria arrived, exuberant, flushed. She was wearing white jeans and trainers, a red cotton top. She moved my papers and sat astride me, straddling me, heels pulled tight into the small of my back. She kissed me deeply for what seemed like a very long time, then lifted her head, shaking the hair from her face. Her eyes were brimming with tears, and everything about her seemed to be encapsulated for a moment in those overflowing eyes: desire, incomprehension, and something akin to fear. She began to talk slowly, her voice uncertain.

'When I'm at work I know that I am going to meet you and yet it's only a few hours since I last saw you, touched your face. But I burn up inside with the thought of seeing you again, and by the time I step onto the street, walk down the Ramblas, I want to... I want to *drown* you. I want to *everything* you. It can't be *this* good, I keep telling myself. Something really shit has to happen. And why do I think that? I hate myself for thinking that. I feel like a monster too, as though I wanted to consume you; no, to drown you, like I said, or better still to drown with you. Drowning you and drowning with you and drowned by you....' She had spoken softly throughout, and then had run out of words.

I stroked her hair and smoothed her forehead, my thumbs gently massaging her temples. Everything that she had said I understood, and felt something similar. Yet we never talked about being incomplete without each other: that was just a silly myth, a trick of the psyche. Both of us were self-sufficient: but together we created a new and subtle alchemy. It showed in our talk and in the way we stood and walked and slept and breathed. She startled me, and my astonishment extended into our erotic life. I had discovered that she could come to the brink of orgasm by my tongue tip-tracing the contours of her ear, or by simply feeling the current of my breath between the soft of her thighs. Her physical effect on me was likewise cataclysmic, and yet she learned to hold me back, to restrain me, to help me take my time.

But it wasn't just in bed that things synchronised so well. Her knowledge about, and liking for, certain music and writers and artists mapped onto my own uncannily. And yet she could, and would, out-argue me on almost any subject. She was maddeningly concise about what she believed and what she didn't. She was bafflingly contradictory and argumentative at times. She loved good food, but denied that she could cook well, saying that she preferred me cooking for her. Once she phoned me from work, saying she wanted to eat a particular kind of fish that she had bought in the market early that morning, and proceeded to give me precise instructions for the complicated sauce by telephone as I wandered around the kitchen, handset clutched between cheek and shoulder, following her directives, chopping herbs, mixing and stirring.

She arrived just as the dish was ready to eat, as she had planned, clutching champagne and a surprise gift: a beautifully bound first edition of Lorca's *Romancero Gitano*.

Sometimes, when she spoke, I struggled to keep up with the stream of her thoughts, the constant backtracking and introspection, the complex self-reflection. And then there were the times that she retreated into a corner of herself that I did not know, and I learned early not to question, although, paradoxically, on occasions, questioning was just what she required, and she needed me to intuit when the one and when the other. And at other times, on the contrary, I almost felt as though I were insulting her with any assumptions I might be making about the way she was, or what she thought.

But here, in this emotional limbo, in a winos' park, with the sun burning down on our shoulders, I held her in my arms and I felt once again the welling tearfulness that had almost overtaken me the first time we made love, this sense of recognition, of precognition. How could we have arrived this far, this fast?

She leaned over and scooped up the beer that had been standing in the dwindling shadow to my left.

'It's not too cold,' I said.

'That's okay.' She took a long swig, wiped her mouth on the back of her hand, then brushed the remaining tears from her cheeks.

'It does me good to cry,' she said. 'I've needed to cry for at least twenty four hours now.'

She laughed, re-circled her arms around my neck and kissed my cheeks. She leaned her face closer to mine and whispered, 'I am wracked with lust.'

'Me too. Absofuckinglutely *wracked*.'

'But it's good to hold on, too.'

'To hold on too. To hold onto. Yes.' I kissed her in return, on the throat, the neck, towards the danger zone of the ears.

She pulled away. 'You'd better stop that. I might disgrace us.'

She took some more beer, swilled it around her mouth, then spat it out.

'True,' she said. 'Beer's getting warm. Let's go for a cold drink, or a coffee.'

We walked down a couple of streets and turned into the Ramblas. The Café de l'Opera was quiet and cool. Its *fin de siècle* décor and cavernous interior provided a welcome contrast from the glare of the early afternoon sunshine. The window seat was free for once, so we sat and ordered coffee. Outside everything was normal. Human statues, birds in cages, bemused tourists, the occasional piece of human wreckage stumbling past.

'There was once a girl, quite an ordinary girl,' Nuria started, staring at me, 'who woke up one morning to find she had grown another face on the back of her head.'

She hesitated while the waiter delivered our drinks.

'It was the face of a boy, or a man. The girl could see this other face by standing in front of the mirror and holding a second mirror behind her head, parting the hair with her free hand. The face behaved badly. It poked its tongue out at her, attempted to wolf-whistle, glugged its lips like a fish.'

She imitated the labial movements of a fish in water.

'The girl was horrified, of course. Overnight she had turned into a freak. For the first day, she refused to leave her room. She lived alone, so it didn't matter too much. At least the face didn't speak, though it sighed, and made chuckling sounds. In fact it chuckled at particular moments, and of course the girl realised that this other face was laughing at her thoughts. A few days went past, and sooner or later she was going to have to confront the world. She put on a headscarf. It was a sunny summer's day. She had made an appointment at her doctor's surgery for eleven o'clock, and she arrived as close to eleven as she could, to avoid having to spend time in the waiting room, in case her new, unwelcome face made some obscene sound. She was lucky. She barely had to wait two minutes before the receptionist called her name.

'The doctor was in his fifties, a real gentleman. She had known him since childhood. He was kindly and discreet. When she took off her scarf to show him the face, he parted the hair and then exclaimed quietly: "*Caramba!* I've never seen anything like this before. Does it hurt?" "No, not exactly," she replied, "if by hurt you mean actual physical pain. But it hurts my soul and makes me want to die. I don't want another face, certainly not this evil thing. Can you make it go away?"

'The doctor was sympathetic but not very helpful. "I'm sorry," he said, "but it looks as though you're going to have to live with this face. You never know, you might get used to it." The face had been on its best behaviour throughout the examination. But as she left the doctor's surgery and stepped onto the street, it sighed, made a sound like a fart, and then chuckled intermittently all the way to the supermarket, where the girl had intended to buy groceries. She didn't hang around. Once she saw the rows of food on the shelves, the bright advertisements for special offers, the customers chatting happily with the check-out staff, she realised that she no longer belonged to the same world as them. She went home, ran a bath and waited for the tub to fill. If she lay in the bathtub long enough the face might drown. And if that failed, she would simply stay at home until she starved to death. She wouldn't open the door to anyone.

'When the bath was full she got undressed and, naked, was unable to resist a quick look in the two mirrors. The face had been quiet for a while, but when she looked closely, she noticed that it bore a strong resemblance to her. This made her feel terrible. The face was smiling faintly, and then began to make its fish-face, with big eyes and a glug-glug-glugging. It knew what she was thinking. It knew everything that she knew. She stepped into the bath, lying full-length. She lay there like a Bonnard nude. The sun went down. She didn't bother to add more hot water. She fell asleep.'

Nuria stopped, looked out of the window for a moment, then drained the last of her coffee.

'And?' I asked.

'And nothing. I don't know the rest. Some stories just end, you know, without explanation.' Then she added, very softly, 'You, of all people, should know that.'

She took one of my hands in both of hers and leaned over to kiss me.

'I have to go,' she said. 'See you later. *Adéu.*'

On the Friday of our second week together I took the afternoon off work and went to see my friend Eugenia. We stood on the veranda of her flat drinking an infusion of mint tea and I told her what had happened since our chance encounter in the sauna; about the meeting with Nuria, and our sudden and intense romance. She listened attentively.

'It's like a detective story,' she said. 'But in fact it contains only one element of mystery. The rest of it is simply boy meets girl. What you are trying to do is link the mysterious element with the non-mysterious element in order to make your meeting with this girl appear utterly synchronistic, a meaningful coincidence. Or somehow pre-ordained. Which of course it might be. But not necessarily in the way you think it is.'

Leaning on the cast-iron railing of her veranda, beside a large pot from which sprouted a prolific and exuberant specimen of plant-life, Eugenia adjusted her steel-rimmed glasses and continued staring down into the street, three storeys below.

'You are certain you did not post this card to yourself?' she asked, an apparently serious question. 'Perhaps to remind yourself of something which you have now forgotten? You can be a very silly boy.'

I was accustomed to Eugenia's condescending epithets, and considered her suggestion without taking offence. It was not as fantastic as it sounded. The consumption of drugs and drink had, in the past, as Eugenia knew, propelled me to actions for which I afterwards held no rational explanation. And then there was the issue of the green ink. The message on the postcard had been written in green – the same green I always used in my fountain pen. The notion of posting messages to myself for unfathomable reasons appealed to me. Perhaps I was slowly turning into someone else. I played along with her idea.

'I think I would have remembered by now,' I answered. 'And I'm not as devious as all that. After all, why would I *post* it to myself? Why not leave the message out on the kitchen table?'

'Because, let's say, you had already left the apartment and couldn't be bothered to go back in. Or you couldn't find your key. You had already written the card, and were holding it in your hand. So you slid it under the door.'

'No, that's ridiculous. Besides, this was written in a tidy, measured hand. Unlike mine.'

'You wrote it in an exceptional moment of lucidity. The *lux divina* passed into your fingers.'

She was playing games now. Again, I didn't mind: it was part of her conversational repertoire to improvise along provocative lines.

'Pure speculation. My mind doesn't work like that.'

'No? How would you know how your so-called mind works? You should have someone video you sometime. Perhaps I'll do it myself, out of love and compassion, of course. You'd receive an education about your "mind" then.'

'Love and compassion. I'll remind you. Thanks.'

'*De nada.*'

Eugenia probably understood me better than anyone I knew, family members included. It was, in part, my friendship with her that had led me to Catalunya in the first instance, and I had spent a week at her apartment when I first arrived in Barcelona. While she had been a source of sustained friendship and support to me, demonstrating a kindly tolerance – love and compassion – for some of my excesses, where others might have lost patience, the details of her own life often seemed obscured by acts of wilful mystification. She was a lesbian, and had been in several relationships with women whom I had met only briefly, and who were rarely, if ever, to be seen in her apartment. Not that she was recalcitrant about her sexuality: she discussed aspects of her past quite openly, but simply avoided talking about her present affairs. She was wary of explicit self-disclosure. She had lovers, but liked to live alone.

In many ways she was typical of a sophisticated *barcelonesa*, but having grown up in the Franco years had seen a lot of changes in the city of her birth. Barcelona was a world capital for human marginalia, a sanctuary for transsexuals, cross-dressers, fetishists and sadomasochists. It was now openly what it always had been beneath the suave exterior: a centre for all the things that Franco had most detested: Catalans (of course), anarchists and queers. But the abiding attraction of Barcelona lies in its relentless powers of reinvention, a ruthless creativity that rubs off on people after the briefest visit. It was no accident that Picasso, who endlessly reinvented himself through his work, began his metamorphoses here. Moreover Barcelona is a port, and if a city is a sedentary place fixed in a specific geography, then a port is always less so, due to the constant flux and interaction that seafarers and rough trade bring with them. A port might be regarded as a city infiltrated by nomads; sailors and immigrants foremost among them. In this respect, we lived in the most nomadic of European cities, and Eugenia was herself a nomad, taking off for long solitary walks in the Pyrenees, travelling for months in the Andes, the Himalayas, the Australian outback. Big mountains and wide open spaces. And whenever it was feasible, she travelled alone.

Eugenia's sculptures and drawings described semi-abstract narratives of shadowy men and women attempting to avoid the impact of imminent catastrophe, and yet incapable of movement, of unfreezing themselves from the context in which they had momentarily been detained. A favourite ink drawing of mine displayed two ambiguous figures, one most definitely a man, the other an androgynous human with a dog's head, stranded on top of a Corinthian column; caught, like cartoon characters, in a freeze-framed microsecond of flight from a monstrous fire-breathing dragon, itself immobilized on the summit of a high pillar. The canine ears, pinned back against the imaginary wind, added to the helplessness of their attempted flight. Those ears seemed to suggest that however fast you might run, escape from the dragon was ultimately impossible. Her sculptures too captured figures in strained postures, turning, as though avoiding too bright a light, too direct a gaze. They almost all were exhibited as unfinished. Everything was only ever a work in progress. But she was happy to let them go, and people paid large sums of money for them. Other than in her work, however, and even there only obliquely, Eugenia's demons, or dragons, were not for public consumption.

From Eugenia's third floor veranda we enjoyed a superb panorama of street-life through the main thoroughfare of Gràcia. As we stood there staring down, two traffic police were in the process of guiding the driver of a breakdown truck in his effort to remove an illegally parked car from the street. The breakdown truck was equipped with a crane. One of the traffic cops was attaching the crane's iron hook under the front bumper of the car; a new, silver BMW. The cops were joking with the driver of the breakdown truck, who leaned out of the window of his cab, reversing carefully towards the BMW. At this point an agitated man appeared from a neighbouring building, and, waving his arms and shouting, walked rapidly towards the three officials. He was balding, red-faced, expensively-suited, and extremely indignant. The cops acknowledged him warily as he approached. He started shouting at them when still twenty paces away. The police, their body language informed us, had been through this a thousand times before, having to confront an angry car-owner at the precise moment that they wished to tow the car away. It was, for them, part of the routine. Once the wheels of a top-heavy civic bureaucracy had begun to roll, the police having summoned the breakdown truck, it was, (we could discern) too late, just too late. The owner of the BMW would have to accompany the police and breakdown car, or take a taxi if he so wished, follow them to the pound, pay his fine, collect his receipt, and only then might he retrieve his car. The car-owner's response was audible, scatalogical and explicit. He remonstrated violently, even producing a wad of money from his wallet and waving it in the face of the officers. But no: it seemed that the paperwork would have to be done in the correct place. The notice of *denúncia* had already been written out. The car's removal was an implacable fact in the merciless rationale of the law. The procedure would have to be followed.

One of the cops signalled to the driver of the breakdown truck, and it pulled away, towing the silver car at a 30-degree angle. The car looked humiliated by its denunciation, tilted at that angle, rolling along on its back wheels. Its owner stared after it in a state of helpless wrath, delivered a final volley of imprecation skyward, and then stepped resignedly into the vacant back seat of the police car. They drove off.

The cackling of a group of gulls in dispute on the facing rooftop brought the vignette to a close. I followed Eugenia back inside, where she stood cleaning her spectacles with a handkerchief. I knew I had something to say, but did not know where to start. It concerned making a new beginning, the sensation that something remarkably good was being allowed to unfold in my life, and that I had a chance to ride with it, to follow a new path with Nuria, a path free of repetition from the dead-ends and fruitless affairs of my life to date.

But I never brought myself to say it.

7. The man in the green suit

I decided to walk home from Eugenia's apartment
rather than take the metro. It was early evening and
the shops were beginning to open in the broad streets
of the Eixample after the siesta break. I skirted the
Plaça de Catalunya and headed down Laietana. As I
crossed the road I noticed a distinguished-looking
man in a pale green suit who was staring at me from
across the way. He had close-cropped white hair,
and an eager, tanned face. I recognised him as the
feeder of gulls from the first evening I had spent with
Nuria in Barceloneta. His eyes were fixed on me.
Unsettled, I walked on. Halfway down the next block
I could still feel his eyes burning into my back, and
I paused deliberately to look in a bookshop window.
Then, turning into an adjacent tobacconist's, I scanned
the street, but could not see the man in the green
suit.

When I came out of the shop, I was confronted by an incongruous sight. A herd of around thirty cows was being ushered down Laietana, a wide and usually congested street. The cows ambled by, swishing their tails against the noise of traffic and the fly-like distraction of blaring horns, their heavy bells clunking in bizarre counterpoint. A pair of rugged, confident farmers guided them with long crooks, steering them down the street in the direction of the sea, presumably in some kind of demonstration against, who knows, the price of milk? I needed to cross again, just as they were passing. As I waited there, I realised the green-suited gentleman was standing at my left shoulder. He spoke to me, without hesitation, in precise Castilian.

'How extraordinary, that we should be here, in the city, with these cows.' He spoke as though he knew me well.

'Isn't it,' I replied, surprised, but also amused, by his forthright manner. 'Remarkable. Do you know why they are here?'

'They are demonstrating. Against their income. The European subsidies that their farmer receives.' And he added, with a smile, 'They hope to meet the President. Mr Pujol.'

'I see.'

'But that is not what I find so extraordinary,' the man continued. I noticed the almost painful intensity of his eyes, a bright blue-green, all the more startling alongside his green suit, which was cut from fine silk. 'What is incredible to me is that we should stand here, you and I, two individuals, to all intents and purposes with nothing in common: stand here, side by side, at this zebra crossing.'

I was nonplussed.

'Why so extraordinary?'

'You will see. You will see. Allow me. Do you speak English, by any chance?'

'Yes, I do.'

'Of course you do. Excellent, excellent.' And he opened a soft leather attaché case that he had been carrying under his arm, and produced a typed manuscript, neatly stapled. He handed it to me. On the title page was written, in bold type, the heading: ANIMAL HUSBANDRY AND THE URBAN MYSTIC: A TREATISE. There was no name, no acknowledged authorship, no address. In the bottom right-hand corner was some kind of insignia, stamped in red, depicting a boar.

'Thank you,' I said, switching to English. 'I like a good read. Is this your own work?'

'Indeed it is. Study it if you wish. We'll meet again, I'm sure. And a good evening to you.'

And he had left before I really had time to register that he had made a little bow to me, there in the street, a bow utterly in keeping with his dress and manner – the bow of a Japanese businessman addressing a colleague of marginally elevated status – but entirely strange in the crowded and stolidly democratic environment of Laietana under the mournful gaze of passing cattle.

When the road was clear I crossed into Avenida Francesc Cambó and began to make my way across Santa Caterina towards my house, but then decided to visit Enrique's bar and have a beer. The manuscript that the green man had given me was like a living entity in my hands: it demanded to be looked at. There were no customers in the bar. Enrique's Basque girlfriend, Ixía, served me. Ixía had a two-year-old daughter, who sat contentedly on the floor behind the bar, attempting to knock the top off a bottle of beer with a plastic hammer. I took a table by the window and opened the manuscript at random:

The care of animals for purposes of food is not intrinsically evil, although it is well-established that carnivorous beings occupy a lower level on the ladder of spiritual evolution. While cattle, sheep, goats, rabbits and chickens might be kept for the sale of their produce, it must be questioned whether it is ethically sound to do so. Persons seeking to attain a higher level of consciousness would refrain from eating any manner of meat, and, by extension, from encouraging others to do so. Therefore the rearing of these creatures, even for sale to others, must be considered detrimental to the life of the spirit. The urban mystic, of whom we speak, must treat all animal life with great respect, above all those animals which are eaten by our less enlightened brothers and sisters. Therefore, do not kill any animal, however lowly: your future life may depend on it.

Cats are an interesting case, because, like dogs, they are not reared for food, but unlike dogs, they serve little useful purpose as guards or as walking companions. Their function in the household in these days of efficient rodent control is open to question. It would seem that they provide something for their owners to stroke, to be comforted by, and to speak to. However, it is untrue that cats are diabolical. They simply unsettle people by the ease with which they snub affectionate advances, and inspire jealousy in the relaxed and libidinous lifestyles that they pursue amid the toiling masses of humanity. They should, if anything, be venerated for their independence of spirit and their spurning of human control. However, their insouciant carnivorousness must condemn them to rebirth at a consistently lower level of incarnation.

I flicked through the pages of the document. It rambled on in the same discursive vein, touching on topics such as veganism, respect for the body, care of the dead and the nurturing of what it referred to as a 'mystic sensibility':

Urban dwellers might consider themselves at a remove from the numinous, depleted of any mystic sensibility, which has always been associated in the collective consciousness with the countryside, especially with mountains and with waterways such as streams and pools. It is not surprising that we consider ourselves disinherited in some way, cheated of a long-lost birthright to commune with nature, and thus to replenish the spirit. But the urban dweller can replicate the life lived in nature by imagining the tall buildings that surround him to be mountains, the busy streets to be raging torrents, and the people walking by with their fixed somnambulant stares to be mere ghosts or sprites, the relics of human memory, deprived as they are of any nourishment that stems from a deep and daily communion with the grace of God.

Insouciant carnivorousness? Somnambulant stares? Sprites? The treatise might have been aimed at a certain kind of fashionably 'alternative' contemporary audience, but it was composed in the tone of an evangelical pamphlet from the nineteenth century. How could anyone be expected to take such stuff seriously at the turn of the twenty-first? And yet I was intrigued by the figure of the man in the green suit, if this was his work. He had singled me out in advance. If this had happened in isolation from the other events of the past few days, I would have been less interested. But our meeting had come about in a sequence of apparent coincidences, not least of which was the fact that I had seen him before, only two weeks earlier, and had remembered him, notably, I supposed, because of the colour of his suit. People impose significance on events when they happen in clusters that, occurring in isolation, they would not; but I was tempted to regard the man in the green suit as a participant in some conspiracy, and I was the target.

I put the manuscript down and asked for another beer. Outside, the street was getting busy. A pair of kids sat on the pavement opposite, sharing a joint. One of them looked about thirteen years old, small and elfin, and the other was a little older. They both wore trainers, blue jeans, tee shirts and lightweight bomber jackets. They acted as though this was all they ever did, hang out in the street, smoking dope. I tried to imagine the smaller one in school, sitting at a desk, being told about electrical power circuits or the history of Spain's serial civil wars. I drew a blank, unable to hold him in the frame. He must have noticed me staring, made a mock-astonished face, and then enacted a curt gesture of masturbation, followed by an obscene flicking of the tongue, and raised his eyebrows in question. I'd not been solicited by a rent boy in the *barrio* before. I looked away and shifted in my seat, turning towards Ixía, as if somehow to confirm (to the boy? – to her?) my heterosexual credentials. Ixía was clearing the froth from my beer with a knife.

'Those two outside,' I asked, 'are they on the game?'

She didn't raise her eyes from the task in hand.

'The small one, yes. The other keeps an eye out for him, as they say.'

'Christ.'

'I know. But it's the nature of things in this *barrio*. What do you expect?'

'Do you still want to be here when your little girl is older?'

She rolled her eyes at the stupidity of my question. 'Shit, no. If we can save enough money we're moving back to the Basque Country. Buy our own bar in a nice part of Bilbao. A nice area. Not like this.'

I nodded, and wondered what her notion of a nice area was.

'You rent this place then?'

'*Claro*, sure. So it's a job to save anything with the rent and so on. And you can't turn your back for a second.'

'Have one for yourself.'

'Thanks. I'll have a small one.'

She brought the beers over and sat down at my table. The toddler appeared from behind the bar, no longer holding the bottle, but wielding the plastic hammer like a tomahawk. She started across the room, arm raised, and then paused to give me a thorough perusal, dropping the hammer onto the floor.

Ixía took a sip of beer, leaving a thin line of froth on her upper lip. She crossed her legs, and settled back in her seat. She had attractive legs, and was dressed entirely in black: tight black sweater, short black skirt, fishnet tights. She wore purple nail varnish and her hair grew straight and thick to the shoulders. She had the sullen, bruised good looks of a city night-owl, and there was a hardness to her face, but there was also kindness in her mouth and her eyes. I offered her a cigarette.

'You live nearby, don't you?' She accepted a light.

'Yeah. Santa Caterina.'

'Why do you live there?'

'Caterina was the name of my first girlfriend.'

'Seriously.'

'I am being serious.'

'I've seen you about. Sometimes you wear pretty smart clothes. I bet you've got a good job, make a packet. Why live here?'

'I like living here. I like living on the top floor. Looking down on the world.'

'Had any trouble from the roof people?'

The roof people. This was an expression I had heard before, never knowing for sure whether such a group really existed. They were said to be a diverse gang of nocturnal vagrants, who lived among the precipitous rooftop masonry of the Gothic quarter. I had not met anyone who had actually seen them, and I suspected they represented some kind of collective paranoia, a category of grotesque outsiders said to dress in capes and hoods. Phantoms of the night.

'No. What do you know of them?'

'Only what I've heard, that they live like birds on the rooftops, that they slink into people's apartments at night and rob them, that they have been known to steal children too, on occasion.'

'They steal children?'

'So I've heard. And though they always bring the children back before sunrise, the child fails to recognise its parents for a week.'

'You believe that?'

'No. Of course not. But that's what they say.'

This facility of the Spanish language to obfuscate what was said, and by whom, sometimes demanded further enquiry.

'That's what *who* say?'

'I don't know. The old women, as always.'

She quickly changed the subject, as though she had been put on the spot.

'What do you do, by the way?'

'I work for a publisher's office. Dictionaries, encyclo-paedias. Fat books. Long words. Small print.'

'I see, a posh job. You're a yuppy.' *Yoopy.* She giggled, and flicked hair that didn't need flicking out of her eyes. The child too laughed briefly, a little machine-gun rattle, in imitation of her mother. She had edged nearer during our conversation, and was standing by Ixía's chair, hovering unsteadily between us.

'And it's hard to tell, but you're a foreigner, yuh?'

'Aren't we all?'

She smiled, but didn't rise to the bait.

'I've heard you speaking English here once before, with a friend. A man who wore many coats. A small man, but many coats, and a *gran borracho*.'

I guessed she was referring to the highly conspicuous Igbar Zoff.

'Yeah, I speak English.'

'You know what he said to me, your friend, in Spanish?'

I dreaded to think.

'*En la boca de un caballo cabe una persona*. What do you make of that? You know, we get plenty of drunks here. Big mouths, dirty tongues. Your friend though, he's just plain nuts. This means something in English?'

I shook my head. It was not an aphorism I knew, in either language. A person will fit in a horse's mouth.

Pure Igbar. Maybe some hallucinatory association with Chagall, though I was more than willing to concur with Ixía's diagnosis.

'You know what I learned? In school, that is.' Ixía grinned and pulled her chair a little closer, resting her elbows on the table. 'In English, wardrobes, tables and pianos have legs, just like people. The same word. You know, in Spanish we have different words for the legs of people, animals, things. In English they're all the same. That's very strange. Can you imagine a piano with legs, I mean a man's or a woman's legs? I just kept thinking of all this furniture walking around the place. I'm crazy too, huh?'

Outside, the two boys got up off the pavement and set off down the street, both walking with the studied idleness of the streetwise. I finished my beer and looked at my watch. I had arranged to meet Nuria at my place after she finished work. The toddler stared up at me as though expecting me to do something spectacular.

'She likes you,' said Ixía.

I smiled at the little girl, ruffled her curly brown hair. She laughed.

'I have to go. Nice talking to you.'

'Until later.' Ixía picked up the empty glasses and set them down on the counter, then turned to lift up her daughter, and disappeared through a bead curtain at the end of the bar.

8. We move about the rooftops

Back home, on the large communal roof terrace, Manu was in a state of sweaty agitation.

'*Funcionarios!*' He spat out the word contemptuously. No expletives were necessary, since for Manu, no other word in the Spanish language could rival it as an expression of useless privilege and narrow-minded obtuseness. He jerked himself from the canvas chair and walked over to the rabbit shed, peering from hutch to hutch and muttering endearments to each twitching nozzle. He turned back to me, cradling a huge grey beast in the crook of his arm, and flattening the rabbit's ears against the shiny fur of its back with a hairy hand.

'Look,' he said, his voice trembling. 'The grandfather of all the little bastards. He's old and a bit slow, but still mean. He'd have your finger off, given half a chance. I call him Attila.' Manu held the rabbit up close to my face, baring the skin away from the mouth to show me Attila's teeth.

'See this scar?'

He showed me a thin indentation along the edge of his thumb.

'That was this beauty. Seven years ago he did that. Can you imagine? He drew blood. I knew then I'd keep him as a breeder, and by God he's done his share of shagging.'

Attila's nose twitched horribly, as if the mention of blood had excited some submerged memory. His strong rear legs pushed against Manu's gut.

'Hey, easy!' Manu rearranged the rabbit in his arms, keeping a tight hold on the head.

'Look at that, will you!'

A pink welt had appeared on the skin of Manu's underarm, where the rabbit's claws had dug in. He displayed the arm to me.

The white wine from Córdoba was on the bench. I filled a tumbler and passed it to him, cigarette drooping from his lip, rabbit folded reluctantly under his arm. His vest was twisted up on one side, so the belly-flab sagged over the waistband of his jeans. The rabbit still looked malevolent, but had stopped struggling.

'You know what they are good for, *los funcionarios*?' Again, the word went spinning across the terrace at volume, incandescent with loathing. 'They are good for impaling through their arses on sharp sticks, and roasting over slow fires. No, wait. That's too good for them.'

I waited while Manu conjured an appropriately grisly end for the functionaries, but when nothing sufficiently vile presented itself to him, he resorted to scatology.

'*Mierda*. May they drown in their own shit.' And he drained his glass, shuffling back towards the shed, tossed Attila into his hutch and quickly slammed the wooden latch.

'So what's the story?' I asked.

Manu scratched his belly and looked at me, exasperated.

'I had a visit from the City's Directorate of Public Health, the ones who have nothing better to do than to make others' lives a misery. Somebody, no doubt that son-of-a-whore Ramos on the first floor or his wife, had made a complaint. They trooped up here, clutching their important papers, inspected all the rabbits, and then fucked off. Two weeks later, I get a letter telling me the rabbits are a danger to the public hygiene. How could they be a danger to anyone or anything? Apart from Attila, of course. So I have a deadline to dispose of them myself, otherwise the city will confiscate them and charge me for their destruction. Their destruction! What's the point of that?'

'Can't you sell them?'

'It's not worth it. I have thirty rabbits. I have them for the pot, or else to give away to friends, like you. I've given you a few rabbits over the past couple of years, no?' He had indeed, and the process of skinning them was still distressing to me even after half a dozen occasions, particularly the sight of their pathetic floppy ears after the pelt had been removed.

'Of course. I realise it isn't a business venture for you.'

'Precisely. Not a business. It's my hobby, raising rabbits. I like to have something happening up here on the roof. Something useful. Some breeding going on.

What could be more productive than having rabbits fornicating on your roof?'

'Nothing,' I agreed, 'could be more bountiful.'

And it was true. The roof garden was a paradise of amorous activity. It occurred to me that there might be some kind of atmospheric fallout from all this procreation. Apart from the rabbits, cats made their way across neighbouring rooftops for regular gang-bangs on this veranda. I had spent absorbing afternoons during the siesta hours watching the passionate antics of one particular pair of cats. It often made me feel horny just sitting there. And I had recently come to realise that my apartment, which adjoined the veranda, was a place which seemed to encourage, enhance and prolong sexual congress in some mysterious way. If the rabbits went, all this might change. I had never before thought about them in this light.

'This is serious,' I said out loud.

'Serious? Of course it's serious. *Coño*, it's doing my head in,' replied Manu.

He poured us both full glasses of wine and sat down on the other canvas chair.

Just then my doorbell rang. I had to go inside my apartment and lean over the living-room veranda in order to see who was there. It was Nuria, as I expected. I dropped her a key to the street door, and shouted that I would be on the roof patio. Within a few moments, she appeared at the top of the stairs. She was wearing jeans, a black silk shirt open at the neck, and the silver necklace. Nuria and Manu had not met before. I introduced them, and summarized, for Nuria's benefit, the rabbit situation and the cause of Manu's grief. Manu then shuffled off down to his own apartment. Nuria and I stayed out for a while, before moving to my place, and sitting on the smaller terrace there. Nuria rolled a joint, blowing smoke into the deepening blue towards the sea, laughing and chatting about her day.

Later that evening our clothing lay strewn alongside the route our bodies had taken from the terrace to the bedroom to the hard floor of the studio. We showered in cool water and retired to bed, simply too content and light-limbed to venture out and address the city night. There was a weightless quality to the air that night, and if we were to wander too far from the familiar sites of bed, bath and kitchen, chances are we would have drifted away like helium balloons across to Tibidabo.

Lying naked on our backs, the sheets kicked off in the heat of night, I made out patches of flaking paint on the ceiling, vertical patterns thrown by street-lamps against the window of my bedroom (barred by previous occupants against intruders from the terrace) and the gentle purring sounds that Nuria made, curled like a cat around a brace of pillows.

I must have been asleep when I heard the sound. A steady, persistent scratching, as though a stone were being rubbed softly on glass, followed by a prolonged hissing. I sat up at once, though at first I could not be sure how long the scratching had been inside my head, or if indeed the sound corresponded to something in the outer world, beyond the bedroom walls. Then the hissing sound was replaced by a muffled clunk, as though something heavy and metallic were being moved carefully on the tiles of my terrace.

I reached down for shorts and slid off the bed without a sound. Behind me, Nuria turned in her sleep, then settled. I crouched so as not to be seen through the window. There was a half-moon hanging low in the sky, and the street lamps cast a vague light upwards. I decided against losing time searching for a weapon. The sight of one might cause the intruder or intruders to react in kind. I couldn't remember whether I had locked the door leading to the veranda. Probably not. I rarely bothered unless I was going out. On all fours I edged around the corner of the bedroom into the studio and reached for the door handle. I pulled myself up and pushed the door open in one movement, jumping onto the veranda with a low guttural shout that was intended to convey extreme menace.

No one there. Not a shadow.

Only a sharp metallic smell that I could not at first identify.

I paced quickly along the tiles, then stepped on the low parapet overhanging the alleyway four floors below, and heaved myself onto the upper terrace, which slanted back behind my bedroom. This large terrace connected with the main communal rooftop patio where Manu kept his rabbits. I padded down the four steps connecting the terraces and circled the shed. The lock had been forced and the door was swinging open. I looked inside, but it was too dark to see anything. I fished in my pockets for a lighter. The flame cast a yellow, flickering light on the rabbits' upturned faces, their noses twitching, frightened. The fact that they were all awake indicated some recent commotion. One of the cages had been broken into and the stick which Manu used to wedge it shut lay snapped in two on the concrete floor. Stepping out of the shed again, I sensed that I was being watched. I was in half a mind to return to bed, but I wanted to find out where the thieves had gone, and, if possible, some clue as to where they had come from. Of course, they could have walked past the open door to the inner staircase and gone down to the street that way. But those stairs echoed, especially at night, and the door that led onto the street creaked loudly. I had heard nothing.

Staying close to the parapet, I crossed to the far side of the patio. There was a drop of a few feet to the roof of the adjacent building, where a flat area surrounded a central raised plinth of tiles, a jumble of chimney stacks and television aerials. Between the brickwork and the tiles I caught a movement, the flapping of cloth.

The wind from seaward reminded me that I hadn't brought a shirt. My skin was goosepimpled and I was shaking. I jumped quietly down onto the neighbouring flat roof, catching my breath on landing, then walked straight towards the chimney stack, and almost tripped over one of them: a slight adult, or a tall child, swathed in black cloth like a Ninja warrior. The face was mostly obscured, eyes staring through a slit in the black headscarf. We stared at each other, he (as I imagined) with nervous concern, I with a charged curiosity. The Ninja was sitting on the floor with his back to the brickwork of the chimney. Then I noticed two others, squatting in the deeper shadows. Nobody spoke. There were two dark sacks on the floor between them. One sack appeared to contain something conical or triangular in shape. The other sack wriggled. I had a strong sense of the absurd, standing half-naked among these three cloaked figures, with their bags of booty. I dug a pack of Camels out of my shorts.

'Smoke?' I offered, in Spanish, taking one myself, and lighting up. I took a deep draw, feeling oddly relaxed now, and in control. I was no longer shaking.

One of the raiders stepped forward and took two cigarettes, without a word. He had on a long coarse smock, wore his head in dreadlocks, tied back with a piece of string. He was muscular, alert. I saw the tattoo of a bird in flight on his neck, and black curved lines were patterned on his forehead and cheeks, in the manner of a Maori warrior. He had sharp, inquisitive eyes. His companion stepped forward, and took one of the cigarettes from him. She wore a roomy knee-length black dress covered with a sweatshirt of indeterminate colour, hanging loose at the shoulders. She had cropped hair, multiple piercings, an upturned nose and smouldering distrustful eyes that were thickly outlined with black Kohl. As we stood there, she began moving her body in rhythmic spasms, as though powered by a personal generator: jumping on the spot, stretching, and swinging her arms, before standing still again and lighting her cigarette from her companion's.

At this point the wriggling bag let out a series of rapid squeaks, *crescendo*. The Ninja slid a hand inside his gown and produced a short, strong stick. Reaching over, he loosened the string around the neck of the moving sack. A pair of ears poked through, and in a flash he had the rabbit out of the sack, grabbed it by the hind legs and, holding it vertical, delivered two sharp blows to the back of the neck. The rabbit's head slumped. Meanwhile, the Ninja's headscarf had come loose, revealing him to be a boy of twelve or thirteen. He rolled back the neck of the sack and placed the limp body alongside another dead rabbit.

'Died of fright, that one,' explained Ninja boy, to no one in particular, stroking the rabbit's fur.

I watched this, thinking of Manu, and the warning from the city council of his rabbits' imminent confiscation. Better, I thought, that they be eaten by this hungry-looking troupe, whoever they were, than removed by the loathed functionaries.

I sat down. They sat down.

I told them I lived in the top flat behind us, and had heard them on the roof. They looked at the floor and nodded. They knew, they said. They knew where I lived, where everyone lived, all over this part of the city. I took this as hyperbole, bravado, but let it go. I asked them if they lived nearby. The muscular young man simply gestured around, palms up, indicating a circle in the air. They lived hereabouts. I probed, gently. They were, he said, part of a larger group, scattered across the Gothic quarter, who lived on the roofs, in disused ventilation systems, in wooden and cardboard constructs on the tops of buildings. They moved about. They were Spaniards, Basques and Catalans; Algerians, Moroccans, Germans, French, Italians, a few British and Irish, a smattering of Latinos. Ric, the athlete, was a Catalan, and did most of the talking. The girl was Irish-Galician, Ninja boy was Moroccan. They spoke a Spanish argot with occasional English phrases and words interposed, terms from the youth cultures of the past half-century mixed in at random and resulting in a bizarre form of poetry. They moved across buildings in the dead of night. They flew, interjected the girl, without smiling. Yes, they flew, agreed Ninja boy, looking up at me.

Ric held the heavy-looking bag aloft.

'Know what this is?'

I confessed I didn't have a clue.

'The stuff of flight.'

He pulled a bulbous grappling hook out of the sack, displayed its sharp claws, then upturned the sack and a length of strong nylon rope tumbled out, falling loosely onto the ground like a coiled hose. A couple of cans of spray paint clanked out also. Ric scooped these up and dropped them back in the sack.

In this way, he explained, they launched themselves from the parapets across the narrow defiles of the barrio, flying and tumbling through the night like a troupe of renegade athlete-monks. Occasionally, of course, they needed to descend to ground level. For stealing vital provisions, for selling looted merchandise, for 'shopping' (buying drugs, mainly hash, but also amphetamines, LSD and Ecstasy). Sometimes simply to cross a wider highway such as Via Laietana. On these occasions they would shimmy down the ropes on poorly-lit or abandoned buildings, move in single file, with wide gaps between them, cross the deserted road at a run, before ascending the nearest appropriate building. No ropes were used for ascent, except for novices or those carrying a heavy load. There was a single criterion for becoming a roof person: the ability to scale, on demand, any building in the city without a rope. The grappling hooks were used only for crossing alleys. They were thrown with such delicacy and grace that they made little or no sound, Ric told me.

'We are artists. *Los artistas de la noche*. Artists of the night.'

I asked Ric why he was telling me all this.

'We know who you are. We've been told to answer your questions, to be helpful. And polite.'

'Who told you?'

'Sorry. Can't tell that.'

'Were you sent to visit me?'

'Not exactly. But if you were awake and followed us we were told not to avoid you.'

'Why were you sent?'

'You'll see.'

'Were you told to give that answer also?'

'Yes.'

'Have you visited my flat before?'

Ric hesitated.

'Don't tell him any more,' said the girl urgently, in English. 'It's not the time or place. Not yet.'

Not the time or place. The girl spoke with a soft Irish accent, Galway, Clare. Ric hissed at her, 'Let me answer the questions, Fionnula. It's my job.'

The girl called Fionnula shrugged, traced patterns on the floor with her foot.

'Well, have you?' I persisted.

'We've been this way before,' answered Ric.

'In a manner of speaking,' added Fionnula quietly, with a subversive glance at Ric.

'Did you deliver a postcard to my home?'

Fionnula interrupted again, with a caustic laugh. 'We're not after posting mail,' she said. 'We leave that to the postman. Why, have you been receiving dirty postcards, unsigned love letters, missives from the Jehovah's witnesses?' She used the Spanish term, *Testigos de Jehová*. She bounced up and down as she spoke, like some demonic toy with a faulty spring.

'Just an invite to an art gallery: a picture postcard,' I replied.

'Oh no, we don't do art galleries,' she said, with finality.

Since the talk had switched to English, Ric backed off, watching the two of us in turn. I suspected, from the intimate way the two of them moved in relation to one another, that they were lovers. Uncertain whether or not to believe the girl about the postcard, and

115

bewildered by her allusion to a more appropriate time and place, I wondered whether I would get anywhere with direct questioning. She was operating according to a distinct set of rules. Or no rules at all. I was tired and sensed they'd told me as much as they were prepared to tell.

'And the rabbits?' I asked.

'Oh the rabbits were incidental. We have to eat.' Ric smiled for the first time, showing off nice gold canines.

'Spoils of conquest,' sniggered Fionnula.

The Roof People. From my talk with Ixía earlier in the day, I had imagined a larger group, extras from a Pasolini movie, clustered round a fire on the top of some derelict property in the old city, turning rabbits on a spit. I had them wearing hats with earflaps and leather jerkins, blackened stumps of teeth or toothless gums, syphilitic noses, cauliflower ears, flattened foreheads, a self-parodying assembly of insane lepers. Nothing that would have prepared me for this rather beautiful trio.

'Why don't the cops stop you?' I asked. 'You must get hassle from them. Helicopters, roof patrols, stuff like that?'

'If there's a break-in we sometimes draw the heat,' replied Ric, whose English had evidently been acquired in North America. 'But we aren't that easy to track down. We move around a lot. And we don't make any noise, as a rule.'

'You woke me up.'

'We meant to. I scratched on your terrace with a stone,' said Fionnula.

Ric scowled at her.

'Why?'

'We wanted to lure you out. The thrill of the chase and all that.' She shrugged.

'You didn't hide very well.'

'We didn't try to.' Fionnula pretended to stifle a yawn. Like a speedfreak ballerina, she was all movement, jogging on the spot, miming kung-fu kicks in the air, and shrugging with every utterance she made. Her defining gesture was the vigorous shrug. The way her sweatshirt hung off her shoulders revealed the straps of her black dress, as if it had been shrugged out of place.

By contrast, Ric seemed cool, detached and serious. He had the air of a commando leader who has led his detachment on a successful night raid. He spoke slowly, in a measured way, avoided smiling. But he was likeable, and had definite style.

Ninja boy kept quiet, and remained seated. He looked like some kind of a mascot, but the way he played with a long-handled knife, spinning and catching it with an easy dexterity, suggested otherwise.

Then again, they were just kids, playing at being outlaws. They inhabited a world in which they were, by their very choice of habitat, looking down on things. The way that Fionnula and Ninja insisted that they 'flew'. A community of Peter Pans, in which the subversion of gravity was the starting point, alongside a rejection of everything to do with the earthbound workaday world. Ironic, I mused, that they based themselves in the old town, centred on those two bastions of provincial power: the Presidential and the Mayoral Palaces. The twin centres of administration. The roofline must have been alive with electric circuitry, CCTV, armed security men, heli-pads even, at least in the vicinity of Plaça Sant Jaume.

Ninja boy tapped my foot and made the gesture for a cigarette, looped thumb and forefinger pressed to his pursed lips, a request that managed to combine subservience with condescension. I handed one down to him and he nodded at me, a grown-up nod between equals, which contrasted strangely with the foot-tugging request.

'Doesn't say much, your friend,' I commented to Fionnula, working on some tacit notion of Celtic solidarity, which she had given me no reason to presume.

'He sings poetry in Berber,' she replied, simply.

Ninja looked up, taking it in.

'Does he have a name? Do you have a name?'

Ninja tut-tutted.

'He has a name, but none of us can pronounce it,' Ric said.

'*Bullanoghiratheriffalachtoyeridobarrandawuyasinstallazazaallaza*,' said Ninja boy.

'See what we mean?' added Fionnula, with a shrug.

Ric slipped into his rucksack, picking up the rope and grappling hook separately. Ninja shouldered the rabbit sack. Fionnula tried to scrounge a couple more cigarettes off me. I gave her the rest of the pack, which she slipped inside a leather pouch, worn around her neck. Then, without another word they left, Fionnula, turning, as they climbed onto the roof of the next building, to poke her tongue out and give me an impish thumbs-up.

As they moved away I saw a fourth figure, a slim girl with long curls, diminutive and unmoving in the pale dusk. She stood waiting on an adjacent rooftop. When Ric had cast his rope across the wider breach to this further building, a distance of some three or four metres, the girl knelt by the grappling iron as if to check its purchase on the brickwork. Meanwhile Ric had tied the loose end of the rope to a chimney stack. Fionnula and Ninja swung down below the rope and pulled themselves over the chasm, arms rotating at speed. Once they had reached the neighbouring rooftop, Ric untied the rope, coiled it into a ball, and tossed it to his waiting companions. He took several steps back, sprinted towards the edge, and jumped, tracing a slight arc against the backdrop of the dark hills behind the city. There was a split second in which he appeared to be suspended in mid-air, and then he landed on his feet, unwavering, on the far side.

A grey-pink waterstain was unrolling in the sky to the east as I watched the small group disappear into a labyrinth of TV aerials, satellite dishes and the piles of orphaned breeze-blocks that littered the nearby roofline: shrouded raiders disappearing into the last vestiges of night. Unseen navigators of the upper zones. *Zonards*. The undead returning to their precipitous daytime graveyard.

Once they were gone it was as if I had hallucinated them, as if I had conjured them from some long-forgotten dream territory of myths about lost children, of kids who run away to join the circus, or who are captured by the gypsies. What was it Ixía had said: that they steal children? Wasn't it they who were the stolen children? I remembered Nuria's gift to me of the *Romancero Gitano* by Lorca, and two lines from the first poem in the book, that speak of the moon lifting a child across the sky:

Por el cielo va la luna
Con un niño de la mano.

Shirtless in the nudging chill that precedes the dawn, I felt the wind keening on my skin. I vaulted back onto the roof of my own building, and trotted up to the top terrace. Climbing back down onto my private veranda, balancing for three or four paces on the parapet high above the street, brought about a rush of vertigo. I thought again of the precarious lifestyle of the roof people. I realised that I was envious of them, envious of their detachment and their appropriation of the unmapped summits of the city.

Then I saw their calling card. On the outer wall of the bedroom, the vertical line a metre long, the horizontal somewhat shorter, had been sprayed a perfect yellow cross.

9. Incident at Sitges

Nuria and I took breakfast on the terrace and I described to her my meeting with the roof people. I had returned to bed and slept deeply for three or four hours after our encounter. I showed her the yellow cross. She frowned and looked temporarily dismayed, then gathered herself, saying it was an insignia that she recognised. The heretics of the Middle Ages known as the Cathars had worn the yellow cross, though she did not remember whether it had been out of choice, or whether the mark had been imposed on them by the Catholic Inquisition which hunted them down. She knew little of their history, but said that in the 13th and early 14th centuries many Cathars had fled the south west of France, where the persecutions against them were taking place, and had found refuge in the villages of Catalunya. She said there were still places with historical connections to the Cathars in the region around Berga. That, she said, was as much as she knew. When I asked her why the Cathars had been branded as heretics she didn't seem to know, and suggested, with a touch of scepticism, that I look in the library after the weekend.

Nuria picked at fruit from a bowl, held in her lap on the hammock. Apricots, slices of melon. She sat cross-legged, wearing a short cotton print dress she had brought with her in a shoulder bag the night before. Her hair was wet from her shower and she had about her a feline, sulky beauty. We had planned a visit to the seaside today, and I asked her whether she would prefer us to take the train to one of the quieter beaches to the north, in the Ampurdan, or choose the lazier option of a half-hour ride to Sitges.

'You choose,' she said, distractedly brushing a fruit-fly away from her bowl.

I looked at her. She seemed to have retreated somewhere inaccessible.

'Is something the matter? Is there anything about these roof people that I should know? That you know? Or that yellow cross?'

She was quiet for a long time, as though struggling for an answer.

'Lucas,' she began, 'there's something I've been meaning to tell you, not this, not what happened last night....' She hesitated, and sighed. 'But it doesn't feel right just now. Can you understand that?'

I remembered very clearly Fionnula's words of the night before: not the time or place. I felt suspicious, but did not know of what precisely, or of whom.

'All right,' I answered. 'But one thing: do you know any reason why my wall should be singled out for the yellow cross? Is there something you know that I don't?'

'No,' she replied.

I stared at her. She held my gaze, and then looked away, over the rooftops.

'Well, in that case,' I said, unconvinced, but feeling it would be wise to change the subject, 'it's getting late to travel far. Let's go to Sitges.'

It was mid afternoon by the time we got there, and the resort was thronging with weekenders taking advantage of the warm weather. Although the beach was by no means empty, it was far from being the sweltering, crowded place it would become by July. The sea water was cold at first, but once our bodies became used to the temperature, it was like a tonic: the first swim of the year, a year in which I imagined taking many such trips with Nuria, perhaps exploring little-known bays in the north, and taking swims in the lakes and rivers of the Pyrenees. We spent a long time in the water, then lay in the sun for a couple of hours, reading. We spoke very little. My thoughts were still taken up with the events of the night before, and when pressed, Nuria admitted she had heard of the roof people, or rather, had heard rumours of their existence, but had always suspected they were just another weird projection of the ubiquitous Other. The boogy people, as she put it. She seemed to be making light of it, treating it as a topic that she wished would go away. She said she'd never known anyone who'd ever met them. She congratulated me, half-mockingly, on my encounter with them. She was in a strange mood.

In the early evening storm clouds started gathering to the north-west, accompanied by long rolls of thunder, and we packed up our things just as the first fat drops of rains arrived. Dressing hurriedly, we made our way across the promenade and into a nearby bar, where we ordered coffee and sat by the wall furthest from the door. Outside the rain pelted down.

As we sat at our table in silence, a woman approached the glass café-front, peering in. Her gaze seemed to linger on our table, on us. She was dressed in a long plastic rain-cape with the hood pulled up, dressed, unlike anybody else, as though she were prepared for wet weather. Having settled her gaze on Nuria and myself, she made for the door of the café and came straight toward us. She was of medium height, with unkempt black hair poking out from under her hood. She stood close by, staring at both of us in turn. It occurred to me that she might well be mentally unhinged and I felt myself becoming tense, ready to move suddenly. Rain streamed off her plastic coat, forming a little puddle by our table. She had a pronounced squint, a feature which contributed further to her wayward, demented appearance. Her dark eyes seemed to have difficulty in focussing, as though she were viewing us through a mist.

Nuria was clearly disturbed by this sudden apparition. She fidgeted with her coffee spoon and looked at the floor. The woman tapped Nuria, poking her shoulder with an extended finger, smiling at her as though in recognition. I winced, knowing how Nuria would hate being poked like a Serrano ham. She turned her face away, biting her lip. Then the woman spoke to her, in Spanish.

'I saw you on the beach. I watched you both. But you, especially. I was thinking, *what can I give them as a gift*? There are so many people here at times. I had not thought there were so many. Lying in the sun. So many. And yet some stand out. Their auras, I mean. I don't see very well, but I can judge an aura. This girl, I thought, she suffers. She doesn't know that I can see. But it is a gift with me, nothing special. Like some people can run fast and others hear the sounds that bats make. What could I give you that would help you, my dear, sweet creature. I don't have much. But you might like this.'

From the folds of her plastic cape she produced a shell the size of a small cat. It was grey and marble-streaked. I looked at Nuria, who seemed to be shrivelling up within her summer dress, visibly shrinking, and, I thought, shivering. She was looking blankly out of the window at the distant sea.

Then everything was abruptly transformed. The woman's disjointed and melodious babbling, which had lulled me into a quiet sense of the speaker's eccentric but essentially harmless nature, had stopped, and the silence that preceded her next utterance was one of dense, suffocating panic.

'It's a shell with an angry voice,' the stranger said, sharply, and as she turned aside, I saw that her whole bearing had changed. She was no longer in the role of quaintly offbeat; instead her face was a smouldering, violent mask. 'Here,' she said, laying the shell down on the table. 'It's yours. Take it.'

Nuria was already on her feet.

'Witch!' she screamed after the woman, who was now heading rapidly for the door. Nuria leaped out of her seat and followed, and I saw her running through the rain in pursuit. The shell lay on the table between our coffee cups. I picked it up and admired it. It was beautifully shaped, with spiral overlaid on spiral, of darker and lighter shades of grey.

I was still inspecting the shell, looking inside its oyster-smooth hollow part, when Nuria returned, short of breath. Her eyes were red and she looked dishevelled. She said simply, 'You can give me that,' and without any explanation she snatched the shell out of my hands and took it outside. I saw her through the glass shop-front as she raised the shell and then brought it down with both hands, hurling it to the concrete at her feet. It was like watching a piece of silent film. I could only imagine the sharp crack as the shell smashed apart. She left it lying in pieces on the sidewalk. Then she came back inside, took some money from her purse and left it on the table for our drinks, picked up her shoulder bag and said to me, 'Let's go.'

Heads had turned in the café during the exchange with the crazy woman, and the solitary waiter was observing things with great interest. He leaned on the bar near the till, and I turned to him, muttering a word of farewell. He nodded back at me.

I followed Nuria outside. She was standing under the canopy of the café, trying to light a damp cigarette. The rain had almost stopped. I should have known better, but was too intrigued by the sudden unfolding of events to hold myself in check. Feeling oafish, I asked, 'What was that all about?'

'Nothing,' she replied. '*Absolutamente nada*.'

'Who was that woman?'

'She was nobody. Nothing. She disappeared. She vanished. There are some people who are nobody. Didn't you know that?'

We walked back to the station without speaking. Sure, the strange woman had been intrusive, with her speculations about the state of Nuria's soul, but she was, after all, probably insane. Through her response to the stranger, though, I had glimpsed an unfamiliar

126

aspect of Nuria's character, and wanted to find out more. But I kept quiet because she evidently had chosen not to talk about certain things today. I felt, in a clumsy sort of way, that I should respect that; that it was expected of me.

When we got back to Barcelona, we were on our way to my place when Nuria said she wanted to sleep in her own flat, as she needed a change of clothes for the morning. She asked me to come with her and stay the night. So we walked south across the Ramblas, and had wandered into the Barrio Chino on the way to Poble Sec, where Nuria lived, when we passed a restaurant that she knew, behind the Boqueria market. She suggested that we eat there, as she had no food at home. Once we were seated in the back room, looking at the menu, Nuria's demeanour changed from one of hostile silence to sudden and silky contentment. She chatted with the waiter, whom she knew, ordered a good wine, and recommended items from the menu. She insisted that she was treating me tonight, and wanted to make up for her behaviour at Sitges. We sat in candle-light, and whatever reticence or sadness had been with her during the day was simply cast aside, lifting a shadow from her face. The room was quite dark, but the flickering light ignited the space between us with a subdued intimacy.

After our meal we set off towards Nuria's place, crossing Parallel, and into the quarter of Poble Sec. Her apartment was on the ground floor. I had visited her here briefly during the week, but had never stayed overnight. It was quite spacious and very clean. All the rooms were painted white, and were decorated with a Japanese minimalism. In the living space were some beautiful small prints and bamboo wall hangings. There was also a futon and a low table of very dark glass, surrounded by cushions. Nuria sprinkled essence of orange into an incense burner, and switched on a Miles Davis recording. I liked being in her home, and enjoyed the sight of her private things, of being surrounded by objects that she touched every day.

We sat drinking mint tea and smoked some exotic grass, then, at Nuria's suggestion, showered together. The warm spray splashed over our bodies, and after she had washed me thoroughly, I took the sea-sponge from her, lathered in a herbal gel, and did likewise, washing her shoulders, her neck, her chest, circling the brown buds of her nipples, sponging her in slow, sweeping cadences. A solo trumpet hovered for an eternity, tremulous and distant, above an underswell of deep strings, as the music followed on the wave of incense. I soaped the hollow space behind her knees, washed her slender feet and toes, a silver anklet nestling above the right foot.

That night we set about each other's bodies with a ravenous intensity. I remember thinking, weeks later, that it must be this way before a woman's lover leaves for war.

10. Dying with your eyes open

The door to the big wardrobe at the foot of Nuria's bed was wide open, and so was the connecting door with her living-room. Two men had manifested like characters encountered at the threshold between sleep and waking. I had a muddled memory of something damp and pungent being held against my nose and mouth. Almost simultaneously, I felt the prick of a needle in my lower arm, followed by the certainty that I could no longer feel or move my limbs.

The men were currently intent on wrapping me in a sheet, trussing me like a parcel. I tried to cry out, but could make no sound other than an inane muffled grunting. My mouth had been bound with tape, but worse, I seemed to have lost the capacity to vocalise at all. I was, in a double sense, struck dumb. It is a pathetic thing to be shouting, bellowing for all your worth, only to acknowledge that you are making no sound at all.

The sensation of being voiceless and limbless might have convinced me that I was still asleep and dreaming, were it not for the fact that one of my assailants had no nose, only the flattened segment of what might once have been a nose, and this detail impressed me as one which had no place in the wistfully erotic dream which I was still attempting to guide and control. He began wrapping carpet tape around my wrists. I fought against each new turn of events, trying to steer the dream back towards my own sleep's territory, but with each development, each unwanted detail, it drifted further beyond my grasp.

At this point I heard a woman's voice, and realised there was a third stranger in the room. Turning my head, which was an effort, I recognised (with no great surprise) the student of Kierkegaard from the Miró Foundation standing over Nuria, who was still lying on the bed beside me. The woman had just removed a hypodermic from Nuria's arm.

Then the second man approached. I was relieved, at first glance, to note that he was facially intact, although he had no neck, his head emerging like a boulder perched between massive shoulders. On closer inspection however, I saw that this giant had only one operational eye, the other nestling motionless in its socket, a shiny black glass orb. Its black brightness was startling, reflecting the light from the bedside lamp. He moved to the woman's side and lifted Nuria's head from the pillow. Nuria's eyes opened. She gazed towards me without seeming to recognise me. Then, almost immediately, I felt myself being raised off the ground and half-dragged, half-lifted out of the door, onto the street, and into the back of a large van. There was just enough light from a distant street-lamp to see that the van contained two long wooden boxes, or rather (and this was cause for consternation), not boxes but coffins. So this is what death is like, I thought: I must remember to do it with my eyes closed next time around.

My arms were strapped to my sides, and I was laid on my back inside one of the coffins. The rear doors of the van were closed. Shortly afterwards, they opened again and the two men carried Nuria into the other box. She lay limp in the arms of the men. Once we were both inside our coffins, a lid was placed over me and I heard a soft, definitive thud as it slid into place. I was now in total darkness.

Some holes had been drilled into the wooden lid of my coffin. I had no difficulty breathing, but it was not long before I felt the onset of claustrophobic panic, followed soon after by a pitiful despondency. I understood that I was entirely unable to act, and with that realisation of helplessness came a tremendous desire to sleep: more, to sink into oblivion. I drifted into a troubled and liminal zone of slumber, my bodily responses taken over by the movements of the van, its gear changes, acceleration and braking, an immeasurable distance covered in darkness.

I felt a growing sense of violation at being driven through the night towards an unknown destination. Dipping in and out of a confused sleep, constantly waking to find that things were precisely as before, feeling the steady throb of the van's diesel engine as it powered along the straight roads, and then its forceful chugging as we began to climb mountain roads which twisted into hairpins, straightening out for a while, only to repeat the process. Up and up. The movement of the van became a familiar extension of my own body, and its shifts of gears and little bursts of speed began to correspond to thoughts, or rather, became the extensions of thoughts. Every detail of ground covered succeeded in evoking a corresponding detail of my life, real or imagined, past or future. I had enough experience with narcotics to recognise this for what it was. I was, in junkie's parlance, gouching out, tracking the fragile borders of consciousness.

I suffered too, a dreadful longing for Nuria, in the coffin next to mine, and wanted desperately to hold her, to comfort her, (and, no doubt, to be comforted). But Nuria might as well have been on the other side of the planet. Trying to make loud sounds through the tape across my mouth was more frustrating than remaining silent. I could only manage a sort of pained lowing, which did no more than convey a vocal expression of the panic I felt.

I had no idea how long we had been travelling when we eventually came to a stop, having been conscious only for parts of the journey. The rear doors of the van opened and I felt my coffin being lifted out and carried smoothly across an even surface. There were voices, but I could not make out the words, muffled as they were by the wood of my box. I was carried down some steps, feet first, and my coffin was again laid down on a flat surface. There was more indistinct conversation, and then the cover of my coffin slid back.

The first thing I saw was an arched ceiling, in ancient stonework. My eyes strained to either side, but I could not lift my head to peer out of the confines of the box.

'Relax,' I heard a man's voice say. 'The drug will wear off shortly, and then you'll be able to move. We'll bring you something to eat and drink. You'll be hungry. But in the meantime, try and rest. There's no point in struggling. You aren't going anywhere.'

The voice was calm, beguiling and slightly husky.

Its owner was leaning over me. His face appeared oddly convex and out of focus. He was middle-aged, had weathered brown skin, with marked crows' feet to the sides of his eyes. He seemed to be in a state of controlled exhilaration. He had an easy but calculating smile, which he applied freely. His eyes were sharp and bright blue, his bronzed head clean shaven, as was his face. He was dressed in a black robe, and had begun to perform some kind of ritual over me, muttering words rapidly in what sounded like an obscure dialect of Catalan. He carried a small wooden bowl, which he dipped into with his fingers and dropped water over me.

Although still unable to lift my head to see out of the coffin, I heard him move to my right, and he began the same dull incantation over what I presumed to be Nuria's coffin. The ceremony did not last long. When the man had finished, a helper moved to my side and gave me an injection. I barely had time to register what was happening to me. I looked up and saw the first man's face once more, peering down. He was gazing at me with an expression that approached compassion.

As I drifted off to sleep, the image of the man's face began to contort, the lines and furrows deepening until his face resembled a freshly-ploughed field. Enormous red flowers, like giant poppies, sprouted energetically through the soil. I could hear the movement of earth, the crackling and shift of topsoil; could hear the sprouting of the green stems, the hum of insects in the air. I had a bug's-eye view of the giant poppies as they swayed against a sky of cornflower blue. I closed in on one flower, and saw, halfway up, a field mouse holding tight to the stem, swaying back and forth. The mouse seemed real enough, but displayed obvious cartoon characteristics, first by winking at me, then by calling out, in a predictably squeaky voice, 'Hey, mister, they're everywhere, you know. You better watch your stepping.'

When I next woke up the room had changed, and the coffin was gone. I was lying in a bed with clean white sheets. My hands and arms were no longer bound. I was dressed in a plain white nightshirt. This room too had bare stone walls and there was a single, small, barred window. On the bedside cabinet was a jug of water and a glass.

I sipped some water, moved myself slowly to the edge of the bed and attempted to stand. I had to hold onto the iron bedstead to balance myself, and was dizzy at first, but then made my way over to the window. A mountain landscape showed in the frame, two or three wind-lashed trees and a distant forest, falling behind the nearer peaks. The sun was a deep red, low in the sky, but I had no way of telling whether it was evening or morning. The landscape was washed in a strange light, so that the grey rocks of the nearby mountain appeared to be rose-tinged. Despite the dramatic beauty of the setting, there was, it seemed to me, a sense of desolation to the country: the bent-over trees in the foreground, the spruce pines of the distant forest, the encircling mountains.

A key turned in the door and the shaven-headed man, whom I thought of now as 'the priest', came into the room. He still wore the black robe and sandals. Alongside him came an extremely muscular attendant with cropped black hair, who was dressed in a leather waistcoat and brown cord trousers. The priest motioned to the attendant, who moved away to stand by the door. He himself took the spare chair, and sat facing me across the table.

'Please,' he began, in English, 'forgive the abrupt way in which you find yourself brought among us. My name is André Pontneuf.' He did not offer me his hand, fortunately. He smiled, though.

'I owe you an explanation, I know. But before we continue, let me assure you that I have brought you here, both yourself and your girlfriend, in your own best interests.'

I found this combination of gall and gentleness both unsettling and insulting, and could not summon up any immediate response to his words. It irritated me that he dressed like a monk. He appeared to me to be the very worst kind of pompous fraud.

'Where's Nuria?' I asked, weary before asking with the need to ask.

'Your companion is safe, nearby. She has eaten and she is resting. You may see her tomorrow.'

'I may see her?' I echoed, incredulously. 'You sack of slime. By what right do you tell me that I may or may not see Nuria?'

The priest looked at me with the expression of a man who had been called many things, none of which would test his composure. He had an urbane, moneyed feel about him, which I found hard to reconcile with his priestly outfit. I could easily picture him addressing the board of directors of a multinational corporation, rather than presiding over a remote commune of mutants and muscle-men in the Pyrenees, which was where I imagined we were situated.

'Please, not so hasty. All you need to know will become clear to you in due course.'

I restrained myself with a scowl. He continued. 'What we have up here is a little community of like-minded people. You do not yet know that you too belong with us, but rest assured, you do. In fact you and your friend are the last two, and in many ways, the crucial elements in our entourage. But I can't expect you to understand this, or even to concede it, at first. I am counting on your memory to do that for you.'

He gave particular deliberation to the word 'memory'. His English, although perfect, had been learned in the United States or Canada, and still had a marked French accent. I had the impression of a sophisticated aesthete with a dangerous sense of mission. I wanted to tell him that I resented being a part of his intrusive and offensive game, and to express my sense of outrage at these violations of my personal liberty, and of Nuria's, but there was little point in me reacting so predictably at this stage. I wanted, more than I was prepared to acknowledge, to find out why we had been brought here, and what lay in store for us, so I conserved my energy and decided to hear what he had to say. I wasn't going anywhere in any case, as he had pointed out; not with his henchman guarding the door, and others like him no doubt employed in a similar capacity throughout his 'community'.

'Where exactly are we?' I asked.

'We are in the mountains,' he answered, somewhat redundantly, with a nod towards the window. 'Let's not get bogged down in questions of time and location.'

'Why are you keeping me under guard, assuming you're a man of God? I couldn't help but notice your uniform. Or do you simply have an overdeveloped sense of dress code?'

Once again, I made a bad job of concealing my anger. I had to calm down. The priest certainly was not rising to this kind of provocation.

'As you are aware, the law prohibits kidnapping.

If you were to leave this place and go to the police, there would be a lot of unpleasantness. Not that I am without friends in the police, though it would be, to say the least, an inconvenience. But it is my belief that once you have listened to what I have to say, and weighed it against your own experience, and memory,' (that word again) 'you will make your own decision, and that decision will be not to leave us. If by some chance you do decide to leave, and no one yet has, you will be entirely free to do so. But by then, you will not, I am certain, consider reporting us to the authorities.'

'You seem very confident of that.'

'I have confidence in the truth, that is all.'

'The truth? Your truth?'

'Truth that has no affiliations to mere personality.' He now stared at me enigmatically, the guru-hypnotist's stare. He was quite good at this, I had to concede. His bright blue eyes fixed on mine, as though casting down a challenge which he did not doubt he would win.

'Can I get this straight?' I asked, pedantically. 'Once I have heard your story, I will be free to go? Both me and Nuria?'

'Precisely. We will, of course, be obliged to lock you in a windowless van for the trip back to Barcelona. But you will understand that, I'm sure.'

'But no more unrequested drugs?'

'No drugs. Last night was an unfortunate necessity.'

I sat back in my chair. I suddenly felt vacant, drained by the events of the past twenty-four hours. But I was also strangely alert. There was, I had to admit, something undeniably interesting about Pontneuf. The man exuded a forceful clarity. He reminded me of one of those early twentieth-century celebrity sages, in the tradition of Gurdjieff and Crowley, even down to the shaven head and the twinkling eyes. His was a pernicious presence, but also a compelling one. My immediate impression was of a paradoxical man; likeable and seductive on the one hand, evidently power-crazed and deluded on the other. I found myself intrigued at the same time as being repelled by him.

Pontneuf placed a loosely-bound folder on the table between us. The cover was untitled.

'I have had this drawn up,' he began, 'as an explanation of why you have been brought here. Similar documents were prepared for every member of our community, after the appropriate research was carried out. Your companion will be receiving one also. They are all of a kind. You will discover that they are concerned with events which took place over seven hundred years ago. Do not let this deceive you into believing that I have constructed some kind of fairy tale for the delectation of an audience hungry for cheap thrills. The events I have laid down are based on established historical fact, and endorsed by the statements of numerous subjects under proper hypnosis.'

I wondered in what sense he meant 'proper' hypnosis.

'My work has been going on for nearly two decades,' he continued, 'and only now do I feel it to be nearing completion. All I ask of you for now is to read, and to take your time.'

And with that, he left the room. The door was again locked behind him.

I picked up the folder and opened it. It was neatly bound with green thread and printed on quality handmade paper. On the title page was a name, nothing else. The name was RAYMOND GASC. I can only summarise the story that it told from memory, since the original has long since gone, but I have retained the gist and tone of it, if not all the details, and attempted to retain the mix of inventive speculation and historical detail that pervaded the account I read that night.

RAYMOND GASC

On a Spring evening in 1247, a shepherd named Raymond Gasc sat watching the horizon from his perch on a boulder. He was from the village of Mélissac on the northern slopes of the Pyrenees, in the region of France known as Languedoc. He watched the land with interest because smoke was drifting across the skyline above the neighbouring village of Caldes, a nucleus for followers of the Cathar faith. Soldiers had come from the north again, three years after the mass annihilation of Cathars at Montségur, and, following the instructions of the crusade, were intent on purging the region of the last vestiges of heresy.

Raymond was a Cathar, and he was, like his co-believers, deeply concerned about the events taking place in the area. Although the persecution of Cathars had been quite thorough in the centres of population such as Toulouse, Béziers and Carcassonne, the outlying regions towards the mountains had remained free to practise their beliefs, and villages like Mélissac had provided shelter for the small bands of *perfecti*, who acted as the spiritual guardians of the faith. For the past thirty years they had lived through turbulence, war and retribution. Now, it seemed, the rich and powerful barons of the north had decided to extend their power southwards, and the best way they could accomplish this end was by working alongside a scared but homogenous Catholic hierarchy.

Although Raymond was illiterate, he had a deep and perceptive understanding of many subjects. He could read these mountains, for example: he knew the weather, the sudden drops in temperature, the likelihood of every wind change. He understood the birds, the animals and the plants that lived there. He could make remedies from roots and flowers. He was reputed to have an ability to work beneficial magic, and had helped many who were sick. He was a popular man in the village, and a lively debater on theological matters, as were many of his fellow-villagers. Like all minorities, the Cathars had a heightened awareness of their own predicament in the wider world, and Raymond was no exception.

The religious movement to which Raymond and his fellow-villagers adhered held a dualistic vision of the world. God and the Devil had equal power in many respects. God originated all things in their pure sense, but the Devil had actually shaped the material forms that inhabit the world, including humanity. Since the ways of the flesh were all the work of the Devil, all creatures formed by coition were products of the Devil also, therefore humanity was burdened with an innate evil which could only be relieved by receiving the *consolamentum*, a form of ritual purification. Once one had received the consolamentum, however, one had to refrain from sexual intercourse, the eating of meat and all animal produce (because animals were the fruit of sexual congress), and follow a holy and rigorously ascetic path. Most ordinary believers never received the consolamentum, and were therefore excused from taking this path, at least until shortly before their death. It was left to the perfecti to lead the way through their immaculate lifestyles. They lived as wanderers and ascetics, often hiding out in the woods and in the higher reaches of the foothills. Villagers would provide for them (in so far as they required providing for, since their needs were few) and give them shelter if they passed through on their journeys. The journeying of the perfecti was a metaphor for the eternal journey of the soul in search of salvation. Many perfecti preferred not to stay for long in any resting place, both for their own safety, and for the security of the villagers who accommodated them. Their itinerant fellowship provided the backbone of the faith, and the frugality and humility of their lives acted as a touchstone against which ordinary believers might measure themselves.

The perfecti preached also, and the constant butt of their condemnation was the Catholic priesthood, with their bishops' palaces, the abbeys bursting with gold, the fat preachers with their concubines, the abuses of the poor and needy, and their constant denigration of the true teachings of the Christ. They singled out the selling of sacred charms and indulgences as a typical indication of the parlous state of the Catholic church. They questioned the notion of Christ's literal corporeality, and regarded the symbolism of the cross with extreme scepticism. As for the sale of pieces of the true cross, which Catholicism endorsed, they regarded it as a treachery of the very worst kind. Since they denied the possibility of a material manifestation of divinity, believing that they walked in the footsteps of an idealised and somewhat abstract Christ-figure, they insisted that only by living lives of purity, chastity and holiness, could they escape repeated incarnation into this world of the flesh (which was the fate of ordinary believers) and achieve everlasting salvation in the kingdom of the holy.

For those who were bound to repeated incarnation in the world of flesh, the kind of life-form that their spirits might next find themselves in depended to a large extent on the type of life they lived in the present. Thus a person might find himself in the shape of an ox, or a cat, or a horse, in a future life, or perhaps a lizard or a crow. It was thought that the spirit living in these animals might have some dim recall of a previous life, and this spirit would strive to attain human form in its next incarnation. But if, once in human form, the person lived the life of a sinner, then he was condemning himself to repeat the cycle of re-birth. Sometimes a previous existence might be recalled briefly by a person in a moment of realisation, as when one felt a familiarity, whether genial or antagonistic, towards a particular person or place. Thus a sensation of déjà vu was frequently explained as the memory of a previous life. There were many stories of perfecti recalling the most intricate details of previous lives.

Raymond set off down the mountainside. He walked with a relaxed but purposeful manner, in a way that seemed to correspond entirely with his natural surroundings. This organic bond between Raymond and nature was also reflected in his relationship with his large white sheepdog, who, with his strength of character and mildness of disposition constituted an exact four-legged replica of his master. Indeed, this relationship was just one example of Raymond's profound organic relationship with the animal world. He had few plans: those that he did have centred on his life in the village, and on his marriage to Clare, his childhood sweetheart. He had never thought in terms of fleeing his own village, of abandoning a life whose rightness and inevitability had become as natural to him as the progression of the seasons in the shepherd's year.

Although the blossoms indicated the onset of warmer weather, it became cold quickly in the evening in these uplands. Raymond knew that if the soldiers were pursuing heretics, it would not be long before they arrived at his village, and he must alert his friends, especially the perfecti, otherwise they would be taken away, interrogated, and forced to retract their faith. They would never do that, of course, and so they would be tortured, and probably burned at the stake in Carcassonne or Toulouse.

Why could the barons of the north and their bishops not let the ordinary people live in peace? It was enough that they took the rich farmlands, built their castles, and imposed their language and customs on the people of Languedoc, without dictating also what they were or were not to believe. And always, the priests came hard on the heels of the butchering soldiers. Raymond had heard stories of the terrible persecutions endured by the Cathars to the north and east of his home, of how they were rounded up in hundreds and slaughtered like geese. Those who survived the tortures and the massacres were forced to wear the mark of the yellow cross on their tunics or outer garments, making them more readily identifiable to the new forces of power and authority in the region. There were relatively few perfecti left in these parts now, and they were the last of the breed.

Raymond arrived at the outskirts of the village. Everything was peaceful. The scent of woodsmoke drifted on the cool evening air. The stone houses felt safe and solid, with their blazing hearths and warm animal smells. He went straight to the home of Pierre, his uncle, who immediately convened a village council.

It was decided that fourteen villagers would leave, in the company of the three perfecti who had sought refuge among them over the past two years and who acted as their unofficial priests. They included Bernard Rocher, the Inquisition's most targeted and sought-after Cathar leader, and also another man and a woman, who had been passing themselves off as a married couple, common practice among the hunted Cathar perfecti. The villagers elected to leave were the adult members of those families most closely associated with the Cathar faith over three generations. It was believed by the more conciliatory (or frightened) members of the community that by informing the Inquisition that all the Cathars had been driven out by the remaining villagers, clemency would be afforded them, and that they would be left in peace. It transpired that this was a mistaken view.

Raymond Gasc was one of those selected to leave, along with his wife Clare. In fact the full list of names of those who left the village that May night has been made available in the parsimonious script of one of the Inquisition's official transcribers in the scourge of Mélissac that followed. It is known exactly when they left and what they took with them. It is known that they were headed towards Castelldenau, well to the south of the Pyrenees, where there already existed small communities of Cathar refugees.

With a few basic provisions and homespun blankets, the fourteen credentes and three perfecti left the village at dawn on the 15th May, 1247. They travelled light, but carried bundles of warmer clothing for the cold nights on the higher slopes of the mountains. Raymond's dog accompanied them, the sole non-human refugee. He circled and backtracked, as though rounding up the straggling procession of now indigent adherents to the dualist faith, as they made their way along the winding paths into the upper reaches of the Pyrenees.

Straggling chains of migrants were not such a rare sight in those times. Victims of the crusades launched against the Cathars over the past forty years had left thousands dead and thousands more displaced and homeless. Often the members of these wandering bands would have been mutilated by the torturers of the Inquisition, their eyes gouged out, their noses and upper lips sliced off. Such were the punishments meted out by the executors of northern French and Papal order on those who would resist the sweep of a rigorous and barbaric religious and political orthodoxy.

By late afternoon the distant forests of the lowlands had receded into an unvarying green swathe, and the exiles' route was defined by more perilous tracks. They were now beyond the upper reaches of the summer pasturelands. Giant boulders were strewn across the mountainsides, lumps of grey rock halted in their downward path during some prehistoric landslide. It was an eroded and windswept landscape, snow-swept for nearly half the year, although at this season clumps of spring flowers sprouted prolifically across even the rockiest escarpments. This was the territory of eagle, wolf and mountain bear, of vertiginous ravines, and of icy streams and waterfalls. It was a route known to Raymond Gasc, at least, who ventured further afield than most other of the villagers, as well as to Rocher himself, who had spent a previous stay of exile in the Cathar settlements on the southern slopes of the Pyrenees. One other traveller, Bertrand Moyet, who had family in the village of Castelldenau, towards which they were heading, three days' march to the south of the highest peaks, would have been familiar with the route they were taking. The group intended staying there until it was safe for them to return to Mélissac, or else remain in exile for the rest of their lives.

*

We might presume, if we follow Pontneuf's story, that the Cathars continued until nightfall and set up camp by some upland spring before continuing their journey at first light the next day. Whether or not they reached the plateau of Puigcerdà, in the shadow of Mount Cadí, is not known. What is certain, from Pontneuf's account, is that they never arrived at their destination in Castelldenau. Nor did they ever return home. Somewhere along the route, between Mélissac and what is now Spain, they simply disappeared. The whole troupe of seventeen souls vanished out of time and out of history.

I read the document with a mix of emotions. I did not understand why I was being given it to read and whether the reading of this account was the sole reason for my abduction and incarceration in Pontneuf's mountain stronghold. I was still angry, but my anger was tempered by the sheer improbability of my situation. Far from being uninterested in the account of Raymond Gasc the Cathar shepherd, I found myself absorbed by it. I could even detect within the tale – but here the power of retrospective knowledge might be affecting my perceptions – a familiar ring, as though it were something I had been told many years before, but had forgotten.

Part Two

These men denied reality to all appearances and any
material manifestation of divinity.
Zoé Oldenbourg

11. The city ghostly in the heat of summer

It was a day of unrelenting sun. Outside Nuria's house I rang the bell for her ground-floor flat. The street door buzzed back at me and I pushed it open. As I walked into the hall, the door of her apartment opened and a woman emerged, pausing in the doorway. She looked set to go out, carrying a shoulder bag, with keys in her hand. She was in her early twenties, dark-skinned with long frizzy blonde-streaked hair, and wore a pale green dress with a red floral pattern. She seemed surprised to see me, as though expecting someone else.

'Oh,' she said, confirming this impression. She looked tense, and waited for me to speak.

'I'm sorry. I came to see Nuria Rasavall. I thought she lived here.'

She relaxed a little, and laughed nervously; a half-laugh.

'Nuria. That was the name of the girl who lived here before. But she moved out in June some time. Are you a friend of hers?'

'Yes.' I was utterly confused. 'I'm her boyfriend.'

I checked the address with her. There was no question of me having rung the wrong doorbell. Besides, this woman knew of Nuria. I decided to spin a story.

'Nuria phoned me from Paris to ask if I could pick up any mail. You see, I'm going to visit her there tomorrow and she thought it would be easier if I brought any letters with me.'

I smiled pleasantly, and tried to look harmless and sincere.

'Well, there isn't much, and most of it looks like junk mail. Hang on a minute.'

She turned to go back inside the flat. I desperately needed to see inside the flat, to confirm that this was not some elaborate hoax. But I couldn't just barge in. As I pondered this, the woman spoke again, just the friendly side of businesslike.

'Why don't you come in?'

I followed her.

The place had been completely re-decorated. Everything of Nuria's was gone. In the living room, the futon had been replaced by a sofa covered in a pale blue spread, and the low table of dark glass had likewise disappeared. I was unable to glance inside the bedroom, since the door was closed. I wanted to see whether the large wardrobe remained there.

In the living room, the woman handed me a small pile of letters. She was exraordinarily trustful of me, which again made me suspicious. Why should she so willingly allow me, a stranger, inside her flat, and hand over a previous tenant's mail, simply taking me on my word that I was who I claimed to be?

'Thanks,' I said. 'I'll make sure she gets them.'

She adjusted her shoulder-bag and tossed her hair out of her eyes with a self-conscious little nod. She smiled, only half as businesslike now.

'You've saved me the trouble of taking them along to the Post Office. You see, your Nuria didn't leave a forwarding address. I phoned the agency to find out, but they said she hadn't rented from them.'

'So you got the flat through an agency?'

'Yes.' She looked at me curiously, and I at once regretted asking. 'I came to look at the flat in the middle of May. Your friend said she'd be moving out at the beginning of June. She said she'd be travelling, but didn't mention France.'

'Of course. It's just that Nuria didn't actually rent the place through the agency. She rented direct from the owner. I forget the name now.'

I was freewheeling now, but the girl seemed relaxed.

'Pons. Something Pons. It was in the contract I signed.'

'You haven't met this Pons have you, by any chance?'

She tutted a negative.

'Is something the matter?' she asked, innocently. I was biting my lip.

Her naïvety was quite beguiling.

'No,' I replied.

Outside in the street there was the blaring of a car horn.

'Oh my God,' she said suddenly. 'Look, if you don't mind I'm going to have to ask you to leave. I was expecting somebody.'

'Sure. I'm sorry to have troubled you.'

151

'Oh no. No trouble. It's just my boyfriend. You see, he's the jealous type.'

She giggled, and with that comment, and that laugh, I immediately discounted her as being in any way connected with Pontneuf's crew. She was too obviously ordinary. I thanked her and left. I opened the door to the street just as a smooth young man in a sharp suit and shades reached for the buzzer. He looked at me suspiciously. I wished him a good afternoon and made for a café.

It was the same, slightly seedy café I had come to with Nuria the morning of our meeting at the Miró Foundation. I sat down at the same table under the plane tree and ordered a beer. It was that time of early evening in late summer when the city has begun to stir again after the narcolepsy of afternoon. The little square was overlooked on two sides by tall houses girded with ornate balconies. A playground was on the third side, backing onto an infant school, and on the fourth, behind the road, ran a low wall behind which lay a construction site in a permanent state of abandonment, where a beaten-up bulldozer had been nuzzling the same pile of sand for as long as I could remember. On the low wall this side of the site some-one had sprayed FUCK in large red letters.

I was caught up in increasingly confused and melancholic reflections when I heard a familiar, disbelieving and inebriate voice calling my name, and turned just in time to be grasped on the shoulder by the unsteady hand of Igbar Zoff. Standing alongside him was the equally well-lubricated but more vertical figure of Sean Hogg.

'Lucas, old pal,' beamed Igbar, evidently overjoyed at finding a potential companion with whom to continue his day's carousing. Sean looked around painfully, weighing up the advantages of this spot under the plane tree as opposed to the several other empty tables, before pulling out a seat and sitting down on my left. He grinned at me, as if recognizing me for the first time.

'Lucas,' he echoed. 'My old *fiend*.' He spat discreetly on the ground in the direction of the plane tree and offered me one of his cigarettes.

'Hullo,' I replied, happy, for the moment, to have had the process of morbid and wearisome reflection broken up by their arrival. They were a pair of amiable drunks as a rule, and never so amiable as on occasions when, such as now, they had cash to spare. It transpired that Igbar had, that very morning, sold a painting for a quarter of a million pesetas, and the two were wasting no time in divesting themselves of this unaccustomed wealth in the only way they knew.

'It was a Japanese collector chappy. Paid cash,' explained Igbar, who with his Balkan bandit's moustache presented a preposterous spectacle, dressed as he was, in jeans several sizes too large, which concertinaed over his laceless trainers. As always he wore a quantity of clothes that guaranteed his body temperature was kept at furnace heat. Now, on an afternoon in August, he wore a shirt, pullover, linen jacket and ragged tweed overcoat, this last displaying loose shreds of cotton where there had once been buttons. The absence of laces, buttons and other fasteners on all Igbar's clothes represented an aversion on his part to closure of any kind, as though Igbar was in dread of tying things up or keeping them shut away. As usual the zip of his fly was ajar, or, as he would claim, broken; fastened by a single coy safety-pin.

The painting that had been sold was one I knew.

It was a spacious canvas that showed an empty deck chair beside a multicoloured parasol on a beach. The sea was blue, the sky a cloudless lilac. Across the painting were stencilled, in red, the names of Igbar's favourite bars worldwide, from Cuernavaca to Singapore. The list provided a detailed geography of inebriation, the letters precise and clinical against the ludicrous beach iconography of the background. Ironically, due to his abundance of clothing, it was hard for me to imagine Igbar on a beach at all, ever. Or in a state of undress for that matter. He was a person persistently and irrevocably dressed, and always in too many and overlarge clothes.

'Where have you been all summer?' enquired Igbar. 'The Hogg and I have called your place a number of times, but no reply. You look pale, Lucas. Have you been over in blasted Blighty?'

'No,' I replied, then hesitated. What had happened to me over the previous ten weeks seemed too close, too suffocating, to recount right then. But Igbar's use of my name provided cover, of sorts. I replied with circumspection.

'Lucas has been locked up in a cell by a madman who heads a medieval religious sect in the high Pyrenees.'

'Blimey,' said Sean, surfacing from some private daydream and voicing the mild and un-American expletive in imitation of his friend. 'That's dramatic.'

Igbar burped. I signalled to the waiter, who came over to the table.

'What'll you two be having?'

'No, I insist,' said Igbar. 'On me today'. And to the waiter he said: 'A bottle of cava, three glasses. And olives. Lots of olives.'

The waiter withdrew, returning a minute later with the order.

'And what about your beautiful companion, the one you came to Alastair's party with?' Igbar continued. 'Was she locked up with you?'

'No. She had her own cell. We did briefly share accommodation, but could not agree on the décor.'

I was beginning to get into the swing of this.

Sean looked at me thoughtfully, as if weighing up the possibility that I might be telling the truth. For Sean, more than most of us, every proposition presented a range of interpretations and choices. The difference was that Sean tended to go through these options with a stupefying pedantry. Chronically and acutely indecisive, Sean appeared to regard life as a sequence of near-impossible quandaries from which escape was rarely possible, but from which temporary refuge might be sought through a self-paralyzing absorption in minutiae, interspersed with frequent and chaotic bouts of drug-taking and drunkenness.

'Tell us more,' pleaded Sean.

'Not now,' I replied. 'Another time. Lucas has Achilles' heel syndrome and is tired of this saga.'

'But you have been up in the Pyrenees?'

I nodded assent.

'And how were you taken in by this sect, these *medievalists*?' persisted Sean, sweeping aside my resistance to questioning and propping his head between his hands, elbows pivoted to the table.

'Okay then. Lucas was not exactly taken in. It was like this. One night, after a day on the beach at Sitges, during which they were confronted by a mad hag, Nuria and Lucas went back to her flat, which, incidentally is just around the corner from here. In the middle of the night a cyclopic giant and a leper jumped out of the wardrobe, drugged them, tied them up, and drove them in a windowless white van up to an abandoned village below Mount Cadí. In coffins.'

'Hang on,' demanded Igbar, his clear blue eyes fixed on me in confusion. 'This is a lot to take in. You said "in coffins". You were in coffins inside the van?'

'Yeah. Coffins with air-holes for breathing.'

'Aerosols?' Sean interrupted, incredulous. 'They don't help you breathe.'

'Air-holes, arsehole. Carry on,' said Igbar.

'Who drove? The man with one eye or the leper?' Sean wanted clarification.

'Lucas has no idea.'

'But,' Sean insisted, 'it makes one hell of a difference. A man with one eye in the middle of his forehead could not reasonably be expected to drive a van at night, even a white one. A leper, on the other hand, providing he held a current driving licence, and had fully adhering limbs, would be able to drive as well as you or I. Well, you, anyway. I don't drive.'

'Shut up you bloody fool. No one said the one-eyed man *did* drive the van. Nor that said eye was centrally located. Man's telling his life story. Important chapter from. Stop interrupting.'

'Okay okay. Keep your many shirts on.'

'Please. Continue.'

'Once the abductees were safely locked away in his mountain hideout the leader came to visit Lucas. His name was Pontneuf, an erudite and unscrupulous Frenchman.'

Sean hissed.

'He was dressed like a monk. He performed a ceremony of re-birth. Much jiggery-pokery and mumbo-jumbo. Incense, water, etcetera. Then, the introductions

156

over, he presented Lucas with a manuscript relating to a group of Cathars from the thirteenth century. His intentions were to recruit Lucas and Nuria into his loyal band of followers.'

It was Igbar who interrupted now.

'Cathars? The Albigensian heresy. Very trendy. Yellow cross merchants. All over the place at the far end of Els Cecs de Sant Cugat and also on a derelict building in Templers.'

I knew this first street, tucked away deep in the Old City. Its name means 'The Blind Men of Saint Cugat'. Templers was nearer the centre, not far from Sant Jaume Square.

'What?' I asked. 'You've seen them?'

'Sure, man. I live near there. A whole row of yellow crosses. I thought, well I didn't think then, but it struck me afterwards as a brilliant idea, that they might be starting a Cathar theme bar. Or night club. Forthcoming events: Saturday night, a burning at the stake. Bring an old flame.'

Igbar broke off into spasmodic chortling which in turn brought on a fit of asthmatic wheezing and coughing.

'You know about the Cathars?' I asked, when he had recovered.

'Quite a lot, actually.' Sometimes Igbar compounded his received pronunciation with the supercilious nuances of the public schoolboy that he had once been.

'I could lend you some books,' he resumed. 'But when I saw those yellow crosses I thought hullo hullo, a Cathar revivalist society? In Barcelona? You see it's been pretty big in the south west of France for quite a while now. Parallel with the renewed interest in all things Occitan. Troubadours, jongleurs, throwing live pigs from the battlements of Carcassonne. That sort of thing. But now, apparently, there is a more widespread revival in the religion itself, communes being set up near Castres, which claim to replicate the simple lifestyle of the original Cathars, with an emphasis on frugality and holiness, compounded with Sixties' fantasies about free love and the more contemporary concerns of feminism and vegetarianism. Apparently one or two wealthy Germans involved – they always get in on the act, eh? – buying up abandoned villages: and if this were not enough, rumours of links with far-right political organizations. Not popular at all with the locals, of course, many of whom see themselves as the direct descendants of the *real* Cathars. More wine?'

I knew Zoff well enough to realise that this brief outburst was probably reliably informed, and what he had said aroused my interest. It didn't quite tally with Pontneuf's unique vision of a Catharist revival centred on the work of a handful of recruits, and resonated more with any number of confused cultists, whose affiliations and followers were concerned with predictable notions of dropping out and adopting alternative lifestyles, whatever the guiding philosophy. But it was the idea that such communes were being set up by wealthy individuals, German or otherwise, that interested me. I presumed that such communities all differed from one another to some extent; that they each reflected the idiosyncratic beliefs of a single, more or less charismatic, leader. I began to wonder how many versions of 'Catharism' existed, and to what extent, if any, they reflected the actual beliefs and practices of their medieval antecedents. I needed to find out more, but already my conviction was growing that there was no such thing as a single identifiable Cathar faith, but rather, that a once-coherent religion had somehow become, centuries later, a melting pot of fashionable beliefs and millenarian fantasies, shaped by the dictates of whichever would-be guru had the cash to buy up a few hectares of land and start a 'movement'.

'So once you'd been initiated into this group, what then?' asked Sean. 'Did you have to bite the head off a living cockerel? Enjoy sexual congress with a Pyrenean mountain bear?'

Sean clearly knew nothing about the Cathars.

'No. Something far harder. Pontneuf asked Lucas to trust him. To believe in him.'

'Pontneuf. The bad wizard. And you say he'd locked up Nuria in a coffin? The scoundrel.'

'The necrophile.'

'The cad.'

I cleared my throat. 'I'm glad to see the story has touched you, boys. But sympathy does not carry Lucas far enough.'

'No,' confirmed Igbar. 'What you want is Revenge.'

'With a capital R,' added Sean.

'In my book, it already has one,' I said.

'You're writing a book?' asked Sean.

'But most of all you want the girl back,' said Igbar.

'Of course he does.'

'And that would constitute Revenge. On the New Bridge.'

'That's what you could call the book.'

'I don't think so.'

'Without the girl there can't be a happy ending.'

'Precisely.'

'And revenge is sweet.'

'Sweeter than a thousand kisses.'

'So when do we get to find out, Lucas? The ending.'

'Lucas is working on it.'

'We have plenty of time,' said Igbar.

'Never short of time,' echoed Sean.

So I told them what I could remember. And ejected myself from the story altogether.

12. Dualistic drop-outs and the eagle's dive

Pontneuf's account of the events that took place in 1247 was long, rambling, and melodramatic. Lucas could not know to what degree his story of the Cathar flight from Mélissac varied in detail from those given to other members of the community, since after reading his personal copy that day, he never saw it again.

After he had finished reading, Lucas fell asleep in his chair, slumped forward over the table. He was still sleeping, his head resting on the manuscript, when the door to his room was unlocked once more, and a young woman came in, carrying a tray of food. She greeted him pleasantly, placed the tray on the table and departed immediately, leaving the door ajar. It was a relief not to be locked in, but Lucas expected another visit from his chief captor. Sure enough, Pontneuf arrived shortly afterwards and led him out of the room, down a corridor, and outside into warm sunshine.

This time the priest was unattended by any strongmen. He led Lucas to a stone bench at the edge of the village square. They sat down.

'I have just left your friend Nuria,' Pontneuf began. 'She is in excellent spirits and you will see her shortly, after she has bathed and eaten. I need to talk with you first, however, and must apologize for keeping you waiting. No doubt you're impatient for the truth. But the truth can be hard to accept sometimes, wouldn't you say?'

Lucas chose not to respond to this inanity.

'Does the name Arthur Guirdham mean anything to you?'

Lucas shook his head in the negative.

'Guirdham was a psychiatrist who practised in the west of England. In the early 1960s he was consulted by a young woman who had, over a period of years, displayed curious symptoms of displacement and anxiety. She claimed to have suffered from terrible dreams, witnessing, among other things, a burning at the stake. Under hypnosis he found that his patient spoke a variety of Occitan, which, as you know, is the language of Languedoc. Guirdham's investigations led him to the belief that a link of some kind existed between a group of Cathars from thirteenth century Languedoc, one of whom, at least, had been reincarnated in a quiet and prosperous region of rural England. He found himself increasingly drawn to this patient's story, and her precise recollections of thirteenth-century life. He did some research, confirming not only the veracity of her story, but his own role within that story. Eventually he came to accept that he, too, had been a Cathar in a previous life, and that his encounter with this patient had to a large degree been dictated by the events of their past lives. Did you know that the Cathars believed in reincarnation?'

Lucas admitted that he barely knew who the Cathars were, other than from the potted history he had read in Pontneuf's pretty manuscript.

'Permit me to give you some background,' continued Pontneuf, apparently oblivious to sarcasm.

'The Cathars believed that an ordinary believer, or *credens*, was subject to innumerable reincarnations, until he or she attained a state of perfection, and would be absolved from further incarnation. The perfecti, or spiritual leaders of Catharism, had by definition achieved this state, and they led by example. Virtuous lives, no meat, sexual abstinence. The ascetic virtues of self-denial.'

Lucas stared hard at Pontneuf as he talked. There was little doubt that the priest considered himself as falling into this latter category.

'Guirdham's findings, although fascinating, are by no means unique. There have been several instances of Cathars being re-born *en groupe*, as it were. I have made it my business over many years to find this out, and to check the evidence. I have concluded that some groups of believers, notably those who were about to face death at the stake, made a covenant among themselves to meet again in a future life. Perhaps doubting their attainment of perfect status, they aspired towards a collective re-birth in a future when their faith might be better tolerated. Guirdham's patient, and Guirdham himself, as far as we can establish, formed the nexus of one such group, though his conclusions have been condemned by some as little more than wish-fulfilment and transference. I met the man. I have no doubts as to his integrity and admire his scrupulous refusal to dismiss his patient's claims in the way that many of his medical colleagues would have done. I myself have come across three other cases in the past twenty years which I can vouch for, including groups of between three and seven reincarnated Cathars. And this brings us to our present community, which constitutes the fifth, and I believe most significant case of multiple reincarnation.

'I say the *most significant* case not out of any vanity, you understand – because I discovered its component elements myself – but because of the records compiled by the Inquisition, relating to its leader, Bernard Rocher. We know that their accounts were thorough and meticulous, detailing their interviews with hundreds of Cathar suspects. However, the records which remain intact and public, compiled in the cloisters of Saint Sernin, are not the only ones in existence. I have discovered manuscripts which have been kept in secret for seven and a half centuries, and are not even in the vaults of the Vatican.'

Here a conspiratorial note of the successful police evader was apparent in Pontneuf's voice: the discovery of these allegedly hidden manuscripts must have signalled a victory of particular importance for him.

'Rocher,' he continued, 'was a man of unquestionable eminence among the Cathar perfecti. He had, like other Cathar leaders, been trained as a priest in the Roman faith: he attended a seminary in his home town, continued his studies in Salamanca, and came from a noble and privileged family, related by blood to the kings of Aragon. He is said to have converted to the Cathar faith after spending three years travelling around Italy with a group of lepers, dressed in rags, and living long periods in the wild, sustained by fungi, herbs and roots. Nothing, I'll grant you, too unusual by the extraordinarily rigorous measures of the medieval epoch. He was known as 'the leper monk', but the Inquisition's papers insist that he was not leprous himself, apart from (as the Inquisitors insisted) in a spiritual sense. His failure to contract the illness after such a long spell among a contagious cohort, was deemed by Cathar believers to be miraculous, and by the Catholics as evidence of his tryst with satanic forces. The Catholics also spread the idea that he gained his sexual pleasures from sodomising young leper boys. These inventive asides, however, were probably inserted at a later stage, when the telling of his story necessitated such unseemly details.

'Rocher was an idealist, perhaps a kind of primitive communist. The era, as I'm sure you know, was strewn with such figures, from Francis of Assisi to John of Leiden. What made Rocher different was the evident fear he inspired in his enemies. Converts flocked to the Cathar faith when he preached. He managed to escape from Montségur at the height of the siege in 1244. All the other perfecti solemnly agreed to go to the stake, but on condition that Rocher be saved at all cost. He was considered indispensable to the successful outcome of the Cathar cause. And among the Papal ministry there developed a belief that if he could not be captured and killed, then his name and deeds must be obliterated from history. That, I was able to conclude from my research, is why his name does not appear in any extant manuscripts. He has been airbrushed from the history of the period.

'I discovered some interesting facts about Rocher. I learned of his parents, his upbringing in the Toulousain, his education. I retraced the steps he had taken, visiting places where he had been. I began to acquire a sense of the presence of the man. After several years, wherever I trod I found the shadow of Rocher. Obscure and remarkable synchronicities began to permeate my life. On a more mundane level, I might offer some of the facts. The composite numbers of our years of birth, 1187 and 1943, both add up to seventeen, the precise number of exiles, fourteen laypersons and three perfecti, who left the village of Mélissac that May morning in 1247. Perhaps the forgotten science of numerology does not impress you, but bear in mind that for centuries before our grossly literalistic era, the skills of the mathematician would have been considered worthless unless explanatory; that is, unless linked to the magical properties of numbers.

'Rocher has been my guiding light and master; or else he would have been, had I envisaged him as an individual distinct from myself. But for many years now I have believed that I am Rocher, and have a simple destiny to fulfil: the founding of a world religion based on Cathar principles. Our community here contains the seed of that vision.'

Pontneuf was in his stride now, his eyes bright with a sense of mission, with the single story that governed his life. His was a remarkable rhetorical presence. Although evidently well-rehearsed, his account was delivered as if for the first time. He was a preacher preaching the faith as well as the storyteller and protagonist of his own fantastical theatre. He was in the process of fulfilling a potential that very few achieve: of fashioning a new world entirely in accordance with his own convictions.

'That disappearance of the seventeen Cathars in May 1247 became the focus of my life. What had happened to them? Was there a traitor among their number? If so, who was it? Moyet, whose family was to provide sanctuary for them in Spain? Gasc, the pantheistic shepherd? Or one of the others, payrolled by the Inquisition, who may have led them into an ambush? Had they been pursued, hunted down and killed? If so, why is there no record of the fact in the documentation of this period? Did they walk, hand in hand, over a precipice and into some Pyrenean abyss? If so, no remains have ever been found which would correspond with such an outcome. Were they then captured by aliens, or otherwise abducted by extraterrestial forces? Yes, I will admit, the possibility did cross my mind, fleetingly. But, alas, I do not believe in such things.'

He uttered these last words in a tone of mock regret, then added, 'I do however believe in the unwavering call of destiny.'

*

We had remained under the plane tree in the little square while I spoke, and the shadows were beginning to lengthen. If my two companions had lost any interest in my story, they were not showing it. Also, in the telling of it, I felt a great sense of release as the stress of the past three months' emotional turbulence began to loosen its hold. Although I was unable to convey to Zoff and Hogg the anger and anguish I had experienced over my enforced separation from Nuria, it was somehow easy to recount this first of Pontneuf's perorations as though it had been delivered to somebody other than myself.

We agreed upon a change of location, and from Poble Sec headed towards the Barrio Chino, by which time our conversation had strayed from the theme of my abduction and into the caverns and cupolas of a well-practised bibulous repartee.

Igbar, after demanding that we eat at a particular Lebanese restaurant, promptly fell asleep with his face in the yogurt dressing that covered his plateful of skewered lamb. Pulling him back repeatedly into an upright position only guaranteed an almost instant nosedive back into his dinner, so there he remained while Sean and I enjoyed ours, Igbar eventually stirring after an hour or so, his face decorated with yogurt and sprigs of coriander, to complain that his meal had gone cold. After a trip to the washroom, and presented with a re-heated ration of food, Igbar began to regain lucidity, if not complete control of his motor senses.

Once fed, we made a quick tour of some of the quarter's more insalubrious drinking holes, attracting attention from the working girls and transvestites who lined the streets on account of Igbar's increasingly eccentric manner of walking. This involved a half-skip, a hesitant pace or two at walking speed, followed by a lopsided sprint into the nearest immovable object. He hummed, or sang while travelling in this peculiar way. I had long since given up speculating as to why he moved in this fashion, since when sober he denied that he did, and when sufficiently drunk to be doing it, he was unintelligible. In any case, Igbar regularly ended the night with a collection of cuts and bruises. The safest thing was to get him inside a bar and hope that he would go to sleep. We headed therefore for Joaquim's filthy den, and managed to find a table at the end of the room, as far from harm's way as possible. By the time he was seated, Igbar was talking to himself quite contentedly in Russian.

Sean and I took up snatches of conversation from previous meetings, about half-remembered friends or acquaintances. And then, out of curiosity, I asked him if he had heard of the roof people.

Sean looked impenetrable, brushed his hand over his receding jet-black hairline, and scowled. His scowls showed he was giving a subject considerable thought before replying. I sat back and played with the rim of my glass, which contained a cuba libre with a larger measure of liquor than I really required. It was hot in the bar, and the fan that whirred above us in lieu of airconditioning made a sound like a chain-saw.

'The roof people,' Sean began lugubriously, 'probably do not exist.'

The torpidity of this place was infectious. I yawned.

'That is to say, they may exist as individuals, or even collectively, and may live on roofs for much of the time, but to use the term 'roof people' of them as a commonality, misses the point. It lends to them not only a degree of cohesion, but also honours them with a mystique, gives them a certain status that they cannot pretend to. It allows the good burghers to tell their children scary stories about them, and others to mythologise them in a way that the citizens of Nottingham might once have spoken of the Men of Sherwood Forest. So they become romanticised by a minority of the population, those who would secretly like to be one of them, and demonised by the majority.'

Sean Hogg took a sip of beer. I had no idea whether he had any knowledge of what or who the roof people were, or whether he was simply improvising.

'Have you ever met any of them?' I asked.

'Well, not exactly. Not up on the rooftops. What would I be doing up there? I might have seen clutches

169

of them down at street level, but if so, how am I to know whether or not they are truly roof people, since being in the street they are not, *ipso facto*, on a roof.'

'Sean. Do you know what the fuck you are talking about or is this just your way of making conversation? I'm interested to know about them. They paid me a visit before I was abducted.'

Sean gazed at me blearily, then grinned.

'Ah, the abduction. I've heard it said that they steal children, like the gypsies. So maybe they steal little children. But not big ugly bastards like you.'

'Okay, forget it. Let's drink up and get this wastrel home. How shall we do it? Taxi?'

'Taxi.'

Outside, once we had commandeered a taxi willing to take the mumbling Igbar and drive him home, we still needed to help him up the stairs to his flat in Carrer Carders, which involved the usual crisis of searching for keys, buried deep in the fastness of his overcoat. As soon as we were inside his flat, Igbar regained full consciousness and demanded to know what we were doing there, insisting on going out for a drink instead. When Sean Hogg produced an envelope overflowing with cocaine, however, Igbar decided that he wanted to hear more of my story. I was willing to comply with this, but felt like buying some brandy to take the edge off the drug. An over-enthusiastic snort already had me rushing, and I could sense the demons of my paranoia galloping fast behind.

I made my way out of the building and then remembered what Igbar had told me about the yellow crosses in the street called Els Cecs de Sant Cugat. This street was on the corner of Carders, within spitting distance of Igbar's flat, as he had said. I had in fact visited a bar at the far end of a parallel street several times for a cheap meal. It was little more than an alley: dark and uninviting, with one side covered in ripped posters and graffiti. I walked on a little way. The end of the alley led into a wider thoroughfare called Assaonadors, where there was an abandoned house, whose windows had been boarded up with rough planks. Several large yellow crosses had been daubed on the house front. I searched closely to see if there were any other marks that might provide a clue. But I did not really know what I was looking for, and it was too dark to see properly, my cigarette lighter only illuminating a small area of wall at a time. Nothing here gave me any feeling that I was on the verge of a breakthrough regarding the Cathars. I imagined the Ninja roof-boy spraying the yellow crosses just for the hell of it.

The bar at the end of the next street, Neu de Sant Cugat, was disgorging its last customers. A small group of them began walking in my direction, talking low amongst themselves. It was around two in the morning. I was aware of what a sinister place this part of town might appear at night, and yet I had never felt much concerned for my safety there. I lit a cigarette as the group of men passed by, still talking in stage whispers. The little tableau, with its hushed voices and dramatic gesticulation, was reminiscent of a Jacobean drama. All they lacked were short cloaks and rapiers.

Fortunately, the owner, Santiago, who was just closing the blinds, recognized me, and shuffled inside the now empty bar to fetch a bottle of Fundador. When he returned I paid him over the odds, telling him to keep the change.

'That building at the end of the street,' I said to him, pointing, as he wrestled with the long pole that hooked down the rolled shutters. 'The one with yellow crosses painted on it. Do you know what it used to be?'

Santiago squinted in the direction I was indicating.

'Ah yes,' he said. 'It's been closed for years now. They're going to have to do something about it, though. The roof timbers have gone. Pity. Until about, let's see, ten years ago, it was a small convent.'

'A convent with nuns?' I asked.

The man looked at me wearily.

'Is there any other kind?'

I had an idea, originating in a desire to follow my last question with a more intelligent-sounding one.

'You don't happen to know what order they were, do you?'

'Order? Shit. No. I'm not a religious person.' He gobbed defiantly in the road.

'Oh well. Thanks anyway.'

I started back the way I had come, clutching my bottle. Then he called out after me.

'But this much I know –' I stopped in my tracks, frozen by an incipient sense of déjà vu, 'it was a refuge for so-called fallen women. Plenty to choose from around here, wouldn't you say, huh? And it was dedicated to Mary Magdalene. They say she is the patroness of whores.'

I returned to Igbar's flat and we made *cuba libres* with the brandy, coca-cola, and a lot of ice. The flat was stuffy and hot, and opening the windows did little more than attract mosquitoes. The cocaine was working well, however: Igbar and Sean were ready for another instalment of my story, and as I got underway the words came with a surprising facility.

13. Pontneuf's perfect pitch

Pontneuf suggested now that they walk for a while, as walking, he said, helped to nourish the talking and receptive processes. Lucas agreed, reluctantly. The truth was, he was fascinated, and mildly horrified by Pontneuf's story. He was certain that he was in the presence of an inspired madman. Pontneuf spoke with the authority of one who was accustomed to being taken seriously, and Lucas was not immune to the sense of gravitas that accompanied his discourse. So they walked. Out of the village and into the rocky shrubland of the surrounding mountains; and Pontneuf continued talking.

'Now is not the time for me to reveal to you precisely what I have concluded in respect of the group's apparent disappearance from the world. Suffice to say, for the moment, that there exist certain openings where the structure of Time as it is normally measured breaks down, and what to the rational mind seems utterly inconceivable takes place. These magical zones are known to so-called primitive peoples throughout the world, and always have been. Modern man has simply forgotten about them, or chosen to ignore them. They enable a transubstantiation of spirit, a clear passage between one state of consciousness and another. I do not for a moment expect you to accept this.'

Then, he added, softly, 'Yet.' He savoured the moment, and smiled, as if remembering the taste of the word, its delicate placement in past conversations with new converts or captives, and their subsequent acceptance of his doctrine. How many had there been? If, as Pontneuf had suggested, Nuria and Lucas were the last two, there must already be fourteen of Pontneuf's acolytes in the community. Presumably not all the people who lived there were among the chosen ones. The mutant thugs who had carried out the abduction, for example. How were these others convinced to stay? What were the details of *their* contract with him? But Pontneuf had taken up his story again.

'I realised that if I was truly who I thought I was, a reincarnation of Rocher, then why should there not exist others: reincarnations of the remaining sixteen refugees from Mélissac? Why should they not exist contemporaneously with me? I went back to the accounts, read and re-read the often scant details about the other Cathars who made that final journey. I underwent hypnosis with an eminent psychoanalyst whom I paid handsomely until he developed an inkling of my true intentions and declared, rather unkindly, that he considered me to be profoundly deluded. No matter, I thought, I would practice auto-hypnosis, and would develop a type of dreaming known to certain esoteric traditions which encourage reflection upon past life-times. I began to *visualise* the human forms which my thirteenth-century friends and followers had been given in their present lives. I studied everything I could find that has ever been written about reincarnation. I visualised those Cathar refugees first *en groupe* as though from a distance, saw them walking through a mountain pass and gradually halting, spellbound, as though simultaneously overwhelmed by a manifestation of the numinous. A moment in which I grasped the holiness of their joint realisation and the absolute necessity of its fulfilment. This was the great turning point in my search. But I could only scan the group; not break through to the individuals themselves. So I went to the village of Mélissac, bought a rundown property, restored it, and began a lengthy process of meditation and visualisation *in situ*. Gradually, one by one, the characters began to take shape. I cannot of course be sure whether those forms replicate the physical appearance of the thirteenth-century originals. What I *saw* during these visualisations were the current physical attributes of those individual souls. I visualised them in particular settings, which eventually led me to them. They were all living, or had recently lived, relatively close to these mountains. I was on the right track. The members of the group had been drawn back to, or else had been reborn in, the vicinity of their last parting from this world.

'I won't go into the details of my search for these lost companions. But as you now know, they were all found, and they have all, up to this point, accepted the truth of their existence in a previous lifetime. They have acquired a new vision of their world, and have, by so doing, fulfilled their destiny. Not that this process has been without its difficulties: families, businesses, schedules, taxes to pay, and so on. But they all came to recognise the truth in the end, and somehow arrangements were made to bring them here.'

He spoke here in terms of unqualified success. But, Lucas wondered, of those identified by Pontneuf as reincarnations of the original group, how many had resisted his argument, had refused to play his game? What happened to them? Were they discarded, left out of the equation? How many had jumped ship from Admiral Pontneuf's merry armada? Pontneuf's reply was just on the polite side of disdainful.

'There have been, and can be, no recreants or deserters from this community. We are bound together by immutable fact and by a common destiny.'

Lucas shied away from this favourite expression of Pontneuf's. 'Destiny' implied a kind of determinism which he could not bring himself to tolerate or even understand. What was more, Pontneuf's use of the term 'deserters' cast an interesting light on his earlier claim that Lucas and Nuria were free to leave the community if they wished to.

They had approached a stream, which, with its surrounding boulders, provided a peaceful music and shade. Lucas sat down between a large, polished-looking grey boulder and the water, removing his shoes. Pontneuf also found a convenient rock, straightening his robes once he was seated. Lucas had many questions to ask, but was aware that by showing too much interest in the other man's story, he might be granting it plausibility. He was, he admitted to himself, impressed by the way Pontneuf had researched and fashioned his project for a caucus of dedicated believers to be nurtured in this community, and he wondered how much money he must have to engineer such a scheme. Moreover he was curious as to the part that Nuria and he were to play in Pontneuf's vision, although, at the same time, he had not the slightest intention of accommodating to any role designated him. But he might, he conjectured, at least humour Pontneuf in order to discover why the two of them had been chosen.

'Where do we come into this then, André? Is it André, or would you prefer Bernard, as in Rocher? Where do Nuria and I fit into your plans? Did you *visualise* us also? And for how long, by the way, have you had me followed? Did you 'arrange' our meeting at the Miró Foundation? Pay off the roof people to spy on us?'

Lucas could feel his temper rising with each emergent question. He had intended, as far as possible, to remain calm and detached, but the moment he opened his mouth he could feel the onrush of an unstoppable anger. Nuria and he were merely figments of some other person's deranged fantasy. They had been delivered here like parcels, to participate in Pontneuf's dance of the dervishes with his dualistic dropouts. Lucas's pride hurt too, because Pontneuf's deterministic vision attempted to undermine the belief Lucas had always held in free will and the overriding dominance of chance. There was a comfort in believing that things came about for no particular reason. It fell in with his atheism and a lifestyle which decreed that nothing much mattered. Being a pawn in someone else's strategy for the setting up of a world religion was one of the very worst things that could have happened to him.

Pontneuf, seated beside him now, turned and smiled. A full, holy-man smile, with eyes twinkling, that was probably designed to convey to Lucas the triviality of personal anger.

'Let's discuss you right now, rather than in conjunction with Nuria,' he began.

'You appeared to me in dreams early on. There was a special glow around you, or rather the person that you were: Raymond Gasc. The reports go into some detail about Gasc. Outwardly a simple shepherd, but obviously an intelligent and pious follower of the faith. He was a popular man, with a strong inner life, and a loyal commitment to his wife and elderly relatives. His lack of children was a source of mystery to many in the village, but I think I have the answer to that. I believe that Rocher had consulted with four people about his intentions long before the escape from Mélissac. They were the two other perfecti in the group, and Raymond and Clare Gasc. He had, even before the fall of Montségur, discovered the potential for selecting one's own reincarnation at a propitious time; had discovered one of the secret doorways to the numinous, and he knew the people he wanted to accompany him on this journey. Moreover, Raymond and Clare's childlessness was part of Rocher's scheme. He knew that they would accompany him to the edge of the abyss, but had doubts as to whether children could be asked to follow them there. He conveyed all this to Raymond and Clare in secret, promising them a new life in a safe future, in which the Gascs could have children who would not suffer the persecution of being born to known heretics at such a dangerous time in history. Better now than in the 1240s, wouldn't you say?'

For a moment Lucas was stuck for a response. This talk of selecting a doorway between lifetimes, and somehow forcing an entry into the last years of the twentieth century, in order to breed children during a more tolerant epoch, had moved beyond the realms of the merely eccentric into unqualified dementia. But there was one element in this account that contradicted the version Lucas had read the night before. Here perhaps was a breach in Pontneuf's argument.

'If the perfecti were exempt from future incarnations, then how come you, or Rocher, as you believe yourself to be, re-appeared with the fourteen credentes?'

Pontneuf was completely unfazed.

'A very good question, and one which I would have provided an answer to in due course. But I might as well tell you now. I believe that Rocher, and the other two perfecti, *elected* to be reincarnated along with their followers. They might even have provided the others with the *consolamentum* before taking their leap, but that would hardly have been necessary, given the group's agreement to re-incarnate together. In any case, true Catharism could not have prevailed into the future without Rocher, and the collective will of the group was that they remain together in the next life: they *were* and *are* reborn at a more propitious time in history.'

Presuming from his silence that Lucas was unable to respond to this piece of idiosyncratic logic, Pontneuf continued speaking.

'But to return, if we may, to your own role in this. You were a principal target for the fulfilment of our community. I *saw* you, as I have suggested, for a number of years, before actually tracking you down. I had come close when you lived in the Aude region of course. You kept appearing to me draped in vines, a peculiarly Dionysian vision. You had the kind of vibrant, earthy qualities that I like in a man.'

Lucas winced at this overt flattery.

'I found out later that you were working as an agricultural labourer in the vineyards round Lézignan, good Cathar country, of course. The Dionysian characteristics were rather dominant in your life at that time, I believe. However, I missed you then, and in hindsight I think it was probably a good thing. You settled down emotionally after your move to Barcelona, became a slightly more serious person, despite remaining a proud and self-important atheist.'

Lucas grunted, not wanting to let this taunt provoke him into another loss of temper. It was important for him to gain a balanced and sober understanding of Pontneuf's peculiar brand of derangement. Besides, the analysis was not inaccurate. He was certainly an atheist, and probably proud. He could afford to let the 'self-important' go.

'I discovered some interesting correspondences between you and Raymond', Pontneuf resumed, 'not out of idle curiosity, but because such details provided a kind of evidence in all the other cases of reincarnation that I had uncovered. The matching birthdays, for example, are not consistently verifiable with all our group, but we know that Raymond was born on 22nd July, like you. That date is highly significant in the annals of Cathar history. It is, as you may know, the feast of Mary Magdalene, who held particular importance for some groups of lay Cathars, as it has done over the centuries for other, shall we say, marginal Christian groups. Mary, the first to see the risen Christ; Mary, who loved Jesus in a worldly as well as spiritual sense. She is revered by the gypsies of the Midi to this day. There is even a folk belief that she and Christ fled the Holy Land and settled in southern France.

'Her feast day, however – your birthday – coincides with the two earliest and in some ways most shocking of the slaughters carried out in the crusade against the

Cathars by Simon de Montfort and his army of northern mercenaries, at Beziers in 1209 and at Minerve the following year. The odds against these events taking place on the same date in consecutive years are massive. "Kill them all: God will recognise his own," ordered Bishop Amaury at Beziers, when asked how his troops should distinguish Cathars from Catholics. The blood-letting was immediate and ferocious. The date became etched in the memory of Cathars throughout Languedoc: the most blessed and the most cursed of days.

'Raymond Gasc was thirty-three years old at the time of his disappearance. Like Christ, of course. And like you, at thirty-three years of age he had the opportunity to pass from his old life to his new. And yesterday he fulfilled that miraculous opportunity to rejoin his co-believers in the Cathar faith, when we gave you rebirth as your true self.'

So, thought Lucas, that was the meaning behind the coffin ride, the closing and opening of the lids, the incantations, the sprinkling with water (to help him grow, like a plant, into his new identity?). Pontneuf interjected on this train of thought.

'We are not taking anything from you, merely offering you a truer vision of yourself, the one to which you were born, but have forgotten. The exercise of the night before last was intended to tug at your memory, to find out if there is anything in you that will answer to the name of Raymond Gasc. I know that you and he are one and the same: I can prove it. We might begin with your affinity with animals, something which you have always been dimly aware of, something which you share with Raymond, of course. How domestic animals always seem to find it comfortable to be around you.'

It was true that cats and dogs seemed to like Lucas. In his childhood he had been fond of horses, though he was a little wary of them now, having been thrown on several occasions. But going back, the summers spent on his grandparents' farm in west Wales, his happiness at being surrounded by the morning activities of milking and tending the cattle and goats; all this would verify Pontneuf's assertion in some way. He liked birds too; could watch them for hours. But this proved nothing.

'You have become a city-dweller,' continued Pontneuf, 'which does not suit you. You have lost touch with that element of yourself which was so clearly drawn in your childhood. And later. Can you not remember how you saved the lambs?'

The words impacted on Lucas like a blow to the solar plexus. He remembered the occasion well. Waiting out in the freezing cold for half the night and most of the following day. He must have been fourteen years old. On the farm near Tregaron. His grandfather, Tad-cu, calling him out of bed at three in the morning. Outside, a blizzard. Driving through the *cwm* on Tad-cu's tractor until they were hemmed in by the snow, then trudging through the drifts, the sky and everything around them an otherworld of pulsing white flakes in the tractor's headlamps. The flock was huddled, terrified, in the top field and Lucas bundled inside a trench coat that suddenly seemed paper-thin, covering himself and the bleating newborn lambs with a tarpaulin. Lucas was to wait for Tad-cu to come back with help. The morning seemed never to arrive; his watch moved on, but beyond this eery, mustard-tinged dusk the day did not progress. The lambs were frightened, and burrowed their faces ever deeper under Lucas's woollen coat, diminishing his own fear. Saving the lambs became his only concern. They formed a little community under the tarpaulin, an oasis of fragile, animal-scented warmth in the total bleakness beyond the improvised tent. When eventually help arrived it was five o'clock, and night again. Lucas was utterly exhausted. But both lambs were alive. He heard the muffled sound of the snow-plough approaching, and then the scatching of the men's shovels on the surface of their little cavern. He stood unsteadily as the tarpaulin was pulled away, holding the lambs snug beneath his coat. Tad-cu, an undemonstrative man, came towards him, eyes heavy with tears.

Lucas cut off abruptly in his silent re-tracing of the memory.

'Have you been digging up my past? Have you been to Wales and *researched* me?'

Pontneuf waved his hand dismissively, tut-tutting. As if such a pedantic course of action were necessary!

'I *visualised* you as a teenager, a very young man, holding lambs beneath an overcoat. Your teeth were chattering in the cold, but you were smiling. You were exhausted. That's all. You've told me the rest yourself.'

So sure of himself. In that instant Lucas both hated and admired him. Here was some evidence that Pontneuf had the powers of visualisation which he claimed to have. But almost immediately Lucas began to have doubts. After all, the older man could, without difficulty, have discovered that Lucas had passed much of his childhood on a farm in Wales. Was it not a reasonable guess that he would have helped out in the kind of situation he had described, at least once? And sheep, of course, the inner cynic added: just mention Wales and it's the first thing many people think of. Lucas decided to test him.

'What else have you *visualised* concerning me?'

Pontneuf hesitated, detecting the scorn in Lucas's question.

'I know of your musical interests, because I found out about your life, to a limited extent. But through my visualisation of the person I thought of as Raymond Gasc, music was an integral part of the picture I had of you. Raymond used to fashion wooden flutes and whistles, not an unusual pastime for shepherds, but he was also a fine singer and composer of songs. One of his fellow-villagers told the Inquisition that his songs were 'lewd and lascivious', which smacks of someone telling the priests what they wanted to hear, that Catharism was a delinquent and subversive sect. But we know enough about the culture of the jongleurs and troubadours to assume that Raymond could still be close to that tradition. This is what you would expect in a rural backwater like Mélissac: last year's songs. Have you by any chance a disc or tape in your collection of songs composed by the troubadour Peire Vidal?'

'That would not be difficult to establish. Your people have no doubt searched my flat.'

'I do not take you for a fool, and nor would I expect you to do the same for me. The reason I mention this particular troubadour is that many of his songs were current in this period. There is one particular song that Raymond used to sing, according to the Inquisition's informant. It is called *La Trystesse de la Dona Marie*. Do you know it?'

Lucas nodded his head. He had a cassette of Vidal's music, recorded by a contemporary French ensemble. *La Trystesse de la Dona Marie* was his favourite song, but he had no recollection of ever telling anybody as much. Furthermore he had not played the tape for months, if not years. Even if Pontneuf's knowledge of the existence of the cassette was easily accounted for, his challenge about this particular song was either insightful or simply inexplicable. Once more, Lucas felt acutely uncomfortable.

'Some years ago I heard the same song at a concert of music by a young French group who made a little-known recording on disc. Perhaps you have it, perhaps not. I assure you I have not checked. But you do not have to believe me. The point I want to make is this. The night following the concert I dreamed about you, exactly as you are, in precise physical detail, singing this song, and accompanying yourself on the guitar. It was the first time I was granted a clear image of you. From that point onward my search became easier. I knew what you looked like. I could have pointed you out in a crowded street. I simply had to wait until the appropriate time, when you would make yourself available to us.'

Lucas felt engulfed by a physical sense of shock and displacement, even more pronounced than when Pontneuf had mentioned the lambs. This was quite simply unknowable to anyone but Lucas. He had been alone, sitting in a farm cottage in the Corbières region, drinking wine and playing the guitar. It was night-time. He had just had a bust-up with Pascale, the only one of his French girlfriends with whom a long-term relationship had seemed a likelihood. In fact it was their differences of opinion on this issue that led to her tearful departure. In typical fashion Lucas found self-pitying comfort in red wine and music, and he had worked out an arrangement of *La Trystesse de la Dona Marie* and played it over and over in accompaniment to his own mournful and inebriated rendering. He could not remember ever singing the song again.

If Pontneuf enjoyed Lucas's moment of confusion, he was diplomat enough not to show it. He stared at him intently for a short while, then abruptly changed the subject. Lucas was left straining after explanations for this impossible insight into a private and obscure fragment of his life, and was unable to provide one.

'It might be news to you, but there is a considerable interest in the teachings of the Cathars at present,' Pontneuf persisted, indifferent to Lucas's frantic attempts at self-collection. 'Many young people, dissatisfied with orthodox religious practices have sought alternative ways to express their spiritual cravings. Most of these alternative religions and cults, I'm afraid to say, are simply disastrous. However, my own teachings on Catharism have not gone unnoticed. I have attracted a following among certain groups of young people, even among those who inhabit the rooftops of Barcelona. Those whom you had cause to speak with the other night.'

Although reeling, as he was, from Pontneuf's previous disclosures, Lucas could acknowledge that this, at least, made sense. It also explained, conclusively, the arrival of the Miró postcard under his door. A scatterbrained collection of dopeheads and petty criminals, street urchins and middle-class dropouts would latch onto the more attractive aspects of Catharism – reincarnation, the relative equality of women and vegetarianism – as easily as a previous generation turned on and tuned into the freewheeling spiritual ecstatics of Timothy Leary.

So why had Pontneuf not chosen a less strenuous way of bringing his religious movement about?

Hundreds of others had done so. People will buy into any creed as long as they consider themselves in some way different or elect. Why insist on the veracity of his vision of a nucleus of reincarnated Cathars, which could surely only categorise him in the eyes of the wider world as yet another Messianic loony? And how to reconcile his detailed and convincing psychic insights with this insane wider project?

But that, Lucas realised, was precisely where Pontneuf's special appeal lay. If he could convince his sixteen contemporary followers of their shared experience in a past life, he was breaking new ground in the annals of religious dissent. And from that starting point, he could insist that the true Cathar flame had never been extinguished, precluding accusations of having cooked up some New Age hotchpotch of ideas for sale to the desperate and disillusioned.

Lucas was by now impressed by this strategy. He began to question his own resistance to the possibility that he was linked to Raymond Gasc and the Cathar movement. He was here, after all, as was Nuria. And he was not resisting as stubbornly as his late twentieth-century persona wanted him to. He could feel the first stirrings of self-doubt.

He summoned a series of rash and desperate explanations for Pontneuf's knowledge about him. He must have simply forgotten later performances of that particular song. Pontneuf had hypnotized him that first night. Or one of his agents had, before the abduction. But hypnotism, Lucas knew, required a willing receptor. And a knowledge of his musical tastes did not suffice for Pontneuf having 'seen' him sing that song, any more than a knowledge that there were a lot of sheep in

Wales could have provided him with the vision of his rescue of the lambs.

Pontneuf got up and moved closer to the crystalline stream. He took off his sandals and stretched his feet into the water. He looked a picture of virtuous serenity: a monk at peace with nature, his God and himself. He rested back on his elbows, lifted his face to the sun, and closed his eyes. A gentle wind blew around them, the kind of wind that at this altitude carries a warning chill. From somewhere out of sight Lucas could hear the mewling of a bird of prey.

But Lucas remembered Nuria, and a long-restrained anger began to simmer. He had been so absorbed in Pontneuf's metaphysical acrobatics that he had almost forgotten the brutal manner of his and Nuria's sequestration and imprisonment at the hands of the man in priest's robes. He realised that he could, if he wished, kill Pontneuf on the spot. A rock raised above the head, a furious release, the crack of a splitting skull. Repeating the action while Pontneuf lay on the ground until his hands became a mess of splintered bone and brain. Never before had Lucas experienced such a spontaneous murderous instinct. It was followed by an onrush of conflicting emotions – uncertainty, fear, guilt – and beneath them that irreparable sense of loss and sadness evoked by remembering the lambs.

Pontneuf's next comment unsettled Lucas further. Raising himself abruptly on one elbow, he looked at Lucas with concern.

'There is no accounting for the thoughts that assail us at critical moments. At the time of the crusades against the Saracens, the ordinary foot-soldiers, the rabble, believed that the Jerusalem they were being sent to deliver from the heathens was one and the same city as that described by John in his Book of Revelation. A glittering bejewelled city which promised the attainment of eternal bliss. But what they found was squalor, disease and death. Those who returned set in place the mood for change, tentative at first, which would turn the twelfth century into the most radically disquieting in history. Until our own, that is. And it was during this period that the seeds of the Cathar faith were sown. So, you see, expectations of immediate gratification during this lifetime are often premature.'

He sprung to his feet with surprising agility, dusted down his robe, then continued talking.

'The Cathars believed that it took multiple lifetimes to achieve the status of a perfectus. It has usually been assumed that the perfecti were then excused future re-birth. However, to my mind, this is merely a point of dogma. As I think I have explained, there should be no reason why one who has achieved perfect status might not select the option of re-birth, if, for whatever reason, he or she felt that there were unfinished business to attend to. That is why we are here, you and I. Unfinished business.'

14. Kataskapos

It was approaching daybreak when I left Igbar and Sean and walked home. The wind blew in gusts around me from the direction of the sea. It had been a hot day, but this wind brought no relief. The blasts of warm air chased the shadows cast by the scant lighting in this part of the city. There were few people around. The drugs I had consumed, and the dislocation of myself from my own story, combined to make my trip home both detached and vivid. In the dark, narrow streets, sound was intensified; every shadow a recumbent night-creature. I remembered those muted voices in the alleyway of two hours earlier and Santiago's: 'This much I know.' The bar owner's words hung in the air long after the explanation that followed them.

When I did pass the occasional pedestrian, the muscles in my neck and shoulders tightened. I became gradually overtaken by an obsessive hypothesis: that the few people I passed were ghosts, led on leashes by the unseen hands of the living, and that I too, was of their number.

Back in Santa Caterina, I climbed the stairs to my flat, grateful that there were no cryptic messages under the door. I checked the answerphone: Eugenia had left a message saying she would be around the next day with Susie Serendipity, and to call her back if I was not going to be in. Let them come, I thought: let them all come. I have a tale to tell.

I went out and stood on the veranda, leaning over the parapet so that I could see the stretch of road directly below. The cobbles were reflected back at me under the street lamp. Somewhere nearby a cat-fight spluttered into action, the preliminary hissing and wailing drifting in malevolent waves across the roof-tops. Up here the warm wind blew in more constant drafts, ruffling my shirt and hair. I stripped off down to my boxer shorts, and lay on the hammock.

What was it about my red-tiled outpost above the city that rendered me invulnerable to all that went on below? I had been living here for two years untroubled by normal social exigencies or their consequences. My sex life had adapted to a pattern of one-night stands since moving from Maragall and Fina's monogamous ministrations. I had become an observer of city life, a cynical frequenter of all-night bars and clubs. A reluctant flâneur. I had stood by, unable to force myself into any kind of action while witness to a street robbery that evening in May; had questioned my inactivity roundly, and yet had still remained incapable of doing anything. Since then the circumstances of my life had changed. My terrace remained much the same, the view identical.

But it was as if everything within my immediate sensory zone had acquired a new intensity, while the boundaries of the familiar world became more indistinct.

I lay there smoking, resisting sleep. When the morning trucks arrived and started unloading outside the market, I dragged myself out of the hammock, and into the bedroom. Once there I pulled the bedclothes over my head and passed out.

That afternoon there was a hammering on the door and Zoff and Hogg arrived, sober and rested, but carrying an immoderate quantity of tequila and cold beer, and demanding the next installment. Shortly afterwards Eugenia and Susie followed, and the five of us retired to my veranda. Eugenia drank herb tea, while the rest of us made a start on the psychotropics with an aperitif of Tequila and more cocaine. I had to bring Eugenia and Susie up to date on the story so far, while Sean and Igbar argued about whether or not to play ambient music. This suggestion was vetoed by the women.

Sean had evidently been thinking about my story.

'Now, I don't wish to prejudice the reaction of the ladies. But Lucas here, or the Lucas that Lucas describes in his story, seems to have been pretty well diverted from his concerns about Nuria after the supposed abduction. Here, I thought last night, was a man in the throes of a passionate affair who has been forcibly separated from his lover. He wanders off on some Arcadian picnic with the evil Doctor Pontneuf and dicusses reincarnation and transcendental philosophy while, as far as he knows, his beloved is, even as he speaks, being subjected to the most horrid improprieties at the hands of Pontenuf's mutants.'

'Mutants?' Eugenia was puzzled.

'This Pontneuf's savages. They all seem to have some physical deformity, an eye or a nose or a foot missing. They're the backroom boys in Pontneuf's house of horrors.'

'Something of a presumption isn't it,' admonished Igbar, 'running the story down at this early stage? Besides, Lucas never mentioned a character with a missing foot, did you Lucas?'

'No. There were no missing feet.'

'Okay. I stand corrected. But an understandable hyperbole considering the unlikely course of events so far.'

'Can you let us be the judge of that?' asked Susie Serendipity.

'Quite so,' said Igbar.

'Fair enough,' said Sean. 'Just airing a healthy scepticism.'

We settled down in the meagre shade of the veranda, spread variously on the hammock (Igbar) and cushions (the rest of us), and I continued where I had left off.

*

Later that same day, though not immediately on his return, as Pontneuf had led him to expect, Lucas finally had his reunion with Nuria. He was lying on the grass near a barn when she approached, dressed reassuringly like a 1990s *barcelonesa* in blue jeans and a white cotton vest, rather than smocked, hippy-primitive, in grey or brown sacking, which seemed to be the couture of choice of most of the residents.

She settled on her knees beside him and they kissed. There was a coy, almost flirtatious air about her that was at once seductive and yet, to Lucas, strangely incompatible with the situation they found themselves in.

'Have you planned our escape yet?' she asked, smiling, as though such a scheme were utterly predictable of Lucas. He was offended by her mocking tone.

'I hadn't planned anything until I could see you. But I for one don't fancy being a willing abductee. It would fit in too neatly with Pontneuf's plans for us. Or rather for Clare and Raymond.'

Nuria watched Lucas carefully as he spoke, twisting a blade of grass between her fingers. She remained silent, however, and he at once sensed a resistance to the tone of his answer.

'Nuria,' he asked, 'what's the matter? Don't you want to leave? The longer we stay, the greater the chances are of us being sucked into this thing, of becoming a part of it.'

Her look expressed more exasperation than concern.

'Can't you see? We're a part of it already. We have been from the beginning, without knowing it. Right down to the circumstances of our meeting at the Miró Foundation. It was all a set-up.'

Nuria pulled a pack of cigarettes out of her jeans pocket, and lit two, handing one to Lucas. He noticed that her hand was trembling. 'Perhaps our being set up is not the best analogy,' she continued after a while, seeming to collect herself. 'I told you before, in Barceloneta, that I felt as though I'd known you all my life. This is not a fantasy, or even a confirmation of Romantic Love. It's a kind of,' she broke off, uncertain of her words, 'inner recognition. I'm only asking you to consider the possibility that what André is saying could be right, and that we might have been together in a previous life.'

'But why do the feelings that we have for one another have to be straitjacketed by Pontneuf's interpretation?' asked Lucas. 'To base one's life on the notion that one is continuing what had been begun in a previous incarnation seems so deterministic, so limiting.'

'It's not *his* interpretation I'm concerned about,' she answered. 'It's what I know in *myself* to be true. Dreams I've had over the years and never confided to anyone. A picture of you I've had in my head since I was eleven or twelve years old. And then there's the other stuff, which we haven't even mentioned yet.'

'What other stuff?'

'Things that André could tell about me. Secret things he could not have known about. My terror of being caught in a fire and burned alive, which I have carried with me always, silently. Arguments I had with the priest at school. You know I went to a convent school?'

He did, because she had told him at their first meeting. 'I invoked practically the entire Cathar litany in religious instruction classes with him. He had called me, only half-jokingly, a heretic. In a religious instruction class', she repeated, 'with a dozen other thirteen year olds! "My little heretic" became his nickname for me. Obviously I didn't know then that I had summarized a dualistic worldview, but that priest made sure I learned the error of my views. Without mentioning Catharism or the Albigensian heresy. He didn't want to nurture my heretical beliefs by grounding them in an historical precedent, by showing that thousands of others had died for harbouring those same beliefs seven hundred years before. He continued using this nickname, "my little heretic" only in private, when no one else could hear. But André knew of this affinity of mine with the Cathars just as he knew the priest's secret nickname for me.'

This disclosure of another of Pontneuf's displays of insight ought not to have come as a surprise. Still, Lucas felt bound to discredit him in whatever way he could. For Nuria, the situation now seemed straightforward, and her behaviour from that point onward only confirmed Lucas's mounting suspicion that she had been completely taken in by Pontneuf. Not that she lost her sense of humour, in the way that religious converts and neophytes are supposed to do. She remained, for the most part, the character that he had known in Barcelona, given to verbal excesses of every kind including sharply observant insights regarding other members of the community (particularly the most slavishly devout); libidinous and occasionally sulky. One thing that she would not tolerate however, after that first meeting, was any criticism of Pontneuf.

That first afternoon at the Refuge, as the community was unoriginally named, they were given their sleeping quarters. The room was spacious and puritan, with a single window giving onto the grass-strewn square and the mountains beyond. It was a pleasant, uncluttered room: a room which (were it not for the double bed) aspired to an ascetic self-restraint. Once inside the room, Nuria flopped onto the bed, and lay on her back, watching Lucas through half-closed eyes.

'Lucas, let's stay a few days and find out some more about ourselves. Or who we might be.' She spoke in her natural voice, with that barely-detectable edge of irony that she often had. 'After all, we've nothing to lose but a few body fluids.'

She laughed, and patted the bed beside her. Lucas sat down on the edge of the bed, non-committal.

'But what about our jobs? Arranging stuff back home? A person can't just disappear.'

'That's okay. I already phoned work this afternoon, using André's cell phone. I'm taking time off. And you were going to have the week off anyway.'

'You've *already* –?' Lucas started.

He was truly hurt: this meant she had presumed Lucas's eventual concordance, at least in respect of staying at the Refuge, before speaking with him. In this she was right, of course. He would not have left her here alone, except perhaps to go and fetch the police. But what would he have told them? That a twenty-seven year old woman had been abducted, but was entirely happy to remain with her captors? They would have laughed at him.

So he sulked.

Nuria shrugged and went on, conceding a little to his mood. 'Look. Why not let's discover what goes on here, at least? There's got to be more than just being reincarnated Cathars. There must be a policy, a strategy. Even if you don't believe in reincarnation you've got to admit it is an interesting situation. And, who knows, you might lose a little of that martyred air.'

Lucas did not respond to the last remark, only making a mental note that martyrdom was a specifically Cathar concern.

'Perhaps you're right,' he said eventually. Secretly, however, he harboured other plans. 'We should stay. As you say, I can fix things at work, since I'm practically freelance anyhow. I'd like to find out what makes our André tick.'

As Lucas discovered over the following days, there was in Pontneuf a considerable element of megalomania, despite his charm. He exerted detailed control over the lives of his followers: in fact the whole community ran according to his plans and dictates. True, there was a 'council meeting' at the end of each day (which he chaired) in which individuals were encouraged to make suggestions for the running of the Refuge, and occasionally to voice complaints, but these were invariably of such a minor kind as to be insignificant.

At the end of the first week, Nuria and Lucas must have given the impression of having reached a similarly conditioned state themselves. They both wrote to their employers, requesting an indefinite leave of absence. Strangely, and in spite of his personal, more subversive agenda, Lucas was seduced by the atmosphere of the Refuge, and while he still held overpowering doubts about Pontneuf, he was swept up by Nuria's enthusiasm. He began to enjoy the sensation of withdrawal from the concerns of the material and consumerist world. Besides, Catharism was undemanding in its imposition of ritual and ceremony. It was, taken on its own, a simple faith, without the central problem of a literal belief in Christ as the embodied Son of God. It was, rather, the ultimate objective which Pontneuf seemed intent on imposing on it that riled Lucas.

Later, he would find it hard to understand quite how easy it had been for him to adapt to the blinkered and delusional way of life at the Refuge. He put it down to two factors: his obsession with Nuria, which he gradually came to accept as, possibly, the consequence of his love for her in a previous existence, and the undoubted personal magnetism of Pontneuf. However much Lucas tried to hate him, however clearly he thought he saw through the rhetoric and hotch-potch philosophy, the man held a sway over him, as he did over all of the members of the community. Indeed, his feelings about Pontneuf sent him again and again into ever-tightening circles of ambiguity and self-doubt.

Daily life at the Refuge unfolded with a repetitive simplicity. There were informal prayers and meditation at six in the morning followed by breakfast. Immediately after breakfast Pontneuf addressed the group, often using a text from the gospel of Saint John. Morning tasks followed, mainly concerned with the maintenance of the land and caring for the animals. The main meal of the day took place at midday, after which there was a rest period, and then either more menial tasks or else a range of designated 'spiritual exercises'. The day came to a close with a council meeting, supper, and evening prayers.

At the community's head was Pontneuf, the undisputed leader and owner of the properties. He employed four 'helpers', two of whom, Zaco and Le Chinois, consented to speak only French and looked as though they had been scraped off the dockside at Marseilles: a tattooed, smouldering, belligerent duo who, incongruously in the peaceful climate of the refuge, appeared to act as Pontneuf's minders. They were assisted by two Spanish-speaking misfits; Francisco, the noseless one of the night of the abduction, and the one-eyed giant, El Tuerto. These four did not attend prayers or take part in the everyday activities of the community, apart from carrying out occasional labouring jobs. They ran errands for Pontneuf, disappearing in pairs in the large van which had brought Nuria and Lucas to the Refuge, or else in one of two Landrovers. Lucas noted early on that the keys were often left in these vehicles, so Pontneuf's claim that he and Nuria were free to leave at any time they wished was apparently not an idle offer.

The two other perfecti were Marta, the Kierkegaard woman who had directed the kidnapping, and her Cathar 'husband', Rafael, a slight, nervous Italian from Lombardy with the harassed eyes of either resolute self-denial or chronic onanism – Lucas could never decide which. These two acted as Pontneuf's lieutenants in spiritual matters. Their role was to lead morning and evening prayers on normal days and to act as counsellors to the rest of the flock.

The community was centred on the council hall. This was a large room comprising the ground floor of one of the main buildings. The floor was covered with straw matting and strewn with prayer cushions. Cathars did not acknowledge the symbol of the cross, believing it to be a corrupt artefact, so the room was devoid of crucifixes or other religious icons. During prayers, Pontneuf, Marta or Rafael would stand or kneel at the front, surrounded by a semi-circle of credentes. The room contained no other furniture, nor any musical instruments. They did not sing hymns or psalms, but recited simple prayers in a monotone, following the lead of whichever *perfectus* was ministering that day.

The meetings, or 'chats', as Pontneuf called them, were a different matter. Pontneuf had indicated to Lucas on his arrival at the Refuge that their own group was not the only one that had been constituted from reincarnated Cathars. He spoke about 'the movement' gaining pace elsewhere, although he avoided any geographical exactitude. He spoke, but again, only in vague terms, of the unique role that New Catharism would play in the overturning of materialism and 'idolatory culture'.

The lack of a coherent structure to his movement, the absence of evangelism or any policy of spreading the Cathar gospel, was, of course, utterly at odds with the notion of developing a world religion, but this was something which nobody appeared to question. It was as if the promise of a world community sharing Cathar beliefs was based wholly within the microcosm of the little tribe at the Refuge. When Lucas mentioned his doubts to Nuria, she shrugged, saying that, no doubt André would provide the means to his chosen end when the time was right, and that all that was required from them as credentes – as, she pointed out, the term implied – was faith. Lucas was staggered that someone as sharp and inquisitive as Nuria could show such blind acceptance. Or rather, the Nuria he had known in Barcelona.

With Pontneuf himself, Lucas edged around the topic with care, while the Prophet of New Catharism expounded grandiosely, both in private sessions and at group meetings, in terms of spiritual fulfilment and the need to convert all the credentes at the Refuge into perfecti before sending them out into the world to preach the faith. This, it was revealed, was the master plan. But no time-scale was ever indicated as to when precisely this might happen. Pontneuf relied instead on clichés and platitudes such as 'when the time is right', or 'when God sees fit'.

In order to achieve perfect status one had to receive the consolamentum, of course; renounce the ways of the world, and dedicate oneself to celibacy, vegetarianism, and the ministry. While all the credentes aimed to achieve this status, there was, insisted

Pontneuf, no hurry. Hadn't they, after all, waited seven and a half centuries in order to be born into a propitious age. Only when they were fully prepared, he insisted, would they have the strength to carry the message in the wider world.

Lucas's growing belief was that Pontneuf was holding something back, something which he alone knew. This withholding of information was not merely a trick designed to enhance his mystique as guardian of secret Cathar knowledge, but something apart. The conviction had been ignited in Lucas on that first day by the stream, when Pontneuf had responded with such alacrity to Lucas's murderous thoughts, and had developed gradually with every prevarication and excuse that Pontneuf made for not ushering his flock more succinctly into an evangelical force.

In early July Pontneuf decided that Lucas needed, as he put it, to 'remember more' about his previous existence as Raymond Gasc, and from this point on, their private meetings acquired a new intensity. Pontneuf proposed using hypnotism to achieve this end, since, he explained, the techniques he himself had mastered for the purpose of 'remembering' involved a long and arduous training. Hypnosis was merely a shortcut to the same objective. Lucas hesitated, but saw no reason why he should not comply. However, when Pontneuf actually attempted to hypnotise him, Lucas began to experience an utter resistance to his efforts, and proved a most unresponsive subject. His repeated assurances that he was not consciously trying to obstruct the process did not convince Pontneuf, who became short-tempered. The loss of his characteristic self-control in this outburst was quite a revelation to Lucas. He began to regard Pontneuf as a man pursuing an unknown but essentially vindictive campaign against him personally. Pontneuf seemed to believe that he, Lucas, possessed, and was withholding, knowledge of Raymond Gasc that was of vital importance to the outcome of his greater vision. In this way, both Lucas and Pontneuf suspected one another of precisely the same thing: harbouring an unshared agenda.

Nuria also became elusive and ill-tempered. Since she and Lucas shared a room and a bed, this was not something she was able to hide from him, nor did she attempt to. For several days, which coincided with a period of sexual abstinence entirely unrelated to the ideals of Catharism, the two of them sustained a climate of mutual indifference, which led to a barely-concealed hostility.

One night Lucas dreamed of loss and betrayal, one of those dreams that persist in the memory throughout the day, leaving a bitter imprint on everything the mind touches. He was travelling on foot in a high and lonely landscape in the company of people he knew he should have recognised. A woman, or rather a conglomerate of women who united fleetingly in the shape of Nuria, was in that company. He was anxious and fearful, because he had made an arrangement to meet some people outside Albi cathedral at a particular time, and he was confused because he was not sure what they looked like. He had been told they would be representatives of some elite paramilitary group. He had no idea how he was going to leave the company he was in, drag himself away from the Nuria figure, and get to Albi. The trains were not running: there was some kind of strike. Nuria was openly and cruelly flirting with another member of the group, who appeared to have a man's body and the head of a jackal, like Thoth, the Egyptian god of the dead. They came to a sharp turn in the path, entering a steep upland valley created by landslides. An armed figure stepped out from behind a boulder. He smiled at Lucas. Other armed men then appeared among the rocks and boulders. The jackal-man turned angrily to look at Lucas, who saw that he was drooling freely, his gums and lower jaw smeared with gore. 'Ah, my dear fellow,' he growled, with the clipped upper-class English accent of a Hollywood villain, 'I see you have invited your friends to our picnic.'

*

'Terry-Thomas,' said Igbar from his perch on the hammock. He was swinging one leg idly over the side, while lying propped up on an elbow.

'Who?' asked Eugenia.

'Oh, nobody you'd know,' answered Igbar, brushing away a fly. 'I don't think he's really export material. A film actor from the 1950s. The archetypal English cad.'

'Plenty of choice there, then,' said Eugenia.

'Some girls do love a cad,' mused Susie Serendipity, in a malevolent tone.

'So I'm informed, sweetie,' said Igbar. 'But I'll have to take your word for it.'

Sean was lining up neat rows of white powder on the gaudily-decorated cover of a volume entitled *Out of Wedlock: Famous Bastards of History*, which I had no recollection of owning. He rolled a bank note tightly, inserted one end into his nostril and vacuumed up a line in one sharp snort, before passing the cargo carefully to me. I ingested in turn, and handed it to Susie.

'Please,' Eugenia said to me, 'carry on.'

*

One day in late July, returning to their room after lunch in order to change for the afternoon's gardening activities, Nuria startled Lucas with a series of accusations: of treating the enterprise of the Refuge with a lack of respect; of being vain and egotistical; of refusing to develop any kind of spiritual sensibility in accordance with his professed adherence to Cathar principles, and of using her sexually to accommodate his attachment to all things material, rather than regarding sex as a temporary obstacle to be overcome in order to achieve the higher purpose with which they had been gifted.

'You're playing some stupid game with me, with André, and with the whole community. It's not as if I can't see through you. You either don't want to progress or else you're simply spiritually stunted. You just want to have sex with me and watch the show. You don't care about what happens to us as a group.' While Lucas took in this outburst, she added, 'André's right about you.'

'I beg your pardon?' Lucas asked, shocked by this disclosure. 'Do you mean to say you discuss my 'progress' with him? Does he tell you about my individual sessions with him?'

Nuria hesitated. Perhaps she was wondering whether she had said rather more than she intended.

'No, of course not,' she said. 'Well, not specifically. But you've told me yourself that you were experiencing resistance, that you had some sort of blockage.'

'I've told you nothing of the kind. I simply said that we weren't getting anywhere with the hypnosis, that André's attempts were unsuccessful. "Blockage" was a term he used to describe it, yes. But I never told you that. So he must have. What else has he told you, in your little sessions with him?'

Nuria paused again, and Lucas knew she had overstepped an agreed boundary. That is, one she had agreed upon, not with him, but with Pontneuf. It was clear to him then that she and Pontneuf discussed more than her personal spiritual development when they were in private.

'Except in the most general terms, nothing at all. André goes on a bit sometimes, as though he's thinking aloud. Doesn't he do that with you?'

'No,' said Lucas.

'Well, I'm sure it's not a big deal. He says things about other people too, but I've never really thought about them much. Whoever said these meetings were strictly confidential? Anyway, it's you he's trying to hypnotise. Can you really not remember anything about your past life? It might provide the clue he's after. You might be holding onto some knowledge that will help us all.'

'You're beginning to *sound* like him,' Lucas responded, his voice rising. 'Pontneuf's parrot. And I don't like the way you two carry on. It's as if you've known each other for years. Did you by any chance have anything to do with him before we met?'

Nuria turned towards him, openly angry now.

'That's a very stupid question to ask, considering your alleged acceptance of the doctrine of reincarnation.'

'I haven't accepted anything yet. Allegedly or otherwise. I've gone along with it this far because I was worried about you.'

Nuria stared at him incredulously.

'What were you worried about, precisely? That I wouldn't conform to some pretty ideal of the kind of girlfriend you would like to have, to feed your ego? You weren't worried about me. You were worried about yourself. It's the only thing you've ever worried about. And your insinuations about André and myself only go to prove it.'

And with that she left the room, slamming the door behind her.

Lucas's suspicions about Nuria and Pontneuf were aroused again the next afternoon when he noticed the two of them talking outside the dining room. He waited, out of hearing, for them to move on, expecting Nuria to return to their room, but instead they set off together towards Pontneuf's private quarters. Lucas followed, at a distance.

Once they had gone inside, he moved around to the side of the building which contained Pontneuf's study, and saw the shutters being pulled to and shut from the inside. This was something which Pontneuf never did in his private meetings as a rule; indeed Lucas had never known these shutters to be closed at all. He crept along the wall, with the intention of listening beneath the window, but was unable to make out any sounds from the room. Instead he felt a hand on his shoulder as he crouched there, and turning, was grabbed from behind by Pontneuf's henchmen, Zaco and Le Chinois. They dragged him around the corner of the house and in through a side door. Le Chinois rapped on Pontneuf's study door, while Zaco held him in an arm-lock. There was a pause before the door was answered by Pontneuf, who seemed angry to be disturbed.

Lucas was shoved into the room by Zaco, and the door was closed behind them, Zaco positioning himself against it. Nuria sat on the sofa, legs crossed, trying hard to look indifferent, but her cheeks were flushed, and her eyes were like small infernos. Lucas's first impression was one of an interrupted liaison, and a dense, dimly erotic atmosphere seemed to permeate the room. In spite of his earlier suspicions and the closed shutters, he was startled by the suddenness of his revelation, and by the sordid and predictable conclusions that he inferred from this afternoon tryst. It was all so at odds with the aims of the Refuge. All so much at odds with what Lucas had considered to be the special nature of his relationship with Nuria, the almost sacred dimensions that their being together held for him, and, he had believed, for her also.

'Well, this is pretty,' Lucas said, finally. 'You two seem very snug. The term *"perfectus"* has taken on a whole new significance for me.'

Pontneuf sighed, while Nuria simply stared at Lucas blankly, then at the floor.

'There is considerably more at stake in our lives here than your pathetic jealousies,' said Pontneuf.

There was a brief silence between them. Outside, Lucas could hear the rhythmic knock of someone chopping firewood.

'Well, *kataskapos*, it didn't take you long to come sniffing around my doorstep. Full of pouting envy and justified rage.'

Pontneuf inspected Lucas closely, and his gaze was devoid of any pretended comradeship, or even of familiarity.

'You really should take time to study your soul,' advised Pontneuf. 'You might find something hitherto undetected by your wayward and undisciplined intellect. If you're lucky.'

209

Lucas found Pontneuf's admonitions tedious in the extreme. But he had no idea what was going to happen next. He was still struggling with the evidence, as he saw it, that Nuria and Pontneuf were having an affair. It now appeared obvious, with the benefit of sudden and inglorious ratification. The amount of time they spent together, their joint arrival, late, at mealtimes; Nuria's recent frigidity, her increasingly unguarded repetition of certain of Pontneuf's stock phrases, and her mindless regurgitation of his ideas. That there was a sexual component to this relationship should not have surprised Lucas. He wondered how long it had been going on; considered with revulsion the notion that it had been going on long before he and Nuria had even met; for all he knew had been in progress (although temporarily suspended) even during their passionate fortnight in Barcelona.

'How long have you two been carrying on this – how should I name it – partnership?' asked Lucas.

Neither Pontneuf nor Nuria answered at first, though they both now stared at him.

'Is that any concern of yours, I wonder?' replied Pontneuf, at length. 'But how about you going somewhere conducive to quiet meditation, so you can think about it?'

He spoke as though responding to a challenge over an article of faith. Just like a priest, thought Lucas. And with that thought, a torturous possibility began to take root. He recalled the story of the priest at Nuria's convent school. Could that simply have been a lie? Was it Pontneuf himself who had instigated everything, had nurtured her as 'his little heretic'; had acted since then as Nuria's mentor, and intermittently but consistently, as her lover?

While Lucas raged in silence, Zaco grabbed his arm and led him from the room. He turned in the doorway and caught sight of Nuria, now looking at the floor again. Outside, Le Chinois took his other arm, and kneed him cheerily in the groin. Lucas doubled over, and the two thugs dragged him down some steps into a basement room. Once inside, they locked the door. He heard them conferring briefly, and then there was silence.

15. Solitaire

'So you were slung in the hole?' asked Igbar Zoff. 'Solitary confinement, iron manacles, what?'

Igbar searched through his pockets for more cigarettes. I handed him mine.

'A dungeon, filled with slimy crawling things?' asked Sean, incredulous. 'Narration slips seamlessly from Gothic fantasy to *The Count of Monte Cristo*.'

'Just so. Lucas himself a slimy crawling thing,' I answered. 'Are there any more drugs?'

'Mandragora, marzipan, migraine medicine, mescaline,' chanted Igbar from the hammock.

'Mescaline, for sure,' I said.

'No kidding,' said Sean, and produced a small package from inside his jacket.

'Christ almighty,' groaned Susie. 'How's he meant to concentrate on what he's telling us with that stuff?'

'Prerogative of the storyteller,' answered Igbar.

'Ancient Celtic custom, as you must know, Ms Serendipity, given your roots. Feed the bard; nourish the tale.'

'I have one of sprites and goblins,' Sean added, handing me the carefully folded foil wrap.

'*You* have one of pure gobshite,' responded Susie Serendipity.

'On reflection, I'll stick to the intoxicants of my ancestors,' I said.

'Wise choice. Put it away, Sean. I for one want to listen, not wrestle with alligators.'

Sean obediently returned the mescaline to his jacket pocket.

'Bones,' said Igbar.

'What?'

'The *bones* of your ancestors,' insisted Igbar, apparently dwelling on his own last contribution. 'The final line of a Turkish imprecation. In which the speaker threatens to fornicate with each and every member of the interlocutor's family, rounding off with the ancestral relics.'

'How unsavoury,' murmured Sean.

The sun had moved out of view behind tall buildings to the west. Susie pulled on a cardigan, and settled herself more comfortably on the cushions. Eugenia was looking at me intently, ignoring the banter. She appeared to be caught up in her own reflections. Tolerant, curious, but not easily distracted.

'Go on,' she said.

*

Inside the cell there was complete and utter darkness. Lucas felt his way around, having barely taken the room in before the door was closed and the light from the corridor shut out. Fumbling along the stone walls, using fingers as eyes, he negotiated all four corners, then came upon the door frame, returning to the place where he had been deposited by Le Chinois' final push. He then remembered that he had a lighter in his pocket, along with some cigarettes. He flicked on the flame and looked around. It was a small room, and it was completely empty. In the upper recess of the wall facing him was a grill consisting of metal bars, a few inches wide, that might have served as an air-hole set just above ground level, but which was sealed off by a sliding metal plate on the far side of the grill.

The flame heated the cheap lighter and scorched his fingers. He returned to the darkness, his eyes immediately conjuring hallucinatory shapes and colours in the sudden blackness. He suspected that the cell had been prepared for him especially. It was intended, he surmised, reflecting on Pontneuf's fondness for allegory, as a symbol of his inner emptiness. He no longer believed that Pontneuf left anything to chance, but that in all he did were implicit messages, secret resonances: he had hatched plans for Lucas long before Lucas had ever met Nuria.

Kataskapos. Lucas could see why Pontneuf had called him a spy. Apart from attempting to eavesdrop on Pontneuf's rendezvous with Nuria, he had, over the weeks, placed himself outside the group, and refused to play along with Pontneuf's efforts to elicit his 'remembering'. But he was also, in Pontneuf's eyes, a spy of a different order, as he would shortly discover.

Lucas sat on the stone floor with his back against the wall. It was damp and cold, and he was dressed only in tee shirt, jeans and sandals. Shivering, he reached in his jeans' pocket for cigarettes, pulled one to his lips and lit it. He inhaled deeply, grateful for the small comfort of smoking, and for the meagre light which the glowing orange tip provided in the obscurity of his prison.

In the course of the next few hours he cultivated a bright and raging hatred for Pontneuf. It had been kept at a distance during the preceding weeks at the Refuge, since he held out hope that Pontneuf's innate character could not be so manifestly corrupt if he had embraced a religion so pacific and harmonious as Catharism appeared to be.

He became convinced that Pontneuf had been unfrocked as a Catholic priest. Perhaps Nuria was an early victim in more ways than one. However, could such a man's sway over her persist into her late twenties?

Lucas' cigarette slipped into the crook between his fingers, burning him, and he spilled the stub to the floor and lifted his hand to his mouth, moistening the skin where it had burned.

Hours seemed to pass by. Lucas knew that prisoners kept in solitary, above all those confined to darkness, were liable to confusion and disorientation. No sounds from the outside filtered through to his cell. Gradually his anger gave way to a despairing sense of resignation. He had been comprehensively gulled. He had allowed his pride and self-importance to blind him to many things about his relationship with Nuria that were now so transparent. It had been clear from the outset that they were being monitored; and yet he was the only one of the two who remarked on it. Nuria never once raised the issue. She responded to Lucas's questions and concerns about the postcard, about the reader of

Kierkegaard, and about the roof people, with a barely-concealed lack of interest. Only the unexpected and dramatic behaviour of the witch in the bar at Sitges had unnerved her, and she had not spoken of the reason for this.

Like a man nursing a sword-thrust through the groin, he lay doubled-up and shivering. He was waiting, and was prepared to wait. The more total his emptiness became, the less the waiting bothered him. He allowed it to envelop him, to make of him a void creature. He was weightless, impassive, and, in a strange sense, nurtured by this emptiness. He in turn nurtured the emptiness so that nothing might touch him. Anything that attempted to get close would vanish into the same void he himself had disappeared into.

He was roused by the rustling of keys in the lock of his cell door. A light came on, and he saw that there was a bare electric bulb above the doorway, evidently controlled by an outside switch. The door opened, and Zaco appeared, carrying a large pitcher of water and a tray, which he placed on the floor. Somebody behind him passed Zaco a blanket. Lucas called out to them to wait but they were gone before he could rouse himself from the floor. The light stayed on, a small consolation. In the far corner of the cell there was a hole in the rough stone floor, which must have been intended to serve as a toilet. Lucas went to the door and hammered on it uselessly for a minute, then settled down to the contents of his tray, which consisted of a thin vegetable soup and bread, and a slice of goat's cheese.

He swallowed the soup greedily, and had begun to nibble on the cheese, when he heard footsteps once more in the corridor. This time there was one person, and the door did not open, but the light was extinguished, leaving him again in sudden and pitch darkness. He shouted after the retreating footsteps in vain, and then finished his bread and cheese in the remorseless silence that ensued. He guessed it was already dark outside, but had no way of knowing. It was certainly colder now, and he wrapped himself in the blanket and lit a cigarette. It was important for him to conserve the fuel in his lighter. Not that there was anything to do in the cell. He simply felt that having access to some light would prevent him from going completely crazy. He was sure they had not intended him to have a light, and that a failure to search him must simply have been an oversight, or laziness on the part of Zaco and Le Chinois, rather than an act of charity.

He could not recall how many times food was delivered to him over the next few days. However, apart from the fragmentation of the hours by unpredictable meals, he was treated to occasional glimpses of daylight: from time to time a hand reached down and the metal grill, set into the wall just below the ceiling, was opened, allowing a trickle of light to enter the room. While bringing him an almost joyful release from the utter darkness, and a hint of fresh air, it was not kept this way permanently and during the night no light entered the room anyway, whether the grill was open or not.

After the first half-dozen visits, he was not sure whether he was being brought an evening meal or a morning meal, since the menu remained much the same. Occasionally he would be given some rice or pasta in place of the soup. The portions were meagre and rarely warm, but sufficient to keep him from starving. A couple of times he was certain they had brought him two meals within the space of an hour, and conversely, he was once left alone for what seemed like an eternity. On that occasion he was so weak he could barely crawl to the door when his food was eventually delivered, and had to chew the bread slowly, aware that bolting it might make him vomit.

Nothing was provided for him apart from the bare meals, for which he was absurdly grateful. While he was able to use the primitive toilet, there were no washing facilities, and he could not spare much of the drinking water for that. After a few days the problem of sanitation ceased to bother him. He could not live without food and water, but he could live with his own stench.

The process of gradual mental de-stabilisation set in early. He had read about political and religious prisoners kept alert and *compos mentis* by their tenets and faith. He had none to resort to. He was completely alone, with no God and no creed. His unexpected flirtation with Christianity had come via the born-again Cathars (whose authenticity he was now in no way prepared to accept) and had ended as abruptly as it had begun. He took no pleasure in contemplating the future, let alone an afterlife, sitting as he did amid the cognitive rubble and detritus of his life, but he was given to occasional outbreaks of demented laughter. This laughter was his only means of communication, and there was no recipient except the bare walls. Frequently his laughter disintegrated into tears. He wept until he was devoid of all feeling, which he supposed was the purpose also of his laughter; to empty himself of emotion. Laughter, tears, then silence. He hallucinated sounds that would have brought him comfort: birdsong; a waterfall; the wind, promising himself that he would never again take these sounds for granted, a promise whose fulfilment was as uncertain to him as his release from this cell. He began to cherish the memories of food, of a comfortable bed, of a sunlit beach.

Inevitably, he pined for Nuria. What he could not come to terms with was her apparent and declared sense of enjoyment in his company, her eagerness to seduce him and be seduced, her perfect enactment of a young woman in love. He revisited in his imagination every meal they had eaten together, every conversation they had shared: above all, he passed hours in the detailed reconstruction of their abundant sex life. These harrowing reflections sometimes led to bouts of prolonged and inspired masturbation, followed by troughs of inevitable and incremental misery. He found it impossible to believe, in spite of all the evidence, that Nuria could have maintained the fiction of being in love as convincingly as she appeared to have done. He tried to convince himself that Pontneuf had hypnotised her, that he had drugged her, that he held some terrible power over her which she was incapable of escaping. But still his doubts remained, a subterranean well of distrust and resentment that he would draw on in his moments of deepest anxiety.

After an eternity of such days and nights, he was awakened rudely from a deep sleep by Zaco and Le Chinois, who carried a mop and a bucket. Zaco indicated that he was to clean up his toilet corner. Le Chinois made idiotic mopping movements, as though explaining the task to one as cretinous as himself. He set about the task enthusiastically – physical work, and the dim light, providing a novel break for him – and when he had finished, sat for a while regarding his new pine-fresh world in silence before hammering on the door of the cell with the mop-handle. Zaco appeared almost at once.

He signalled down the corridor and within a few seconds Nuria was in the doorway. Zaco stood aside and let her in. He must have stayed by the closed door, as his footsteps could not be heard echoing down the passage.

Lucas looked at Nuria in surprise. She seemed anxious and jittery. He had certainly not been prepared for this visit. She reached up and touched his hair, and he instinctively pulled away from her.

She slid down the wall to the floor, and sat there, knees pulled up to her chest. Then she began to apologise profusely and tearfully. She said she had had to bribe Zaco to allow her to visit, a comment which incited Lucas to sneer about the nature of such a bribe. She sighed, but made no retort. She told him that only since his incarceration had she truly come to realise how much he meant to her. He became angry. For days and days he had been bottling everything up in solitude, and now Nuria had appeared, seeking out his compassion and understanding.

'What's gone wrong with your plans?' he asked. 'Can't the old man get it up? Or have you got tired of being a Christian? Well?'

He looked across at her. Her arms were hugging her knees and she was rocking to and fro. She looked up at him and her face was wet with tears. He clicked his tongue in annoyance.

'I get weeks, a month, who knows how long in this shit-hole...' he began.

'Three weeks,' she muttered. 'Twenty days. I counted them.'

'...and rot here in oblivion, but the moment you get an attack of guilt, long overdue I should add, you come running to see me, overcome with self-pity. What, or who, exactly, are you crying for?'

221

She brushed her face with the sleeve of her jersey, then looked him in the eyes.

'Please. Stop. They're going to kill you, Lucas. You won't believe how crazy things are getting.'

He suddenly felt sick. He had suspected something very bad was going to happen, but to hear it put so bluntly into words still came as a shock.

'What? Why?'

Nuria spoke softly and quickly, her voice breaking with a convincing tearfulness.

'They're going to have a show trial. They're going to try you as Raymond Gasc and find you guilty of treachery, of selling out Rocher and his followers to the Inquisition. André's told the others that Raymond betrayed the whole group in 1247 because he, Raymond, believed that Rocher and Clare were conducting a – you know – clandestine affair. There was an ambush in the mountains on the second day out of Mélissac. Raymond had informed the Inquisition of the group's route.'

'But what of the leap into the unknown? The pact. The Cathar disappearing trick?'

'It never happened. But he's told everyone slightly different things. The one thing that remains constant is that there was an agreement of some sort, that the group would fulfil their common destiny in a future incarnation. According to the current version, everyone except Raymond was taken back to Toulouse and burned alive.'

'I've been arguing with him for days,' she continued. 'I think he knows I've turned against him. Ever since that day you were slung in here, I've been trying to find my way out of this mess, and back to you.'

She got up off the floor and put her arms around his neck, nestling her head against him, holding on tight.

She was still shaking. He felt himself soften, and started stroking her hair, experiencing in rapid succession most of the emotions he had endured over the past three weeks: anger, bitterness, sorrow, and now this sudden warmth.

'How are they going to kill me?' He asked, finally.

A few seconds' quiet. Then she said: 'They're going to burn you at the stake.'

16. In which the 'past' closes in

Lucas stopped stroking Nuria's hair at this piece of information. Those few words put everything into perspective. He was at the mercy of a power-crazed psychopath, obsessed with living out his medieval fantasy. As the prospect of his imminent death made its nest in the battered cave of his understanding, Lucas became absolutely terrified.

Before he had a chance to respond, however, Nuria spoke again. 'I'm going to help you escape. If we succced, and can both get away, will you promise to try and trust me again? I know it's a lot to ask, after what's happened. God, I'm so sorry. And asking favours of a condemned man, it should be the other way around, no? But certain things have happened since you've been in here. I can't go into them now, no time.'

Lucas didn't feel up to promising her anything. But then, nobody else was volunteering to help him out, and if the situation was as Nuria described, he was going to need a lot of help. He left her request unanswered.

'How can you trust Zaco not to tell Pontneuf you've met with me?'

'I can't, but it's my only option. Actually, of the four of them, Zaco's the best, or rather the least moronic. And he owes me a favour.' She glanced at Lucas's face and continued rapidly, 'I helped him out once. He went absent without leave one day, hunting wild boar with some of the locals. I covered for him.'

But Lucas wasn't taking this in.

'Can you tell me precisely what they're going to try me for? I need to prepare myself in some way.'

'You will be tried as a traitor to Catharism, a papal spy. He's deadly serious. I think he's probably mad.'

'Well, that's bloody useful.'

Nuria got to her feet.

'The thing with André is this: he thinks he can rationalise everything, while disregarding any rational criticisms of himself. He's been, I don't know, ruling my life. But I simply can't take it any more. My compliance has seized up. Hell, I'm so fucking confused. Look, I have to go. I'll be missed. The trial is today, in the evening.'

'I've no idea what evening means.'

'Of course. No light. It's morning now, around eleven. Listen: I will cause a distraction during the trial or immediately afterwards. I'll sort something out, even if it does mean getting help from Zaco. You must get as far away as possible. Head west at first, then down through the forest. I'll meet you, let's see, it's August the fifteenth today. God, I don't know when. It might not be possible for me to go straight back to Barcelona, but I'll get there. But we *can* be together again, I swear, if you could bring yourself to forgive me. But whatever you do, don't come back for me. And don't get the local police involved. André claims he has them eating out of his hand. Here, you'll need some money. Take this.'

She handed Lucas a roll of bank notes, and his bank card, which she must have retrieved from his wallet. She also gave him a full pack of cigarettes and a lighter, his old one having expired days before. He stuffed the money and the card deep in his jeans pocket. As he did so, it occurred to him that if Nuria were really telling the truth about her plan, she was putting her own safety at risk.

'But what if they find out that you've helped me to escape? Pontneuf would know immediately. Won't they take it out on you? Collusion and conspiracy. Christ, they'll probably burn you instead!'

Nuria stared at him very hard. 'No,' she said, unhesitatingly. 'André wouldn't lay a finger on me.'

He said it before he could stop himself: 'That's funny. I thought he'd already done more than that.'

Nuria began to get angry, her cheeks flushing, then drew herself up.

'It isn't like that. One day I'll try and explain everything. I guess I owe you a lot of explanations. But you just have to trust me. Please let's leave it there for now.'

But Lucas had been starved of any sort of contact for so long, and there was so much he needed to know. He couldn't bear for her to leave, and should her plan for his escape misfire, possibly not see her again.

'No, Nuria. You've been holding stuff back from me for far too long. It was obvious that morning after the roof people came. Was that a sign then, that cross? That the plan would take place that night?'

Nuria looked at the wall, nodding her head.

'Christ almighty. And for those two weeks that we were together in Barcelona, were you seeing Pontneuf then, too? Were you *fucking* him?'

'Oh dear God. Lucas. No, I wasn't even seeing him. Or anybody else. You, you... *idiota*. I was trapped, or rather *inhabited* by him. A younger him. Like carrying a second face on the back of my head. Do you remember?'

Lucas recalled the story she had told him in the Café de l'Opera.

'I believed what André told me to the extent that I agreed to take part in the Miró Foundation meeting. I never told you this, although I always meant to. Gradually it seemed to lose importance, after that day we met. You see, *I* had received a postcard *also*, identical message to yours, except mine had a picture of the sculptures on the roof garden.'

'Why didn't you tell me this before? No wonder you found the story of my own postcard so amusing.'

'I wanted to. I even tried to, twice. But I had promised André not to tell you. He had such a grip on me. I had become dependent on him in a way I simply can't find words for. I don't know. How can I explain to you something that you've never known? It's just not explainable. Of course I knew the postcard had come from André. Perhaps mine was also delivered by the roof people. There was no postage stamp. André had a connection with some of them a while back. I got the feeling that things didn't work out the way he planned; they were free agents, didn't succumb to his charms, but accepted his money. A few still do, apparently. In any case, he used me to lure you to him. I had no idea what precisely he had in mind, and I certainly hadn't counted on falling in love with you. That wasn't part of André's plan.'

'Couldn't he have predicted it? Knowing what he knew of Clare and Raymond Gasc? If we are their incarnations, aren't we *supposed* to be in love?'

'The one thing the fortune teller can't predict is what's right under his nose. André's ego is so massive that he probably thought he could control everything. That's his biggest flaw.'

'Tell me, Nuria. Are you sleeping with him?'

'No,' she said. 'It's never been like that.'

Nuria stopped, suddenly looking weary. She was not exactly presenting herself as a victim, which was some relief under the circumstances; but Lucas could tell, or thought he could tell, that she had been through a terrible personal struggle that stretched back years. Pontneuf had in some way marked her, had been active in forging the person she had become, and the imprint was still there.

An insistent rapping on the door brought Lucas back to his own ghastly reality.

Nuria started, then turned towards him.

'Whatever happens tonight, promise me you won't give up on me. That we'll meet up again. When we're both ready. Will you?'

He had nothing to lose.

'I promise,' he said.

'Remember. Just be your usual charming self at the trial.' She almost smiled. 'They're going to find you guilty whatever you say.'

'Is that meant to reassure me?'

'I'll make certain you have the chance to get away. That's my promise.'

And with that, she put her arms around him and hugged him tight, brushing her lips against his throat. Then she knocked sharply on the door. Zaco opened it at once, and his face appeared in the doorway, leering. Lucas could have sworn he winked at him over Nuria's shoulder as she left. The door remained open only for as long as it took for her to slip out, then closed quietly.

That was the longest day Lucas had ever known, waiting in his cell for the summons to whatever fate Pontneuf decreed for him. He had a meal of soup and bread shortly after Nuria left, brought to him by Le Chinois, and then was left alone. He paced the cell, something that he had developed into a fine art during all those dark days. He knew precisely where the walls were, through a kind of internal radar device, and was even able to sustain a fractured jog around the square room. He practised push-ups and sit-ups. He sank into a fit of deepest despair, followed by jubilant fantasies of escape and of meeting again with Nuria in Barcelona; of the two of them taking up their lives where they had left off. Finally he wrapped himself in his blanket, slipping into bouts of restless sleep. While he had not fully absorbed Nuria's warning that he was to be burned at the stake, at times, between snatches of sleep, he felt the full impending dread of such an outcome.

He woke with the scratching of the key in the lock, and was on his feet before the door had opened. The light came on, dazzling him as always, and Zaco, Le Chinois and the cyclops, El Tuerto, entered the room. Le Chinois carried a length of rope, with which he proceeded to tie Lucas's hands behind his back. The cord dug into the flesh of his wrists. The three of them then led him down the corridor, Zaco ahead, and the other two bringing up the rear. They climbed the stairs to ground level, and walked outside. It was a clear, crisp evening, with a sharp breeze. The fresh air was like a balm, despite the chill. Lucas breathed in deeply. The mountain air tasted so good following his incarceration underground and days of breathing in the rank smell of his own sweat and excrement. He would have liked simply to stay there in the night air, enjoying that brief moment of relative freedom, but his guards hurried him along. They crossed the edge of the village square and Lucas could just make out the shadowy bulk of his funeral pyre in the darkness. They entered the council hall building by a side entrance which connected with a kind of antechamber to the hall itself. Adjoining this antechamber was a small bathroom, where he was told to strip and shower. His bonds were released for this purpose and he was handed a bar of soap. The shower was cold, but it was a relief to feel clean after so many days without washing. After he had dried himself, and put on tee shirt, jeans and sandals, El Tuerto handed him a white smock, a garment which was half country yokel, half mortuary. Lucas pulled it over his head, an action that made him feel condemned in advance of the trial (which, if Nuria's predictions were correct, he already was). Once dressed, his hands were again bound, but this time in front of his body. El Tuerto led him into the antechamber and told him to sit in a straight-backed chair, then positioned himself behind it.

Lucas could hear a murmur of voices from the hall, a sound that swelled in volume by the minute. Occasionally individual voices could be heard against the general hubbub. It must have been time for the evening council meeting, but everyone would have known that something out of the ordinary was going to take place tonight, since normally such meetings were awaited in reverential silence.

It was not long before Le Chinois and the disfigured Francisco entered the room to fetch Lucas. They led him into the hall, which had been set up as a courtroom. Pontneuf presided at the head of the court, seated at a long table with Marta and Rafael, the two other perfecti, on either side of him. There was a designated space for the prisoner between two smaller tables facing this triumvirate of judges, to which Lucas was directed, with his minders standing slightly behind him. They were situated half-way across the hall from the judges, and the rest of the community was seated to Lucas's left. The only exits were the one on his right, from which he had emerged, leading to the antechamber, and the main entrance at the back of the hall, the other side of the thirteen credentes. There were no negotiable windows in the hall. He scanned the group, looking for Nuria. She was nearest to the wall, on the far side, looking straight ahead. It was clear to Lucas that they must avoid eye contact.

Pontneuf was looking through a pile of manuscripts when Lucas was shown to his place, and only glanced up briefly, without indicating anything other than a businesslike preoccupation with his papers. Watching him seated there before this makeshift court, Lucas remembered his first impression of the man. He had thought him then to be a pompous fraud, and Pontneuf was never more so than at this moment, pretending to read, while lording over this assortment of religious crazies, slavish catamites and moronic thugs.

Pontneuf wasted no time on introductions.

'This special court has been convened to try the accused of the betrayal of our group, and of Catharism at large, to the forces of the Antichrist. Shortly before the fifteenth of May 1247, as Raymond Gasc, he

232

passed information to our enemies, enabling them to capture us during our flight across these very mountains.'

Here he gestured melodramatically toward the world outside the walls.

'How precisely this was done, and through whom Raymond Gasc conveyed this information, is, in part, the business of this court. Also, and more importantly, we need to receive an initial declaration of his innocence or guilt, and, when the trial is completed, an acknowledgement of his actions, if not an actual confession of guilt, before sentencing by the court can take place.'

He paused.

'Not guilty,' Lucas said.

Pontneuf grunted.

'We are tolerant people, and it is a right of the accused to deny these charges, if, in any way, he can substantiate these denials. For our part, conversely, we have to provide evidence of his guilt and compliance in what we can prove to be a gross act of treachery. I have in front of me an original document made at the time of the crusade against us, in which Raymond Gasc refutes all teachings of the Cathars, especially those of the renegade priest Bernard Rocher. Some of you have already seen this document.'

He held up a leather-bound volume, no doubt a part of his 'previously undiscovered' library from Toulouse or Carcassonne.

'In it, and I quote, "Raymond Gasc passed information to our officers that the heretic Rocher was currently living in the commune of Mélissac, but that he, and several of his followers were planning to escape within several days of this meeting. When asked, he described the likely course of their route.

233

Soldiers were sent to cut off the heretics, and they were apprehended, chained, and returned to our prison at Toulouse, where they were kept until the commencement of their trial."'

Pontneuf read, or appeared to read, the old French text in an appropriately grave manner, but, Lucas thought, he might as well have been reading from a Batman comic. This did not constitute evidence of any kind, even if Lucas agreed (and it was a monumental 'if') to 'being' Raymond Gasc. There was no option for him to argue against the case, only to pose counter-claims. Even this was probably a waste of time. He began wondering what precisely Nuria had planned for his escape. He had a thug a couple of feet behind him at each shoulder, and both exits were a long way away. He tried focussing on the number of paces he would need to reach the ante-chamber door. Meanwhile Pontneuf provided the audience with gory details of their thirteenth-century counterparts' torture and incineration, emphasising, for those who might still be in any doubt, that they had all died together for the Cathar cause.

'To whom did you pass the information regarding the flight from Mélissac?' he asked Lucas.

'Seeing as you have the Inquisition's report in front of you, I would suggest that you know the answer to that yourself. Personally I have no idea, since you are addressing me as "you" on the assumption that I accept your designation of me as Raymond Gasc. I do not. My name is Rhys Morgan Aurelio Lucas.'

Pontneuf grimaced.

'Very well then. Let us begin again. Do you deny that in your previous life as Raymond Gasc, you aided the inquisitorial forces in their pursuit and capture of a group of Cathars from the village of Mélissac?'

'I will do more than that. I deny any knowledge of having had a previous life, either as Raymond Gasc, Christopher Columbus, or anyone else.'

'And your plea of innocence is based on this fiction?'

Lucas laughed. How Pontneuf had the temerity to claim that his, Lucas's, version of himself was a 'fiction' defied all expectations of reasonable sense, let alone those of a court of law, even one as characteristically kangaroo as this.

'Is it not normal procedure to *begin* a prosecution by identifying the accused?' Lucas asked.

'It is. But in this case you are being tried for actions committed by yourself in a previous life. Therefore your current identity is of little interest to the court.'

'So I am being tried only for my alleged actions as the person you call Raymond Gasc?'

'Correct.'

'Then I can offer no defence other than my plea of innocence, since, as I have stated, I do not acknowledge being or ever having been Raymond Gasc.'

'So be it,' Pontneuf answered slyly. 'You will therefore be tried *in absentia*, as Raymond Gasc. You will, however, as Rhys Morgan Aurelio Lucas, be expected to attend.'

Lucas let this bewildering logic go unremarked. He could see that nothing he said that refuted the charges made against Gasc was going to make any difference. He could, however, try another tack, one which he had surreptitiously been nurturing since his first long talk with Pontneuf by the mountain stream. But he would hold fire on this until an appropriate moment presented itself. Meanwhile Pontneuf enumerated further allegations against the poor Raymond Gasc, whose treachery had evidently been the source of considerable grief to Bernard Rocher, ending as it did his plans for escape and re-settlement in the more accommodating climate of Trans-Pyrenean Catalunya.

'For the information of the court, I can confirm that the Inquisitors' report relates that, at a secret meeting, Raymond Gasc confided the precise details of the group of heretics' escape from Mélissac. The Inquisitor's account reads –' (and here Pontneuf returned to his leather-bound files, perusing the text through a hand-held magnifying lens, like a myopic but benevolent scholar) '"the shepherd Gasc did give cause for me to believe that he would renounce the heresy known as Catharism, and would lead a proper Christian life following confession and absolution. Since the information which he gave to me proved correct, and resulted in the capture of the heretic Rocher and his followers, I would recommend to the Inquisitor General that Gasc's life be spared and whatever outstanding penance is demanded of him be weighed against the honourable course of action he has pursued in meeting with me, at such risk to himself. Gasc also pleaded with me that the life of his wife, Clare, be spared, since he believed Rocher to be an agent of the devil who had poisoned her mind against both himself, Gasc, and the true teachings of our Lord Jesus Christ."'

He passed the manuscript to his right, so that Rafael could confirm the content of the passage he had quoted. Rafael followed the text with a long quivering finger, then nodded his head sadly. He struck Lucas as a pathetic figure, lugubrious and servile. Lucas couldn't imagine from what deathly cloister Pontneuf had recruited his services.

'Need we know more?' Pontneuf questioned the small crowd of credentes now, who sat like a huddle of eager schoolchildren, awaiting his verdict. 'Would any one of you care to speak in defence of the actions of the accused?'

Nobody spoke.

'As I supposed,' resumed Pontneuf, 'since these actions are indefensible. A report in the hand of the Inquisition stating clearly that Raymond Gasc renounced his faith and betrayed his colleagues.'

'May I speak?' Lucas proposed, when it seemed to him that Pontneuf was finished.

'Please. Do.' Pontneuf offered, suddenly magnanimous.

'In your previous life as Bernard Rocher, did you live impeccably according to the tenets of the Cathar faith?'

'As well as any man might.'

'You obeyed the vows of chastity?'

'What is this nonsense? Yes, I did.'

'So you would deny the charge that you were conducting an illicit sexual relationship with Clare, the wife of Raymond Gasc, at the time of the events we are discussing.'

Pontneuf guffawed. The disciplined monk who had serenaded Lucas with his vision of a new world religion was entirely absent from this court.

'I would refute such an idiotic claim unreservedly. It is true that while still a young man, and before my conversion to Catharism, I had lain with women. Yes, I had carnal knowledge of them, fornicated, ate of the forbidden fruit. It was common practice among the Catholic clergy then, and ever shall be. As present day readers of newspapers can verify.'

Pontneuf could barely contain his amusement at the accusation. He continued, enjoying himself rather more than Lucas considered apt, considering the gravity of the punishment he had in store for him.

'While working among the lepers of Lombardy I was gifted with an understanding of the true nature of the world, and made my conversion to the Cathar faith. From that moment I never felt the pangs of lust, nor ever ate the flesh or produce of creatures. To suggest that I lay with the woman of whom you speak, Clare d'Aubrac, who married you, Raymond Gasc, is a gross calumny. Your mindless jealousy, which you placed, and continue to place, before any other consideration, cost the previous lives of all the good people you see around you, burned horribly on the pyres of the Inquisition. A fate which tonight you will share, none too soon.'

What had happened to Nuria's plan, if she had one? Lucas glanced at her, but she was looking straight ahead, unmoving. He realised that in order to prolong this performance, he was going to have to improvise, relying only on his own blurred intuitions about Pontneuf/Rocher.

'So what of Rocher himself? Where, among your "documents" does it state that he perished in the flames, along with all his followers? It doesn't, does it? You yourself have told me that Rocher's name had been "airbrushed" from all official accounts of the crusade against the Cathars. And in your own, private account, what specific mention is made of him? Clearly he has not vanished from there too. Is it not true that Rocher escaped the trials unscathed? How could such an important Cathar fish escape the Inquisition's net? Why don't you inform your so-called court that this was so? Was there a secret deal done with his noble relatives in the court of Aragon? And that he "disappeared" or was "airbrushed" from the official accounts on condition that nothing more was heard of him? I put it to you,

André, that your precious manuscript is either a travesty, a fake, or else a later document, designed and drawn up to protect the real outcome of the trial of Rocher, which was an embarrassment to certain figures in the ecclesiastical community. To be explicit: can you furnish the court – here Lucas allowed himself a dismissive wave of the hand towards Pontneuf's miserable crew of sycophants – with any evidence at all that Bernard Rocher died at the stake? Can you?'

Lucas had no idea where this stuff was coming from, but it seemed to be having a very bad effect on Pontneuf's temper. He sat back in silence, magisterial in his big chair, but his eyes had narrowed and he wore an expression of fierce contempt.

However, Lucas never had the pleasure of hearing his reply.

Before the lights went out, there was an explosion, which seemed to come from one of the outbuildings. Lucas guessed the generator had blown. Whatever Nuria had engineered had taken place successfully. All he had to do now was move, and fast. He could feel the first contact of a minder's hand on his shoulder and he twisted free, sprinting towards the nearer exit. Darkness, he felt, after his three weeks' confinement, was his element, and until someone found a candle or a torch, he had the advantage. He had also, through some subliminal process, been working with numbers throughout the trial, measuring distances and counting steps. He knocked somebody over as he counted three strides before diving to the floor, where he knew there to be a table, then scrambling to his feet, counted four, five, six strides to the exit.

He head-butted his way into the stomach of a body, which he guessed from its bulk was that of El Tuerto, who gasped, winded, and crumpled to the ground. Since Lucas knew that El Tuerto had been standing in the doorway, he leaped over the body and into the antechamber. If the outer door was bolted, he would be trapped inside this small space, with his hands still tied in front of him, but the door gave with a push, and he jumped clear, into the moonlit square.

Part Three

On Saturday nights in Plaça Reial you can almost hear
the viruses mutating.
Robert Hughes

cuando me buscan nunca estoy
cuando me encuentran yo no soy
el que está enfrente porque ya
me fui corriendo más allá
Manu Chao

17. The art of descent

Sean was looking at me suspiciously. Eugenia was smiling. Susie was drawing in a sketchbook with coloured pastels and Igbar Zoff appeared to be asleep. It was evening, and the air was cooler than it had been the previous night. I got up and used the bathroom, then began to make tea. But my mind was still racing with the cocaine and the unfolding story: I needed some kind of ballast. Tea would not be enough. The tequila was finished and I had no taste for beer, so I asked Susie Serendipity to finish preparing the brew and I went down to the corner store and bought a bottle of Fundador. Stretching my legs did me good, and when I returned I expected my friends would want to make a move. Susie had placed a thick candle on the floor in the centre of the terrace, and it gave off a soothing scent of cedarwood.

During the course of my storytelling, my voice had become strained. I sat up in the hammock and drank hot lemon juice with a generous slug of brandy. Igbar, cross-legged against the terrace wall amid a sea of cushions, had taken the short-stemmed pipe from his coat and was ramming the bowl with a soft and sticky putty. Opium was a rarely-encountered luxury at the best of times, but evidently his windfall had caused him to cast financial caution aside.

'Here, let me do that,' offered Sean, as Igbar succeeded in spilling the contents of the bowl for a second time while attempting to light his pipe.

'So you got away, huh?' questioned Susie, who, since it was now dark, had put her sketchbook aside. 'How long ago was this?'

'Oh, two, three days now,' I replied, with a smile.

'Hang on, man,' put in Sean, match poised above his opium pipe. 'Are we supposed to *believe* all this? I thought you were just telling us a story, to uh, pass away the hours.'

'Ignoramus,' Igbar interjected. '*Just* a story? Any story is just a story. What makes one any more *just* a story than another?'

'A true story,' responded Sean, 'is not *just* a story. This one has lurched through too many tests of plausibility to merit the epithet "true". Lucas is even giving us a range of narrative styles. He's obviously pissing us about. That's why he insists on referring to himself in the third person. A true story,' he repeated, with drugged determination, 'isn't just some screwball therapy session for unrequited love. A true story is a true story.'

'A mindless pleonasm, peasant. No story is any truer than any other to the receptive mind.'

'Oh, fuck's sake, you two: grow up,' said Susie Serendipity.

Sean looked up and caught a mosquito in his hand, wiping the residue of the insect on his jeans.

'Little bastards,' he said.

Eugenia sighed, shifting her position on the mattress.

'*Famous little bastards of history,*' mumbled Igbar to himself, before taking a lungful from the pipe. The atmosphere on the terrace was transformed into one evocative of a Bangkok opium den: pungent, sharp, sweet and resinous.

I finished my drink and lay back in the hammock, accepting a fresh pipe from Sean.

'And then?' said Eugenia.

'There's not a lot to say,' I said. 'I managed to escape from the Refuge, under cover of darkness. They sent out a Landrover after me but I headed for the woods, unbound my wrists, and followed a track down the mountain. By the morning I had reached a village, got a lift to Berga, then a bus back to Barcelona. I left a message for you, Eugenia.'

Eugenia nodded. 'And how about Nuria? Didn't you arrange to meet her back here?'

'Assuming she could get away, yes. We didn't exactly *arrange* anything. But coming home, I was out of my mind with worry. I felt like a refugee returning to the bombed-out remains of a previous life. I'd half-expected the place to be ransacked but as far as I could tell there had been no break-in and all my stuff: papers, books and music collection were as I'd left them. The answerphone was jammed, of course. I sat on the bed and began to panic. Here I was, safe and comfortable, while Nuria, for all I knew, was facing some horrendous punishment for aiding and abetting my escape. In spite of her assurances that Pontneuf wouldn't harm her, I was unconvinced. I felt as though, after all, *I* had been the one who'd betrayed *her*, and that by not going to the police at the first opportunity, perhaps in the village where I'd been that morning, I had put her life in danger. But she had told me not to go to the police. I didn't know what to do. So I went scouting around her old flat, and that's where I bumped into Zoff and Hogg. In Poble Sec.'

Across the narrow alley in the next block of flats, a neighbour was strumming a guitar. A song of intimate despair carried towards us before stopping abruptly, as though the singer had forgotten the remaining words.

I glanced at my audience. Susie was stretching on the mattress, Sean shaking his head and looking up at me awkwardly.

'A most unlikely confabulation, if you ask me.'

'Nobody did,' said Susie Serendipity.

Eugenia said she had to leave, but would call me soon. As I showed her out, she made no reference to my story, even though she had known more than any of the others about my romance with Nuria. She seemed unusually pensive.

Igbar, by contrast, was ebullient, and proclaiming that the night was still young, was set to celebrate whatever came to mind: my escape from Pontneuf's pyre, his spontaneous proposal of marriage to Susie Serendipity (rejected), the sale of another painting (yet to be transacted) or whatever other possible justification presented itself. The promise of the mescaline was tempting, but I was not sure my already-beleagured brain could have coped with such a demanding hallucinogen, especially if it involved, as seemed likely, a night of bar-crawling and the inevitable accompanying chaos. Besides, I was weary, and so ushered Igbar and Sean on their way. Susie left with them.

The next day I decided to visit the church of Santa María del Mar. It had always been my favourite among Barcelona's many churches and I felt anonymous but undiminished, sitting for an hour under its massive arches and high, vaulted roof. Why this place might mark the beginning of my quest for Nuria I did not know, but I was convinced that any systematic investigation was going to lead me nowhere. I had to rely on chance, or serendipity, on simply awaiting promptings from the unseen and the impalpable.

Returning home, I paced the floor of my flat, flustered and frustrated by this impasse. Nuria's assertion that we would find one another, somehow, seemed a shallow promise given the absence of any trace of her in the city where she had lived. I decided to try and call her family home, finding the number in directory enquiries.

Nuria's mother sounded anxious and suspicious. I spent a while reassuring her with a representation of myself that was at once concerned but non-predatory. I claimed to be a friend of Nuria's from her London days who had visited Barcelona only to find she no longer lived at her old address. I exaggerated an English accent to this effect. I had known her family lived in Maçanet, and was calling to see if they had any news of her whereabouts. After various false starts and many questions about me, she eventually burst into tears, telling me, huskily, that she had not heard from Nuria for nearly three years and that if I found her, to please ask her to get in touch with her as a matter of urgency. I was, she said, to tell her that she was forgiven for the things that they had argued about in the past, and that she hoped Nuria could forgive her mother for the terrible things *she* had said.

I might have sounded sober enough to convince Nuria's mother of my good character, but no longer wanted to be. I had finished the last of the brandy with breakfast and so went down to the general store on the street corner to buy another bottle. While there I wandered through the market, bought some fresh anchovies and picked up a copy of *El País* from the kiosk, although I had no desire to read the newspaper. Simply buying a paper lent an aspect of normality to my actions, however spurious.

Back in the flat I prepared the anchovies, dusted them with flour, and fried them in oil. Leaving the fish to cook, I made a salad and cut some bread. Then, just as I started to eat, there was a knock at the door. Barefoot, and wearing only shorts, I crossed the studio to see who was there. It was Manu, my neighbour, leaning indolently against the door-jamb, a *Ducados* poking from his mouth. He greeted me as though we had last spoken only the previous day, rather than ten weeks earlier, and invited me to join him on the patio.

Bringing my plate, and piling another with the remaining fish for Manu, I followed him onto the back patio, explaining my long absence by saying I had been working in London. As soon as Manu picked at the food and began to speak, I braced myself for a further installation in the Saga of the Rabbits, which was still not concluded, in spite of an ongoing flow of threatening letters from the Municipal Health Authorities. Manu was by turns melancholic and belligerent, and it was evident that he too had been suffering his traumas since we last spoke.

'And to make matters worse,' he confided, seated on an upturned crate next to his shed, offering me the relative comfort of a broken deck-chair, 'to make matters worse, we have poachers.'

An interesting term to use in an urban context.

'Not regularly. I can't pretend the thieving bastards have decimated my stock, but a couple go missing every week or so. And it's definitely people, not cats.'

I didn't mention the visit from Ric, Fionnula and Ninja boy. Manu would no doubt regard it as an act of betrayal on my part if I had told him that I'd let them get away with two of his rabbits without protest. But I was curious to know whether he had heard anything, then or at any other time.

'They say,' I began, disingenuously, 'that there's a group of kids who live out on the roofs...'

Manu interrupted before I could finish. 'You've heard this too? If they're homeless, God knows, I wouldn't deny them a rabbit or two for the pot. Rather them than the sons of whores at City Hall exterminate the lot with a court order.'

'What have you heard?'

'Shit, all kinds of stuff.' Manu scratched himself vigorously. 'One person tells you one thing, another something else. I've never seen or heard a thing. I even spent a night up here with the shotgun in July, but I got too comfortable and went to sleep.'

He straightened himself on his crate. More scratching. Manu had been drinking but was not drunk. He was never exactly drunk: his lassitude, his prime defining characteristic, merely became more pronounced the further he was from a state of sobriety.

'Manu, do you have crabs?'

'*Joder*, it's a possibility.'

'You should have yourself checked out. And you never told me you had a shotgun.'

'It's a secret. I don't have a licence.'

'What do you keep it for?'

'Intruders.' I pondered for a moment the notion of Manu as armed vigilante, squat and pot-bellied in his stained vest and crumpled shorts, fag askew in his mouth, an ancient shotgun poised. It was an improbable image.

'But when you came up here you fell asleep, right?'

'*Pues... no sé*. Not straight away. I was kind of... resting. I wasn't going to shoot anyone. I just wanted to give them a fright. The gun was for self-defence.'

'But you didn't find anything out.'

'Not exactly nothing.'

'What do you mean?'

'It, uh, gives me shame to speak of it.'

He waited a moment, then added confidentially, 'I've told no one this, you understand?'

'It's all right, Manu. Secrecy assured. Word of honour.'

I could see he was steeling himself against my ridicule.

'Well, it's simple. They came that night. I waited up for them and went to sleep.'

'So while you lay snoring in your deck-chair, shotgun in your arms, they stole your rabbits?'

'Oy, *hombre*; you mock me. This is not a mocking matter. Your word of honour, remember?'

He was only half-joking. I bit my lip.

'So what did they do while you were sleeping?'

'How the fuck do I know? Flamenco dancing on my *cojones* for all I'm aware. Maybe that's how I got the crabs. *If* I have the crabs. But whatever else they did, they stole two rabbits and left that thing in the cage.'

Here he waved his hand at the door of the shed. I hadn't noticed before then, but nailed to the door by its oversize ears was a child's soft toy: a grey rabbit wearing dungarees and a lopsided grin. I suppressed my laughter. Pinned up in that way, the rabbit resembled some kind of juju talisman, as if warding off all who would enter the rabbit-shed.

'And,' he continued, 'they stuck a flower, a carnation, in the barrel of my gun.'

I smiled. 'That's nice,' I said. I could picture Fionnula, the girl with multiple piercings and the snub nose enjoying that moment.

'Nice?' roared Manu. 'They made me look like a fool. Whose side are you on anyway? Damn hippies.'

'So they left you the cuddly bunny to replace the live ones, and you crucified it on the door. Was this meant to keep them away?'

A long pause.

'I thought it may have that effect, but they've been back twice since.'

'Oh. And taken more rabbits?'

'Yeah, but like I said, I don't mind that so much. It was being outsmarted that riled me.'

I reflected that outsmarting Manu was not an arduous task.

'And what's new with the civic authorities? Why haven't they taken the rabbits away if they're a threat to health and safety? It's months since you had the first letter.'

'Ah, you know. Letters might get written, but nothing ever gets done around here for two months in the summer. I have a court summons tomorrow week and I'll turn up, guns blazing. Maybe you could come along. I'd appreciate that.'

'Sure,' I said. 'That's no problem. Just remind me of the date nearer the time.'

'To tell the truth I'm sick of it all, the whole story. Sick of the rabbits, even. It's a matter of principle now though.'

So, I thought; he doesn't mind the night raiders eating his rabbits but doesn't like to be outwitted. He has accepted that the City will almost certainly confiscate and destroy his rabbits, but will fight the case on principle. Here was a man driven by a very definite code of what was what: something I seemed to lack, in spite of my recent experiences. Perhaps I simply didn't care enough to care at all.

We sat on the roof for a while, and when, after half an hour Manu went downstairs for his siesta, I returned to my own flat and settled on the hammock.

Two days later I rented a car and drove to Berga with Eugenia and Igbar. I suppose I should have been more careful: perhaps I should have informed the police after all, reported Nuria missing and made the trip with a police escort. After all, these people had threatened my life. But at first I only intended spying on the Refuge from a distance, as if to reassure myself that it really existed. In the forty-eight hours that followed my account of the abduction and imprisonment, I had come close to convincing myself that I had dreamed the whole thing up. I was suffering from an irrational belief that no matter how long I explored the area, I would never be able to find the Refuge again. So I bought a large-scale map and identified where I thought it must be: a huddle of tiny rectangles on the edge of a high plateau.

Igbar, who had chosen to dress like a pimp for this excursion to the mountains, nominated himself as navigator, but after a couple of inventive detours in search of a hostelry that might provide 'breakfast', he was replaced in the front seat by Eugenia. Igbar resigned himself to smoking a succession of thin joints in the back of the car and demanding pit-stops for liquid refreshment.

A half-hour's climb beyond Berga, nothing about the landscape was remotely familiar. We made a wrong turning up a mud-track, leading to a lake that didn't correspond with anything on my map, and then returned to the main road, where a village was signposted, nestling behind a clump of hills. We drove into the village square and parked by the church, opposite the only bar, which advertised a *menú del día*.

'That's the ticket,' said Igbar. 'A hostelry.' He implored Eugenia. 'A spot of lunch? A jug of wine and thou?'

'We have the time?' She looked at me.

'We have the time. It would be good to eat.'

'Time. Yes. Is good to eat,' blathered Igbar.

In the small bar the plump, eager landlady ushered us past solitary drinkers and a blaring television, to a windowless back room. One table was occupied by a group of local men, who took their time surveying us as we sat down. The rest of the dining area was empty.

Towards the end of our meal Eugenia began chatting in Catalan with the men at the next table and steered the conversation discreetly towards the object of our search. However, fortified by a second bottle of wine, the importance of the oblique approach in village affairs was lost on Igbar. He launched himself towards the neighbouring table and demanded outright the whereabouts of the Refuge, fixing the men with a bleary stare. He swayed over their table, grey hair sticking on end, eyes bloodshot with ganja, splendid in his off-white linen suit, black shirt and a bright red and white polka-dot kipper tie.

'We're looking for a castle where unspeakable things have taken place,' he slurred in Spanish, and leaned heavily on the table. 'A place with dungeons dark and deep, run by the heretic Pontneuf.'

The silence that greeted this did not prevent Igbar from continuing. To my annoyance, he was indicating me, with a generous sweep of the hand. 'This man of wretched appearance was taken captive and tortured at a property near here. A heinous and pusillanimous act of cowardice.'

Igbar dug his hands deep into the pockets of his linen jacket. The Catalans looked at him warily. Igbar was out on a limb here. I sensed impending disaster. One of the men, a hirsute mountain type, leaned towards Eugenia and myself and raised his hands in a request for explanation. I made the universal gesture for insanity, and indicated Igbar with a pitiful expression. The man grabbed Igbar by the shoulder and steered him back into his chair, drew up his own, and introduced himself. Although he knew of the Refuge, he hadn't been there in many years, certainly not since the land had been bought by Pontneuf.

In turn, Eugenia explained that she was a journalist working on a story about cults. She produced a press card she had acquired from one of her contacts which seemed to convince him. Eugenia was good to travel with. The man turned out to be affable enough behind the customary Catalan taciturnity, and, over brandy, he gave us clear instructions on how to reach the Refuge.

Back on the road we found the track, a few kilometres out of the village.

'There, I squeezed it out of them, what?' said Igbar, stretching out on the back seat. 'You need to take a direct approach with these native types.'

After climbing for half an hour or so, the track levelled out onto the *altiplano*. I recognised the markers of the now familiar landscape; the boulder-strewn pasturelands, the forest stretching away below, and the overshadowing presence of the granite peaks. We stopped behind a small ridge a kilometre from the settlement and scoured the landscape with the binoculars Eugenia had brought. The place had been abandoned. None of the vehicles – the two Landrovers, the white van in which Nuria and I had first been abducted, and a larger truck – were in their accustomed places, and there was not a soul in sight, unless, Cathar-style, you included the animals. Even most of these appeared to have gone, apart from some hens, who ran towards the car when we pulled in. A solitary untethered goat bleated at us from near the entrance to the barn.

'This the sorcerer's lair then?' asked Igbar. 'A goat, a few chickens. Quite a cheery spot. Chap could retire here. Grow some veg. A little weed. Vino from the valley down below. But where are the bloody heretics?'

'The heretics have fled.'

'As they would. Heretics flee. Inquisitors pursue. Soldiers pillage.'

'And loot.'

'Nothing much to loot here.'

There was not. I headed for the council hall and looked inside the ante-room where I had been prepared for the trial. There was nothing there.

In the centre of the square lay a wide circle of ash, the remains of the bonfire that had been intended for me. In Pontneuf's office, books, files, even the rugs from the floor, had been taken. This all suggested a thorough evacuation planned over time, which meant, beyond any doubt, that Pontneuf had always intended to quit the site on completion of his task there: my trial and execution. The members of his community had no doubt been packing away their few possessions and cleaning the property while I was still imprisoned in the cellar.

'Anything wrong?' asked Eugenia.

'This whole place gives me the creeps,' I answered, 'but I want to look downstairs.'

The door to the cellar was also unlocked. I led the way down steep steps, and into the corridor. Hearing the echo of our footsteps down the passage reminded me of the only sound I had heard during the long days and nights of my imprisonment. It was dark, and once I had found a light switch, it did not work. Then I remembered that the generator would probably still be out of action. I flicked on my cigarette lighter and scanned the interior of my cell, but there was nothing there for me except unwanted memories. I explained to Eugenia that this was the room I had been kept captive.

'*Qué asco!*' was Eugenia's single comment.

'How vile, indeed,' mused Igbar. 'Most definitely Dumas.'

There was another room at the end of the corridor with a bed and mattress. A French porn magazine lay on the floor beside the bed; the only evidence of a lapse in the otherwise immaculate withdrawal of Pontneuf's troops.

Outside, Eugenia and I followed tyre-tracks through the mud for a kilometre or so. The vehicles had taken a route northward from the settlement, heading for a breach in the mountains that led towards France. Once we could see where the tracks led, it seemed pointless following them further. Returning to the Refuge, Igbar was wading through the ashes left by the bonfire. This wrecked any chances of getting the police involved: they couldn't carry out a forensic report on such sullied evidence. I had begun to feel depressed, and while I appreciated Eugenia and Igbar coming along to keep me company I now wanted nothing more than to be alone.

We drove back to Barcelona and Eugenia at first attempted to make conversation, but soon gave up, as I had turned silent. Igbar snored in the back. We stopped for coffee in Berga and I apologised to Eugenia for my sullen mood. She sighed and said she understood, but she did not.

The next two weeks saw the slow return of Barcelona to its routine swing after the dead heat of August, but September brought no news of Nuria nor her whereabouts. I longed for her with what amounted to a physical pain, and was tormented by her words to me when we had last spoken, promising one another that we would meet up as soon as we could. She had no reason to say that, unless she had meant it. Each day without news from her deepened my anxiety, until I realised I was leading my life solely in expectation of some kind of contact. Anger and frustration gave way to a sense of gloomy desperation.

I could not summon the slightest inclination to return to paid employment, and although I was aware that my savings were dwindling, I dropped unsteadily into a state of inertia, self-pity and sloth. It was pathetic testimony to the hollowness that I had encountered within myself during and immediately after my time at the Refuge. I did not dwell on my shortcomings however, but became immersed in a wilful intoxication with whatever the city had to offer. I stayed out at nights, wandering from bar to bar, sometimes in the company of friends such as Zoff and Hogg, more often with people I met on the night. As well as drinking continuously whenever I was awake, I indulged freely in an eclectic range of narcotics and psychotropics. I managed a couple of desultory one-night-stands with women I met in nightclubs, but realised as soon as the alcohol and drugs wore off that I was only pursuing shadows of Nuria, and could not wait until my new partners were gone from sight. A third encounter involved someone who, in my befuddled state, I took to be a woman, but turned out to be a person with a large penis as well as spectacular breasts. Illuminated by a silver nitrate moon, which beamed directly through the window of my bedroom, the hermaphrodite's glorious and hallucinogenic body inspired me with wonder, but no immediate desire to touch. Nor could its owner arouse me, though whether this was due to frigidity on my part or simply the fault of chemicals raging in my blood, I could not be sure. We compromised with cups of coffee and a joint on the veranda while Paolo/Paola told me his/her life story in lively Brazilian-accented Spanish, and then left to seek out a more fulfilling relationship elsewhere.

One particularly sodden evening I even called up Fina, my ex-girlfriend, with the intention of angling for some kind of sexual encounter, but she hung up on me as soon as she realised who was on the line.

Occasionally, I spoke on the phone with Eugenia, but she and I had always based our friendship on mutual confidences and shared meals, innocent of deceit, and we had joked together that even if she had not been a lesbian we would have been unwilling to compromise that friendship for the sake of a physical relationship. However, our visit to the Refuge and my late-night calls to her began to put a strain even on that valuable friendship. Eugenia's practical suggestion that a return to work might at least salvage some self-respect seemed to me to cloak a reprimand. During one such call we arranged to meet the following evening in the Plaça Reial. It was a Saturday night that belied the oncome of autumn, after a solitary day of warm sunshine, and everyone, it seemed, had taken to the streets. I had been similarly heartened by this change in the weather, and, rising late, had even felt inspired to pick up the guitar for the first time since my return to the city. After an afternoon spent undisturbed, loafing and reading, my torpor had diminished sufficiently for me to take a walk, making my way unhurriedly across the barrio in the direction of the Ramblas. Taking a left off Ferran, I wandered into Plaça Reial and sat in a cushioned aluminum chair.

Even those who have never been to Barcelona suspect that such a place as Plaça Reial exists. It boasts some up-market cafés and night-spots now, suggesting a degree of gentrification, but still retains a shadow of lingering depravity for which it was once renowned. I was staring at the beautiful lamp standards that dominate the centre of the square, designed by Gaudí, and decorated with the insignia of Hermes, when Eugenia joined me shortly after nine. Almost at once she expressed concern about the way I was leading my life. The air of thoughtful abstraction that I had been attempting to cultivate while waiting at the café did not convince her, and she announced that I had begun to look like an irredeemable degenerate. This was hardly perspicacious, but to my annoyance, she added to the unwelcome insight by suggesting a retreat at a Buddhist centre she sometimes visited, near Narbonne. My irritation must have been more obvious than I intended, and my evasiveness was apparent even to myself.

'I know you're trying to help. But personal oblivion has its attractions, and consciousness frightens me, because I keep making connections with all the things that happened over the summer. I see Pontneuf's agents lurking on street corners. In bars, pretending to read the newspaper. A part of me knows they're probably nothing of the kind, but sometimes I'm not so sure. A stranger looks at me suspiciously and that's enough to drive me into hiding for days.'

As I should have known, Eugenia did not accommodate to this kind of talk.

'If that's really where you are, you should do something about it. Not let your world disintegrate around you. I've been worried about you, you silly boy. You hardly ever call me, and when you do you're usually incoherent. I realise you had this big upset in the summer, but perhaps it's time to put that aside, leave it behind. Put yourself into something else. Remember, in the spring, you offered to write something for the catalogue of my exhibition in Madrid next year? Have you given that another thought? I know I'm thinking of myself here also, but it might give you a chance to get out of this mess.'

I nodded. It was true that I had been enthusiastic about the commission at the time she had suggested it. But that seemed like an aeon ago, and right now the prospect of any kind of creative work filled me with panic. I told her this. I was simply unable to concentrate on anything while consumed by my quest for Nuria.

'I don't know where to begin looking. I guess they all went over the border into France. And since I never knew who the other people up there really were – they had made-up names based on their Cathar identities – there's no way of tracing them. Pontneuf's done just what he originally claimed his bunch of Cathars did in the thirteenth century – vanished into thin air.'

'So. Precisely my point. They've disappeared. You can pretend they never existed. An illusion, a bad dream. So, as they say, get a life, start something new.'

'Nuria existed.'

'Okay, Nuria existed. But not as the person you imagined her to be. You created her over those two or three weeks here in Barcelona. And then you found out that she was not the person you thought her to be. You have to un-create her.'

'But that last day up at the Refuge, she helped me to escape. I honestly felt she had changed back into the person I had known before.'

'It could have been part of the act. Can't you see, Lucas? The whole thing was probably scripted. And Nuria was a part of it. The trial itself was a ploy, a trick. The guy who fixed the generator, Zaco, did it with Pontneuf's connivance. And when you ran off into the night they didn't come after you with lights and dogs and guns, did they? They were never going to burn you alive.'

'But why go to all that trouble? It's ludicrous. You can't tell me that the whole thing was set up in order to give me some kind of a weird experience, or to give Pontneuf a thrill. Like some psychological experiment gone wildly off-beam. Are you serious?'

'You're the one who's intent on attaching a specific explanation to it,' she said. 'I'm not saying *why* it all took place, just suggesting that there might be an alternative explanation to what you believe happened up there. A different kind of fiction to the one you're proposing.'

'You're saying that my perception of those events is deluded?'

She framed her response carefully. 'Let's imagine,' she started, 'that there's a novelist called Lucas, who has an idea for a book. Not a bad idea, good enough for him to get started on it. It describes his life in a modern city, his falling in love with a young woman, and their subsequent abduction by a crazed cult. His story takes a shift of direction, however, when we learn that the abduction wasn't really what it appeared to be, but that the girl was compliant with the abduction all along. It becomes a tale of betrayal and paranoia. This serves the fiction well: the cult happens to believe certain things about a medieval religious group and reincarnation, and our hero begins to half-believe them himself. His lover is already committed, has been ever since she fell under the cult leader's influence years before. Let's also imagine, let's pretend, that parallel to the writing of his story, the novelist Lucas happens to meet and fall in love with a young woman and is unsure that his feelings towards her are as fully reciprocated as he would like. He therefore begins to insert his doubts into the story he is writing. At the same time he imputes characteristics typical of his fictional heroine to the girl that he, Lucas, has fallen in love with; and characteristics of his real-life lover begin to infiltrate the person of his fictional heroine. The elements of betrayal and paranoia already implicit in the plot are compounded by more sinister developments. What is more, the cult's leader is revealed to be quite insane, and possibly murderous. But the novelist can't let go of the possibility that the girl he has met in the real world might turn out to be the love of his life, so he has his fictional heroine help his protagonist to escape. However, once he's escaped, and returned to the city, his character is filled with feelings of desperation and loss. He pines for the fictional heroine, just as the novelist Lucas pines for the girl he met one day in an art gallery. The rest you know. You're living it.' Eugenia shrugged. 'As I say, it's your life. And at the moment you're making, what is it in English? – a dog's breakfast of it. I don't think my interpretation is such a bad one. And it gets you out of a fix.'

'No it doesn't.'

'How so?'

'Because I don't believe in it.'

As for Eugenia's suggestion that I go on some kind of retreat, I recoiled. Religion, I said, was the last thing I needed just now. I would, I said, with the stupefying logic of the obsessed, prefer to carry on as I was and see where that took me.

Where it took me was downwards and in upon myself in ever-diminishing spirals. I was tracing the rough edges of the soul's Sahara, and could not resist the pull towards its scorched and barren centre. I was overcome by a debilitating sense of absence. Of absence and being absent. When in company I would begin sentences and fall into silence after only a few words, having lost the thread that connected language with mental function. I would wander from room to room in my flat looking for things which I was either carrying in my hand, or had just put down on the table in front of me. My sleep pattern went haywire, sleeping either not at all for days on end – fuelled with cocktails of cocaine, amphetamines and alcohol – or else spending days under a blanket, getting up only to replenish my supply of drink. Since I would awaken at odd hours, days and nights lost their defining characteristics and I began to inhabit a perpetual twilight. I stopped buying and cooking food. On the rare occasions when I did leave the flat, I often ended up in places I had no intention of going when I had set off. My feet would lead me away from Santa Caterina in spite of my dread of bringing some unforeseeable catastrophe down on myself. As the autumn settled in, with winds blasting down from the north, I ventured out less and less.

18. The fire-eater

Every few days I would become incredibly hungry, and because I could no longer bear to cook for myself, would head for one of two or three cheap restaurants in the barrio which I visited by turn. Among these was Santiago's place in Neu de Sant Cugat. One early afternoon in October, when the morning's rain had been blown inland by the wind, I decided to go there to eat, having spent a bad night with persistent sweats, rising late to try and fend off the (by now daily) onslaught of the shakes by downing a litre of red wine. Finishing the wine, I immediately felt hungry and decided to go to a restaurant, but having lately sensed an attitude of disapproval in the Galician who owned the nearest restaurant, I opted for Santiago.

As I approached the abandoned building in Assaonadors daubed with yellow crosses, I noticed a figure hunched on the low stone steps leading up to the door. A thick matted thatch of dirty blond hair resembling a coarse rug, poked out through a blanket. From somewhere inside the hair came a voice asking me for a few *duros*, a little change. When I slowed my step, puzzling out the exact configuration of this human shape, it shook its hair, revealing itself to be the reckless fire-eater, whom I had seen that evening in May, when I first met Nuria. Simple association with that distant day lent the man special privileges, so I dug into my pockets for some loose change.

I dropped the coins into his outstretched hand and he muttered a brief word of thanks. I stood unsteadily in front of him. By stopping walking, I had suddenly become aware of the precarious status of my sense of balance, and of anything approaching sobriety in my own demeanour. I also recognized, to my surprise, that I was desperate to conjure an exchange of some kind with this vagrant.

'So, fire-eater,' I began slowly, as though waiting for the words to formulate themselves rather than rushing them towards anything as conclusive as a meaningful utterance. 'We meet again.'

The beggar blinked up at me, without a glimmer of recognition. I felt myself to be oddly advantaged by this. My tone became celebratory, and almost vindictive.

'You told me once that you knew me. You *knew* me. And clearly not in a Biblical sense.' It was a pathetic joke. 'But now,' I continued, glimpsing the sudden and unwanted mental turmoil that I was inflicting on him, 'I know who you are, while you, *evidentemente*, have not the monkey's arse of an idea who I might be. Correct?'

The fire-eater nodded glumly, nonplussed. Perhaps he was waiting for a punchline, after which I would, with any luck, disappear, and he could slope off to buy wine with his earnings. But the unexpected meeting had for some reason planted a seed in the inner recesses of what remained of my mind. I saw the fire-eater as yet another link, a cipher in my quest for the Truth.

I gave him some background.

'Granada, let's say three years ago? This spring, here in Barcelona, I forget the name of the square. You are a symptom of perpetual return. But whose? Yours? Mine? Who knows? What I mean to say is, you confirmed the prognosis of a May evening. You sniffed out my dreamy lust for her. I in turn smelled the promise of her juices on your rancid breath, along with petrol fumes. You sought me out, dog-man, though you don't remember. I am now doing the same to you. Tit for tat. Trouble is, the one doing the seeking is always barely conscious. Hardly makes for purposeful interaction, do you think?'

The beggar was trying, with some effort, to stand up, probably with a view towards escaping this madman's diatribe. But while I sensed in him this imperative for flight, now that I had my prey within my grasp I was not about to let him go that easily.

'Hey, mister sniffer dog, where's your doggy mask? And where do you think you're going? I was just getting started. Renewing a friendship. Let's talk of old times. Have you seen a ghost? Or just lost your nerve? Is that why you're not out there doing the dragon stuff?'

I pushed him back down into a sitting position. Not hard, but hard enough to unbalance him, so rather than sitting down he flopped back and was now sprawled on his back across the two steps in the doorway. He glared at me from this undignified position.

'Sorry, *amigo*,' I apologized, without much conviction. 'Didn't mean to send you tumbling. But it isn't time to go. Haven't finished yet. Unattended business. And not too steady myself this morning. Just to make sure of something, I have a favour to ask of you.'

'*Vino*,' gasped the beggar. His solitary word. A non-sequitur, sure, but at least an active attempt at communication.

'Okay, *vino*. Tell you what. I'll buy the *vino*, and throw in a meal if you think you can take solids without chucking up. But first I want to look at your chest. Your lovely tits. *Las tetas del dragón*.' I reached down to the top button of his coat.

The beggar brushed away my hand, and looked up, exasperated. Then, suddenly, with a breathtakingly full smile of rotting and broken teeth, he unbuttoned his coat and shirt to display the red and green dragon engraved on his chest.

'See this?' he said, in his painfully articulated English, as though dredging the bottom of a vast lake in search of a few remaining fragments of the long-wrecked ship of language. 'I share with you the sign of the dragon. *Le plus beau du monde*. I am the man of *foc*, as you suggest, *mon semblable, mon frère*.'

He looked up and down the street cautiously while re-buttoning his coat.

'*Now* we have a drink, *amigo mio*?' He held out a mittened hand for me to pull him up. I obliged.

'You just want to drink? Or eat something,' I tried again.

'Soup maybe. First *vino*.'

'Okay, but I want information from you, got it?' I insisted.

'Yeah, that's cool. Just don't get heavy, man.' This came fluently, as though it were a well-practised refrain.

'Where the fuck did you pick up your English? Heavy? Man? The road to Katmandu?'

I was now ravenously hungry, so my first obstacle was getting him into the bar without being asked to leave. I guided him quickly to one of the tables at the rear, in the section reserved for those who wanted to eat. So far, so good. Once seated it would be harder to evict us. Fortunately, Santiago had begun to regard me as a regular. He seemed in a good humour, and came to take our order himself.

I asked for soup for the fire-eater and a set menu for myself, which consisted of a pasta dish, a meat course, and a salad. Wine was already on the table.

The fire-eater looked around the bar uninterestedly, drained a glass of wine, and immediately poured another. This too he swallowed in one gulp. The third he poured slowly and held in both his hands, sipping from it at intervals while he spoke.

'This same same crazy boy, come midnight, *tu comprends*? *Arriba* among the candelabra no the rooftops no the stars. *Les étoiles*. Catch me if you can. But only if competent in the art of flying. Same other crazy boy maybe sometime. He talk with forked Walkman. Blah blah blah. *Mais moi, j'aime bien les Parisiennes*. When? Last night; no, night before; no, night before that. *Todo por triplicado*. That's what he said, *más o menos*. Everything in triplicate. Want a kinky time? No thanks, kind sir. I'm the Emperor of ice cream and will bide my own. You want, he said, you want play game with me? You musta be *lunático*. No go, no cigar. Bigtime. Up there, *arriba*. *Comme les oiseaux. Les hirondelles du soir*. Now to Africa. *En suivant le soleil*. Here come the sun. You know Beatle song? Let's it be. *Chacun*, every boy and girl, not so much flying, *commes les hirondelles*, diving yes, the grace of god, *merde*, I never saw these things, but dreaming yes. Above the house of the yellow cross. Gone now.'

He paused to wipe his mouth and refill his glass. Just then the soup arrived, along with my food. I didn't want to break his flow but needed to know more about the place where I had found him.

'Tell me more about this house of the yellow cross.'

'Tell me more tell me more,' he mimicked, moving his head from side to side in what I assumed to be a parody of John Travolta in the movie *Grease*. There was something disturbing about the fire-eater's familiarity with any such item of popular culture, even if years out of date.

He slurped his way noisily through half the bowl of soup, dunking bread and swigging more wine. Then he picked up his monologue again.

'The house of the yellow cross. A nightmare in every room. Waiting. They move behind closed doors. *Silencio*. I never saw them till that night. I could not recognise the sounds their feet made. And one, *Francais*, *le responsable*. Eyes like knives. Soft voice. *Qu'est-ce qu'il est? Un cura*? Priest-man? Up on the roof. Stars so bright. *Comme les diamants*. Ha ha. But he is not laughing, he makes signs, brings me big sadness. I don't want bread, only *vino*. Blood of the God. Hiding, *je m'en cache*. I see the wine. I want it. Bad night. Who are you? he asks, this same same guy, louder now. *Moi*? *Le pauvre petit prince. Prince de La*

Macédonie. Look at the nose, the lips. I am of real blood. Royal, *sanctus spiritus* etcetera. And then, *une ange*. I swear to God. An angel, *là-haut*, among the *cheminées*. I saw the face of Mary Magdalene. Why me? No answer. None. Dancing, *doucement*. Like a trance. I see in Konya also one time. You know this? No matter. *Rien*. They make a fire, there *arriba*, *sur les toits*. Burning what? *Je sais pas*. Nothing, everything. It sparks and roars, but *doucement*, gentle like the dancing girl.'

He drifted into some private memory, eyes closed, hands clasping the now empty glass. I let him stay there for a while, forked my salad. With his eyes closed, I could more readily read his face. The deep lines folded across his face, those below the eyes rooting out and joining broader crevices that ran through the thick stubble on his cheeks. His was a face most profoundly occupied, one in which the accumulated debris of a lifetime was somehow revealed openly in these searing ducts.

'Tell me about this girl,' I said. 'The dancer.'

The fire-eater looked up in surprise, so lost in his own internal perambulations that he was temporarily unaware he had an audience.

'The girl? Not any girl, tits, pussy, ass. What you want, picture? For *faire le rumtumtum*? *Wanging*? Huh mister, what you are, a *wanger*? This not a girl for make play, I tell you, this an angel. Come down from *el cielo*. Yes.'

The beggar harrumphed into his soup, then spooned out the remains into his mouth. He looked at me accusingly.

'*Vino*,' he ordered. '*Más*.'

I relayed this message to a young man helping out at the bar, who came over with a fresh litre of the basic red. I was about to pour when the fire-eater took the bottle from me and went through the same ritual as before, downing two glasses straight off, and pouring the third meditatively, letting it nest between his cupped hands while continuing to talk. I remembered what he had said: '*todo por triplicado*'. Everything in triplicate.

'You want words. I give you message from the amber light, straight up.' He stared at me now, with an almost comic intensity. The wine had emboldened him.

'Yes I know you longtime. You call me dog-man. But I am dragon. You see me breathe fire? That is my message. This my words, slowly slowly. Fire is better. Dog-man nothing. There, on the roof, where they jump high, swing yes, from top to top. No look down. Lose your head, same same. Always same but not crazy boy. Man now. I need to find the angel. See her more times, just to watch, *capisce*? But never again. Up there, I never see her once again. But I have the knot of doing, undoing. The knot, the knack. I learn quick, so quick. But one day I fall, too much *vino*. Snap the back. Hospital, here in the city of *maravillas*. Captain Marvels. Weeks too long. Hot food, no *vino*. Every night too they bring quackers. Quackers and cheese, *fromage*. This I hate. I steal money, down to the bottom of the hospital there's a bar. Much cognac. They give me robe, hospital jama. No sleepers. I am in bar *totalmente borracho*, in my jama. Sleep on floor. They wake me up, I kick the place to shit, but tired, *trop trop fatigué*. *Muy cansado*. Call *policia*. Big *fasaria*, fuss. Later time, sleep, hell, back in room. Evening. More quackers, more fromage. Let me out, I tell them. Back not good, but walking okay. Then they let me go. I never see nothing no more. Not people, not the angel.

272

This same spring and summer. All nights and days looking, but not seeing nothing.'

He slammed his glass down on the table and burped loudly, grabbing the bottle at once and refilling. A couple of heads turned our way. I wondered vaguely how long it would be before he got us thrown out, but knew that it could take some doing to get evicted from these Gothic quarter bars. I too was feeling quite drunk again, though the term was beginning to lose any real meaning since I was never truly sober – either in a state of withdrawal or else topping up, or else over the top, in which case I usually went into blackout. But there was an unpredictability about my companion that suggested he was capable of causing extreme offence, as I had witnessed all that time ago in Granada.

I just needed to get one thing straight. If, as he appeared to be claiming, he had briefly joined the roof people, was it before or after I had seen him breathing fire in May? It seemed of great significance for me to know this. The limp that I had witnessed in May, if brought about by his fall, would suggest an earlier date for the experience he was describing. But if the angel he described was Nuria, as my obsession required, then her disappearance over the summer could be accounted for. When had he seen her (if it was her) dancing on the roof?

'Tell me, when you were in hospital, when was that?'

'Oh much time. Too much time. Before, after.'

'Was it before or after May this year?'

He looked at me incredulously as though being expected to know such a thing was quite beyond the powers of any human being.

'Before, after, during. My back hurt, but not so bad I couldn't walk.'

273

'Listen, mister fire-man, I need to know. When did you last see the angel?'

He gaped like a fish coming up for air, then the corners of his mouth twisted into a disconcerting smile.

'Ah. I know. I see you. You too want an angel you can call your own. You want to nail me down with days and dates. Times and days, weeks and mumps. This when, that when. Now and never. Before and after. *En avant et aprés*. During now and never. So you can go back there and make her disappear. Never never never never never. *Jamais jamais jamais*.'

He had begun to shout, and was now badly deranged, leaning across the table towards me in a state of rage. He stood and waved his arms in the air as he spoke, continuing his tirade toward the restaurant in general.

'I come here, *Messieurs*, sit and give the words requested, demanded. I eat my soup, wipe my mouth with clean serviette, drink wine from a glass like a jennulman. I want from you nothing, none of you all. *Nada*. All time is hassle, hassle. I wait all my life for the angels to come and never once I see one. Now one come and everything is shit. I shit on you all. *Me cago en todas partes, en la casa de Dios y en vuestras casas también*. I shit in the house of the God and in all your houses also. I piss on your floor. I call you all wangers. *Mira mira! Je suis le plus beau du monde!*'

He tore open his coat and shirt to display the rearing dragon, turning this way and that so the whole of the place could see him. The bar was crowded with men, mostly workers on their lunch break. While heads were turned towards the fire-eater, none appeared to be overly concerned. A couple of men seated behind him scowled, and a man standing at the bar cast us a canny glance, as though he had seen all this kind of thing before. But there was an air of expectancy in the room now, and people were waiting for this foreign maniac with the long dirty hair to either leave or else be thrown out.

I wanted to pre-empt our ejection by paying the bill and leaving, but a general weariness had spread through my limbs, and I was rooted to my chair, waiting for the next development. In spite of my own despair, I felt compassion for the fire-eater and his troubles. But at this point the madman picked up the half-empty second bottle of wine and started swigging from it, staring wild-eyed around the room as he did so. Then, pulling its neck abruptly from his lips with a sucking noise, he brought the empty bottle down with a crack on the table's edge, leaving a jagged weapon in his right hand. I let out a groan, fearing the worst. Then, with astonishing athleticism, Santiago leapt over the counter and made his way towards us. Simultaneously the two workers at the table behind the vagrant made a move to grab him, one of them twisting his right arm sharply behind his back. The remaining half of the bottle dropped to the floor and shattered. My dining companion offered no resistance, indeed, he seemed to have gone limp in the arms of the two men as they escorted him quickly towards the street door. Meanwhile I counted out some notes and handed them to Santiago, muttering a slurred apology as I did so. He merely nodded in response, and shrugged his shoulders. He told me I could stay if I wanted, but that the other guy, the lunatic, must never come here again. I thanked him, and left hurriedly, wanting to catch up with the fire-eater. I was sure he had broken the bottle with the intention of harming himself rather than anybody else. I could see the next move coming, as he would turn the sharp end towards his own chest and twist the glass into the flesh.

Out on the street I felt the sudden gust of a chill wind. I looked both ways up the street but there was no sign of the fire-eater. I searched the alleyways around the area, the immediate locality of the abandoned house, and then back up to Carders, where he would probably have gone in quest of more drink. But he had disappeared, and I knew then that I would not be seeing him again.

19. Meeting with an angel

As colder weather settled in, I carried a wasted, dissolute look, wore the same clothes for days on end, and ate very little. I hit the sea-bed during a protracted drug and drinking binge, a jag of hellish intensity, with Igbar Zoff and Sean Hogg (whose latest sale had been a moderate success). During that period I did not return home at all, in spite of my apartment being only five minutes walk from theirs; crashing instead on their floor and picking up each morning, or afternoon, where we had left off the night before.

Being with Zoff and Hogg was like eavesdropping on a marriage between two people who spend most of their lives arguing with each other, but cannot break out of the loop of mutual blame, and therefore it becomes a part of their identity as a couple. My mind was so blank much of the time that their interminable rows became as irrelevant to me as the indefinable colour of their sofa. We were all eventually reduced to drinking cheap Spanish gin and red wine, Zoff's money from this more recent sale having mostly gone and nothing new on the horizon. On the third or fourth day of camping out on their floor, I awoke in the early afternoon, automatically reached out for a bottle of wine as soon as my eyes were fully open and looked around me. What I saw gave me cause for alarm.

Hogg was lying on his back, spreadeagled on the sofa, wearing a pig's mask over his face, which had slipped away to reveal an ear and one eye, belonging – I ascertained finally – to himself, Hogg, rather than the pig. Across the room from me, Igbar Zoff lay on the floor, also on his back, but (and this was an unprecedented sight) stark naked, with his arms and hands poised on his chest in the manner of a dog begging, hands flopping at right angles to the wrists. His limp penis lay across his crotch, a sad worm among the scrawny tangle of his pubic hair. He was breathing with tiny irregular snorting sounds, and occasionally moving one hand up to his face and brushing an invisible fly from his nose. I heaved myself upright and surveyed the room. Empty gin bottles lay strewn across the floor, punctuated by plates and saucers containing the decaying remnants of food and countless cigarette stubs. Books and magazines were scattered on the carpet and furniture, and on one unfolded magazine was a rectangle of glued-together cigarette papers and a small pile of tobacco. I picked up a loose chunk of hash from the floor, and put it on the coffee table. A wine-stain had formed around a knocked over bottle of undrinkable *vino tinto*. On the carpet, there were hunks of stale bread spread with a pâté that resembled human excrement; a coke can punctured with tiny holes, coated in a dark resinous wax, and a brightly-hued cowpat of vomit. I gagged, rushing to the toilet just in time to reach the bowl, on my hands and knees, where I spent the next five minutes making noises like a dying ox. I washed my hands and face in cold water and put my head under the tap for a full minute, massaging icy water onto the back of my neck, and into my eyes and ears. Shocked into wakefulness, I returned to the living room, where neither of my companions had yet stirred, picked up the bottle of wine and took another long slug. I brushed the debris off an armchair, sat down and lit a cigarette. A smell resembling ammonia wafted over from Igbar's direction and I realised, without surprise, that he had rolled over onto his side, and the rug beneath him was soaked in fresh urine. I sat there for a while, finished the wine, and smoked a second cigarette. Then, as quietly as possible, I picked my way across the floor towards the door and let myself out.

It was the last day of October, the night on which the spirits of the dead were supposed to roam the earth – not that I would have noticed. Tomorrow would be November, and All Saints, a fiesta day. It was bright and sunny, but with a chill on the wind. I wandered down Carders, and, feeling invigorated by the fresh air, stopped at the first likely bar and tried to eat some bread and cheese, washed down with coffee. When I had finished I continued in the direction of the sea, but with no particular objective in mind. I passed a cash machine and looked at my bank balance. I was behind with the rent, and had only sufficient cash remaining for two or three weeks' subsistence. I withdrew money anyway, realising it was impossible for me to consider the future as anything more than a hypothesis in my current frame of mind, and headed for a bar I knew that specialised in seafood tapas and pink *cava*. The bar was noisy and filled with excited voices. Barça football club must have had a home match on that day: many of the customers were turned out in blue and red striped shirts. There was a satisfying atmosphere of exuberance in the bar. I had several *cavas*, and by the time I staggered out, the short-lived day was already turning to dusk. I walked past the central Post Office, re-crossed Laietana, and headed towards the church of Santa María del Mar.

As I neared the church I began to feel that I was being drawn towards it like a nail to a magnet. I realised that it had been my intention to come here since leaving the flat in Carders, and that my dawdling on the way had been, in a sense, necessary, because only now, in the failing light, was the time right for me to enter the church. A peculiar sense of anticipation guided my final steps and when I stepped inside I experienced a physical sense of relief.

At the far end of the vast church, near the altar, a wedding ceremony was in progress, but the sheer scale of the place meant that even with a congregation of a hundred or so, the gathering took up only a fraction of the total space. A handful of spectators stood behind the pews at the rear of the church, near the door through which I had just come in. As I walked past them, towards the aisle on the right, one of them, a girl in her late teens, with shoulder-length Botticelli curls, turned towards me and smiled. She could not have seen me come in, and I was treading quietly, one of a handful of visitors, several of them tourists carrying cameras or camcorders. But she turned abruptly, looked straight at me, and smiled, as though she had been

280

waiting for me. Her smile was the most arresting and breathtaking expression of joy that I had seen in my life: it was a smile simply bursting with light. It managed to convey compassion, humanity and sensuality from the raw nucleus of somewhere imponderably good. Her eyes lingered on me for a moment longer, and then she turned around, apparently to watch the wedding.

I was stunned into complete sobriety, while my insides filled rapidly with hot foam. I walked a few paces on, then stopped and sat on the low inner wall that marked the border of the outer aisle. I looked over at her, where she stood beside one of the giant pillars, her attention now focussed on the events taking place at the other end of the church. The service, which was in Catalan, was being relayed by loudspeaker, but the priest spoke quite softly and the distance was such that an echo of his actual speech could be heard a fraction of a second after the same words came over the speakers. When the music started a minute later, the same thing happened, the sounds doubling back on themselves, making the folksy accompaniment of guitar, piano and cello collide with the melody taken up by the rather unconvinced singing. But the watching girl was apparently enjoying herself too much to care: she rocked back and forth on her heels and toes in undulating, subtle movements; not actually dancing, but unable to stand still either. There was something of the street urchin about her. She was very slim, wore black cotton jeans, white trainers and a grey hooded fleece. She had a dark complexion and glowing, mahogany eyes, made all the more striking in contrast with her golden-brown hair. At a guess, I would have said she was of gipsy blood, but she was without the sullen arrogance of the southern *gitanas*.

While I was sitting there, feet crossed, wondering how I had been reduced to a human wreck by a single smile, she turned around, with the music droning on in the background, and set off decisively towards the main door, away from me. I felt desperately sad that she was leaving, but realised there was nothing I could do to prevent it. As she reached the revolving door, she stopped, turned sharply in a perfect pirouette, looked straight at me, and then came towards me, not walking but dancing. She danced as though barely touching the ground, and although the distance from the main doors to where I sat must have been twenty metres or so, she appeared to take only three steps, or jumps, both arms lifted vertically, and twisting with a little shimmy on the second beat of her three-step dance. Her movements resembled a balletic version of the *jota*, the wild and jubilant dance of Navarra. Her eyes remained fixed on me. And she smiled her smile. I felt as though my chest were about to burst apart with sheer gratitude. She slowed in front of me, and with the slightest gesture of her head, beckoned me to follow. Still dancing, but with arms lowering to her waist, she headed for the side door, just down the aisle from where I sat.

Of course, I followed. After a few seconds' hesitation. I had remembered the fire-eater's words: 'I swear to God. An angel...' words which, at the time, had indicated nothing more than an overexcited imagination. Now I too, I could have sworn, had seen an angel. But when I got to the door and stepped outside, I could not see her. A sea-mist had arisen, and as I stared through the murky light of the street-lamps it occurred to me that if witches were abroad, it would be tonight, on Halloween, of all nights. Then I caught a glimpse of her, at the far side of the small square which was designated as a memorial to the dead of Catalan insurrections in centuries past. She beckoned to me, and I skirted the little square towards her. When I reached the corner where she had been, she had again moved on, walking quick and light-footed down the narrowing streets. As I hurried to catch up with her, heart pumping, she stopped again, beside a garbage trolley, lifted the lid, and retrieved a black, lightweight rucksack. Twenty paces on, with me alongside her, she stopped again, away from the beams of the nearest street-light, and unzipped the rucksack. Without looking at me, or saying a word, she took out a grappling hook, identical in design to the one that the roof-dwellers had shown me back on Santa Caterina, attached to a length of strong nylon rope. She unfolded its claws by flicking the instrument away from her once, and cast the piece of iron high into the air towards the top of a three-storey building next to which we were standing. Her movements were expert and unhesitating. She pulled hard on the rope two or three times to ensure that the hook would hold fast, and again, without a word, scurried up the ten metres or so to the rooftop, kicking twice against the wall of the building as her weight on the rope caused it to swing into the stonework. Once at the top, she disappeared for a few moments. Then she returned to view and must have lain down, as I could see only her head, neck and arms hanging over the edge of the flat roof. I assumed she had tied the rope to some fixed object, since she now gave me the thumbs-up signal. She was waiting for me to follow.

At that moment the street was empty, but I could see the need to act quickly, since somebody might pass by, on foot or in a car, at any time. Alternatively one of the building's residents might come out into the street, or have heard the movements on the roof. Either way, if I was to follow, I had to climb up that rope.

I grabbed it in both hands, and hoisted myself a couple of metres off the ground, wrapping my feet around the rope in the way I remembered being taught at school. From then on, progress became slower. The truth was, in spite of my moment of apparent mental clarity in the church, I was still drunk, and even if I had not been, I would have been toxic from earlier that day, only having gone to sleep, or passed out, at around seven in the morning. My body wasn't used to this kind of exertion. I had reached the first floor when I slammed against the shutter of a window. There was a light on inside the room. I heard somebody shout, and with legs flailing, attempted to gain a toehold on the window-sill. My arms were aching and hands red-raw from clinging to the rope. I knew that within a matter of seconds I would be discovered, unless I scrambled quickly to the top of the building. But all the strength had gone out of my arms, I was beginning to shake, and at that moment I made the mistake of looking down. The street was only five or six metres below me, but in my condition the distance seemed treble that. Flooded by an acute sense of vertigo, I had a fleeting vision of myself lying crumpled in the road below with a smashed skull. There was an urgent pull on the rope as the angel beckoned me. I stared upward and saw that she was making frantic climbing gestures, placing one hand above the other in sequence, urging me to hurry.

Instead I panicked, slipping rapidly down the rope, and landing on the pavement with a muffled thump. I had landed on my arse, and immediately felt acute pain shooting through my body. My hands stung. The rope was pulled out of sight at once, and I peered upwards again through the thickening mist to see the angel looping the last of it around her arm. In the dim light I could just make out her wave of farewell. Then she blew me a kiss, and was gone. I realised with absolute certainty that the girl on the rooftop was the same figure I had seen in the grey light of dawn, against the chimney-stacks of an adjacent building, when Ric, Fionnula and Ninja boy had taken their leave of me back in May.

Hearing the street door being unlocked from the inside, I sprang to my feet and bolted in the direction I had come. A man shouted some abuse after me, but did not give chase. I found a bar on the square fronting the great church, brushed myself down, and went in.

I was shaking so badly that I needed both hands to down the first brandy. With the second I found myself a seat at a corner table, took off my leather jacket, and my nerves began to settle.

The events of the last twenty minutes had caused a tumult of contradictory emotions and fears to erupt in me at once. I had been so easily persuaded to follow the angelic girl, without her uttering a word, that I had risked my life in the attempt. Only my ineptitude and unfitness had prevented me from now being high above street level in the company of I knew not who. I had so effortlessly convinced myself that the angel was the personification of purity and good that it had not occurred to me until now that she might have been an emissary of Pontneuf, especially if, as I believed, she was the dancing girl referred to by the fire-eater; the girl who had danced at the incendiary ritual on the roof above Assaonadors. In short, I had become bewitched, and only the painful landing on the roadside had brought me back to my senses.

On the other hand, my fears might have been totally unfounded: she may even have been a messenger from Nuria, or else no kind of messenger at all. Presumably not all angels are necessarily messengers of anything.

As I left the bar, I brushed against the figure of a man, who seemed to be hesitating in the doorway. I turned to mutter an apology, but he had already gone inside. Through the glass I saw him take a seat at the table I had just vacated. He wore a green overcoat, and a red silk scarf. He was staring at me, and making a gesture for me to return inside. I recognised him as the man who had stopped me in Via Laietana, the day that the cattle were being herded through the city centre.

I didn't think twice. Re-entering the bar, I took the free seat opposite him.

The man facing me had a sophisticated and charming manner. I could picture him as the owner of a shop of rare and antiquarian books.

'I was hoping we would be able to meet again,' he said, after ordering tea for both of us. 'Perhaps it would have saved you a lot of trouble if we had done so months ago, but it is pointless to pursue such possibilities in retrospect.'

He smiled for the first time: a thoroughly convincing smile that solicited nothing. I began to feel comfortable in the presence of this man, and was only mildly alarmed by the manner in which he plunged directly into his account.

'I do not want to bore you with a great deal of unnecessary personal history, so I will try to be direct. I have been aware of the activities of a man known as

André Pontneuf for a considerable time now. I knew him personally once: indeed, considered him a close friend, if not my closest. We studied law together, some time before his decision to apply for the priesthood. I was best man at his wedding. But there was always an edge to him, something that acted like a warning beacon to me. His is not an entirely benevolent guiding spirit, let us say. But we shared an interest in the Cathars, one which led him, to my mind, to erroneous and harmful conclusions. I don't think I need to tell you what those conclusions were. Not long ago, he had a group of followers here in Barcelona, and led them into all manner of strange and misguided beliefs. This need not have bothered me: there are cranks of his kind operating in every city in the world. He was, at the time, still in the process of, shall we say "collecting" his little band of reincarnated Cathars. One or two of them were to be found among those vagrants known locally as the roof people.

'Unfortunately I became involved, although quite involuntarily. You see, my granddaughter, María del Mar, became involved in his group, fell under his sway, and I had to put a stop to it. She lost both her parents at the age of twelve, in an aeroplane crash. At the time of Pontneuf's activities here she had already been exposed to a variety of dubious cultish influences. She was an only child, and her parents meant everything to her, as did she to them. She became, briefly, an acolyte of Pontneuf's, though I hardly think she knew what he was about. My granddaughter is not in any way dim-witted; far from it, but she possesses an otherworldly quality that at times makes me wonder whether she is really here with us at all. Moreover, since her parents' death, she has lost the power of speech.'

He answered my unvoiced question. 'She has become a mute.'

This onslaught of information had shocked me, for the second time that evening, into a sudden and unexpected sobriety. I remembered the fire-eater, and his infatuation with the dancer on the rooftops. I was in no doubt now as to the identity of the angel I had so recently, and unsuccessfully, pursued.

'Anyhow,' continued the man, 'without false modesty, I do have influence in this city and I put a stop to Pontneuf's activities among the homeless, the phantom-seekers and the vulnerable within the Gothic quarter. That of course, was a while before I accosted you in Via Laietana, Lucas.' It was the first time he had used my name. 'In fact I'd spotted you once or twice before. I don't know...' here he paused to sip his tea carefully, before resuming, 'I felt a certain affinity towards you, which I simply cannot explain, and I sensed – and I believe events proved me right – that you were in some kind of danger.

'When I saw you in Laietana I knew I had to make contact, at the very least. The document I gave you: a hobby of mine,' he confessed, almost shyly, 'composing these pamphlets against everything I consider wrong in this society of ours. I suppose it's my own eccentric and milder equivalent of throwing a brick through the windows of McDonald's restaurant.' He laughed gently. 'Allow me to get to the point. I fear I have been rambling, a bad failing in a lawyer.' He cleared his throat. 'I am aware of who Pontneuf thinks he is, and of who he thinks you are, Lucas. And your friend, Nuria too. I wanted you to know that his activities, and your ordeals, have not gone totally unnoticed.'

I needed to speak, but hardly knew where to begin. So I began with what was uppermost in my mind.

'Do you know where Nuria is?'

'No, I'm afraid I do not.'

I sensed that this was a man who needed to be approached with more subtlety. 'Do you know,' I continued, trying hard not to sound too insistent, 'what has become of Pontneuf and his Cathars?'

He stirred his tea.

'No. Although I imagine he has returned to France. He is a powerful man. France is his home. But he has connections on both sides of the Atlantic.'

'So you know of the community he set up in the Pyrenees? You know of the Refuge?'

'As I said, I am a lawyer. I have friends in the police force. One in particular. A senior officer who has also had the misfortune to have a family member involved in some kind of millenarian cult, not related to Pontneuf's own brand of insanity. I have heard that Pontneuf's little community has, er, *dispersed*.'

'And are you, as a lawyer, in a position to tell me anything you know about Nuria?'

'As a lawyer, no, I can see no problem. But for different reasons, I hesitate. Firstly, I simply do not know where she is. Secondly, because her involvement with Pontneuf is such that...' Here he broke off, and resumed stirring his tea, 'It would be irresponsible of me to pass on to you information about which I am uncertain. So I will tell you what I know, but on condition that you do not breathe a word of this to anyone, including Nuria. You see, I know her family, and they would regard it, her mother in particular, as a breach of confidence.'

I could see no difficulty in agreeing to that.

'I lost contact with Pontneuf shortly after his marriage. This is not uncommon. People move on after they marry, lose touch with their old friends. I lost my wife when she was young, and our only child was killed in a plane crash as I have explained, while still quite young herself. If it had not been for my formal adoption of María del Mar, following her parents' death, I would no doubt have settled into solitary life as a widower. But Pontneuf's marriage ended in an entirely different way, when he deserted his family for his brief career in the priesthood. He left behind, as it happened, two small children, a girl and a boy. Thereafter they took their mother's family name, Rasavall.'

He raised a hand to silence my spluttered profanity. 'Her mother would not even have her ex-husband's name mentioned in her presence after he had abandoned them, though she continued to accept his generous payments to the family, made through their lawyer.' He cleared his throat again, and looked mildly embarrassed by this last admission. 'So the re-union of father and daughter, years later, caused a great deal of pain to the forsaken wife. The son, who was younger than Nuria, and had no memory of his father, sided with his mother.'

I wanted to speak, to voice at least the beginnings of a question, but found that I had nothing at all to say.

'That is all I am able to tell you. Whatever transpires between yourself and Nuria is none of my business. I cannot help you, though I would like to. Nuria, like her father, has vanished before. More than once. It's possible she has inherited his proclivity for wandering. I have no idea where she is.'

I settled back in my seat, ordering a brandy from the waiter. My ten minutes of sobriety was losing its novelty value.

But the man had not finished. It seemed he had another agenda, which I could only dimly recognise as being relevant to my current situation. He had shifted key, and was talking about the Cathars in an almost conversational manner. I was barely listening, finding it difficult to absorb all the new information I had just been given.

'I find the subject of the Cathars particularly interesting,' he was saying, 'for my own reasons, which may or may not be of concern to you, Lucas. Perhaps you will feel you want to leave such things behind you. It is not for me to say. However, if you are interested in pursuing any study into the history of the Cathars, or should I say, any involvement with the Cathars that Pontneuf imputes to you, or to Raymond Gasc, please contact me and I will try to help.'

He handed me his business card. It informed me that his name was Xavier Joan Vidal i Vilaferran, and that he held the title of Baron. The address was on Carrer Provença, in the Eixample district.

20. La caza del conejo

One evening in November I was walking home from Poble Sec, having spent the morning and early afternoon doing some detective work. Following my meeting with the angel and her grandfather, earlier in the week, I had spent the day camped opposite Nuria's old address, spying on her house. I had alternated between a cafeteria, a convenient bench, and the window seat of a run-down bar, from all of which places I was able to see the front door of the building. There had been plenty of time to absorb the information that Nuria was Pontneuf's daughter. I couldn't pretend that it made me happy, but it made a kind of sense, and certainly helped to explain Nuria's behaviour towards me up at the Refuge, if not to justify it. It did nothing to help me understand why she accepted the task of reeling me in for her father in the first place, nor could I assess whether her apparently passionate feelings towards me had been genuine or feigned, or an ambiguous mix of both.

Nothing happened to raise my hopes that either Nuria or Pontneuf had any contact with the apartment I was watching. The young woman who had taken Nuria's flat left with her boyfriend and returned alone at midday, setting out again shortly after three o'clock. I recognised nobody else among the residents who came and went at various stages throughout the day, and when the woman left the house the second time, I had had enough.

On my way home I made a detour, on impulse, to the little square where Nuria and I had sometimes met for lunch. I could see from a distance that our bench was empty. This gratified me slightly, as though some residual magic from our time together had remained attached to the inanimate world of benches, but the feeling did not last. I sat down, allowing my memories of the place and all that it signified to reduce me to a state of abject misery, and, when approached for a cigarette by a menacing young vagrant, I didn't linger, but made my way down the Ramblas and up Ferran towards Sant Jaume Square.

I arrived in the square at the same moment as a white van, which pulled up at a little distance from the Mayor's palace. A policeman stood outside. Businesses were just re-opening after the long lunch-break. It had been a crisp autumn day, and the sun was now low, casting an amber light over the square and the softly-tinged stone buildings. The street lights were not yet on.

A man in overalls had got out of the van, and, with his back towards me, opened the vehicle's rear door. I turned away for a moment to avoid an oncoming motor-cycle and when I looked again, the area between the white van and the city hall was swarming with rabbits. The man was carrying a short-barrelled and ancient-looking shotgun, and, I realised to my horror, that he was Manu, my neighbour. At once I recalled the date: it was the day of Manu's trial, which he had asked me to attend. Of course, in my state of utter self-absorption I had forgotten to go to court to support him. By now there were at least thirty rabbits hopping randomly outside the building, with more still jumping from the van. The solitary policeman had reached for his walkie-talkie, keeping a close eye on Manu while he did so. But there was no way he was going to stop what was about to happen. Manu started blasting off into a cluster of rabbits. Fur and blood spattered the cobblestones, and other rabbits stopped in their tracks, sitting up petrified on their haunches to observe the mayhem. Others fled, while others still had found some pots of cabbage-like plants outside the front door of the city hall and were busily munching on the leaves, unaware of the catastrophe that had overtaken others of their number. Manu re-loaded clumsily, spilling cartridges from the top pocket of his overalls, but had enough time to let off another double salvo, this time obliterating the cabbage-eaters. With this second explosion the square emptied out fast, pedestrians and tourists rushing for cover in the streets leading towards the cathedral and back down in the direction of the Ramblas. At the far end of Sant Jaume there was similar confusion.

Simultaneously two groups of armed police converged on Manu and the rabbits, four emerging from the city hall, and another, larger group from the direction of the presidential palace facing it. Looking around, I realised I was the only civilian remaining in the centre of the square. I began walking towards Manu at the same time as the second group of armed police dived to the ground and took up firing postures. I also glimpsed a marksman on the roof of the palace, aiming down at the square, and imagined there were others similarly positioned.

A voice from a loud-hailer ordered Manu to stop firing, to drop his weapon and to stay where he was. Manu looked around with a satisfied grin at the carnage on the cobblestones. Rabbits scurried away in all directions, some even returning to the van and jumping in through the open back doors. Manu held two cartridges in his hand and was holding the shotgun in the broken position, about to re-load. When he heard the order to disarm he seemed to notice the police for the first time.

'*Joder*!' he bellowed, obviously intent on enjoying his fifteen minutes of fame. 'Fuck you. Fuck the mayor. Fuck the pope!'

The policeman with the loudspeaker repeated the order for Manu to put down his weapon.

Then Manu spotted me. Automatically, he raised his gun arm in greeting, calling my name. His expression was one of bemused relief. At that moment a single shot rang out, and, not thinking of my own safety, I ran towards my neighbour. He had dropped the gun and fallen to his knees, clutching his shoulder and grimacing. Within a couple of seconds we were surrounded by a circle of armed police, who stood with guns pointing towards us. I was relieved to see that Manu only had the single wound. If the marksman had been aiming for the upper arm, he had done a good job. Blood was seeping through the blue overalls, and Manu, still kneeling, was muttering a stream of Andalusian curses.

We were both bundled into the back of a police van, which had drawn up in the meantime, and driven to police headquarters on Via Laietana. We had to wait for a police surgeon to come and look at Manu's wound. He was given an injection and the wound was cleaned. The bullet had gone clean through the biceps.

We were then separated, Manu being taken to the hospital for treatment to his wound, while I was led into an office and subjected to a range of preposterous questions concerning any affiliations I might have with terrorist organizations. I explained that Manu was my neighbour and I had happened to be passing across Sant Jaume Square at the time that he arrived to carry out his massacre. I gave a summary account of Manu's unhappiness over the issue of his keeping rabbits, and his, to my mind, understandable view that he was being harassed by the city authorities. I said, after further questioning, that I did not believe he was mentally unbalanced, but conceded that he may have suffered an attack of temporary insanity. I thought I would then be released, but the officer requested that I provide the name of a witness to my good character, some kind of guarantor to my bona fide status as a member of the human race. Under normal circumstances I would have given the name of the publisher for whom I worked, but since my return from the Refuge I had not had any contact with him and was reluctant to get him involved in this bizarre incident. Then I remembered the Baron: he was a lawyer *and* he seemed well-disposed toward me. I still had his card in my wallet and showed it to the police officer. He looked at the name and raised his eyebrows.

Within twenty minutes the Baron Xavier Joan Vidal i Vilaferran had swept into the police station with the quiet authority that his patrician name and profile demanded. He vouched for my good character and dismissed the incident of the rabbit slaughter out of hand. It was established that I was not under suspicion of being Manu's accomplice in crime so I signed a brief statement to that effect, and the Baron asked me if I could spare half an hour with him. He led me out of the building to a nearby café, where he discreetly chose us a corner table.

He ordered tea and sat down opposite me.

'How are you?' he began. 'You look terrible. Sick. Are you sick?'

I shrugged.

'It's been a difficult time,' I said.

The Baron paused, as if wondering whether to pursue the issue of my health, but then thought better of it, and moved on to the subject he was clearly anxious to speak to me about.

'I heard yesterday that your friend Pontneuf has been located by the Canadian Police. It would appear he has a group of followers over there. The police are keeping their eyes on him, but he hasn't done anything illegal. I have faith in them. Don't they say "the mounties always get their man?"'

I nodded, slightly bewildered by the Baron's rendering of the English adage. 'Technically, if I were your lawyer, and we were to consult the Spanish police, we could apply for an extradition order on the grounds of your abduction and illegal imprisonment, although it might look rather odd so long after the event. Would you be interested in pursuing this?'

I hesitated, before answering. My main concern

was that if Pontneuf was brought to trial, Nuria would be implicated as an accomplice. I didn't want this to happen. 'No,' I replied. 'If Pontneuf were to be charged it would be a lengthy process. He's sure to have the best legal advice available. A lot of unpleasant details about Pontneuf's past would have to be dragged up and I suspect the Church does not willingly share the contents of its files on reprobate priests. The case would go on and on. Newspapers and all that. And what of Nuria Rasavall? Although I believe her to be a victim of Pontneuf's deranged beliefs, a court might not see it that way.'

I paused for a long time, trying to imagine the disruption and upset this would cause to my chances of ever being with Nuria again, and of her tearful mother up in Maçanet following the lurid news reports. 'Her family might suffer also,' I added, offering him a chance to volunteer additional information. I was curious how he could serve the interests of the Rasavall family at the same time as providing me with the offer of prosecuting Pontneuf. But when he did not respond, I continued. 'People like Pontneuf always float to the surface. He'd probably avoid extradition, and there would still be an age before all the evidence could be got together. So the short answer is no, I'd rather not press charges. Thank you for asking.'

But while I said this, I was also thinking of the content of my story, and of Sean Hogg's insinuation, weeks ago, and Eugenia's more gracious suggestion that the whole episode, as described by me, was a fiction. Pontneuf and his lawyers would no doubt find an alternative explanation to completely discredit my version of events.

The Baron was silent for a moment, then smiled at me.

'There was something else,' he confided. 'Along the lines I was pursuing when we met the other week. About Pontneuf and his belief that he is Bernard Rocher.'

'Yes?'

'I have, over the past few years, been able to lay my hands on copies of texts that do make mention of Bernard Rocher, but he was nothing like the man that Pontneuf has made him out to be. I thought you might be interested to know this.'

He looked at me quizzically, as though wanting permission to continue. I decided to help out. 'Pontneuf insisted that Rocher was regarded with such reverence by his fellow perfecti that he was even encouraged to escape from the siege of Montségur,' I said. 'In order to preserve the faith intact.'

'I see,' said the Baron. 'It's much as I thought. André was forging a cult based on an erroneous or delusional reading of history. You see, the Cathars set no store by individual achievement of the kind he attributes to Rocher, and regarded humility, poverty and freedom from the bonds of the material world as the only aspirations a perfectus should hold. Therefore, while certain perfecti did leave the besieged stronghold of Montségur undetected by the crusaders who had surrounded the place, they were sent out on specific and fairly straightforward missions such as the breaking of bread, or administering the consolamentum to local believers. It would have been unthinkable to allow a single, evangelical and egomaniacal priest to escape the fate of his fellows at the stake, to save his own skin in order to engineer an unfeasible group reincarnation among his own selected group of followers.'

300

'So,' I said, 'the "evidence" of Rocher's importance within the Cathar movement which Pontneuf insisted upon was a fabrication?'

'Precisely. Bernard Rocher was a renegade from both Catharism and Catholicism. His was a sect within a sect. He made up his own rules. He was not well-regarded by his fellow Cathars, nor was he airbrushed from history by the annalists of the Inquisition. But he was protected. His aristocratic background was rather elevated. He claimed kinship with the Kings of Aragon, to whom the Lords of Languedoc, including the Count of Toulouse and many others in the region, were vassals.'

'So what became of Rocher. And of Gasc?'

'At the intervention of these royal Spanish cousins, Rocher was spared burning at the stake after his capture. Unlike his sixteen followers, two of whom were also perfecti. The group, it was true, had been betrayed by Raymond Gasc, a shepherd of Mélissac, who claimed that Rocher had bewitched his wife, Clare. Rocher had had, according to the scrupulous accounts of the annalists, improper relations with her. Rocher, for his part, denied these accusations, claiming that Clare Gasc was in fact his own daughter, conceived during his years as a student, before he was constrained by the laws of chastity.

'The outcome of the trial was that all the Cathars of the group except Bernard Rocher and Raymond Gasc were burned at the stake. Gasc pleaded for his wife Clare to be pardoned also, on the grounds of Rocher's bewitchment of her, but was unsuccessful. Precious little consideration was given to the possible innocence of women in the Catholic Inquisitorial worldview. After all, had not Adam been beguiled by Eve? So Clare Gasc burned, alongside her fellow villagers. Rocher was handed over to the Kingdom of Aragon, where, to appease relations with the Vatican, he was confined to life imprisonment. The conditions of his imprisonment however, are strange indeed. With a rare display of irony in their sentencing, the Inquisition required that the heretic Raymond Gasc was to act as Rocher's gaoler, and never leave the place of his charge's incarceration until the latter was deceased, on pain of death. A dual imprisonment then: the once faithful follower now the keyholder to his master's cell. The place chosen for their detention was the tower of Vilaferran. Of which I,' the Baron added, with a gentle smile, 'am the heir and owner.

'I would happily lend you somewhere to stay if at any point you wished to spend time out of the city. This tower, *La Torre de Vilaferran* might be of particular interest. It is a pleasant place, quiet and remote. Please come and see me should you wish to take a break, get some mountain air. I will instruct my secretary with the necessary details, if I myself am not available. In the meantime, why don't you go home and get some sleep?'

Then, as though imparting this information for the first time, he added, 'You look rather unwell.'

I caught sight of myself in the mirror the other side of the café. Circles under the bloodshot eyes, long unkempt hair, face unshaven for a week. He was right.

'I have to check what's happening with my neighbour. Tell his wife what's been going on.' I stood and pulled my coat on. 'I guess he's in big trouble.'

The Baron made a gesture of indifference. 'If he knew what he was doing, he's a criminal; if he didn't, he'll probably be declared insane. Either way, it doesn't look good.'

He returned with me to police headquarters and we spoke again with the officer who had interrogated me. He told us that Manu was under police guard in one of the city hospitals. There was nothing to stop me visiting him briefly, as long as I was accompanied by another police officer, or a lawyer.

'I'll take you,' interceded the Baron, to my surprise. 'It's not far out of my way.'

We drove to the *Hospital Clínic*, as the University hospital is known, in the Baron's chauffeur-driven Mercedes, and stopped near the front entrance. Manu was being kept on one of the upper floors. The policeman guarding him put down his newspaper when we came in, and waited outside the door.

Manu was sitting up in bed, his arm in a sling. He was dressed in pale blue pyjamas with the hospital's name displayed on the breast pocket. He sighed up at me, glanced at the Baron, and decided to ignore him. I pulled up a chair while the Baron remained standing at a little distance, his back to the window.

'Oy, you missed the trial this morning,' he started, accusingly.

'Yeah, I'm sorry. I forgot. Something cropped up.'

He stared at me a moment.

'*Coño*, you look terrible.'

'Don't *you* start. I know.'

'Who's the cop?' This loud enough for the Baron.

'He is not a cop. He's a lawyer.'

'Is he?' Then, to the Baron, 'Pardon me, Chief. You will understand my slight aversion to policeman just at present.' He nodded his head towards the bandaged arm.

The Baron made light of it. 'Nothing compared with the aversion rabbits must have towards you.'

'I know. I was wrong to do what I did. But I had to express myself. My blood was boiling.'

He turned to me, grimacing.

'Would you do me a favour? Pour me a glass of water?'

There was a jug of water and an empty glass on the bedside cabinet. I poured out a glass, and put it in his free hand.

'They let me call my wife,' he continued, 'but she must have been out. If you're going home, do me another favour and ask her to bring an overnight bag.'

'Sure. What's going to happen to you?'

'I don't know. Probably go to prison for a few weeks. A fine if I'm lucky. I don't know which is worse. In the court this morning, they granted me bail. I doubt they'll make the same mistake twice.'

Manu stared at the end of his bed. He was washed out with the excitement and painkillers. 'You know the worst of it?' he went on, after a while, 'They wouldn't even hear me out properly, in the court. They kept cautioning me for using disrespectful language and blasphemy. Can you imagine? "Respect?" I said, "You want my respect? What kind of respect have you shown me? I was only exercising the rights of the Spaniard to keep rabbits."

'They kept going on about hygiene and health and safety. "Your honour," I said, "why do the drains in Barcelona smell so bad?" He waved his hand at me, the jerk. One of those superior little waves. "I'll tell you why they stink, the drains of Barcelona," I said. "HUMAN SHIT," I said. "The shit that is shat every day. My shit and yours. I assume, your honour, that you shit also. Everyone shits. Not just my rabbits." He banged on the desk then. Contempt of court. I got this massive fine. One fine for refusal to comply, another for contempt. Two fines. They said the City would remove the rabbits within twenty-four hours. So I got home, changed, went to get you, but you weren't at home. Managed to get the rabbits in the van before the death squad came. Only rabbit killing today is going to be done by me, I thought.'

He stopped, evidently exhausted by the effort of giving his account. 'Listen, *hombre*, I'm going to get a kip. Remember to tell my wife, huh?'

I got up to leave.

'Okay Manu. You just take it easy now.'

He looked up at me through half-closed eyes.

'Don't worry. That's exactly what I'm going to do. *Hasta luego.*'

'*Hasta la próxima.*'

The Baron followed me out. The policeman at the door went back inside as we left, wearing a rather downcast expression. I told the Baron I would find my own way back to Santa Caterina, and we shook hands. I needed to be alone. I bought a bottle of Fundador and went back home, stopping off at Manu's flat on the way. His wife was in, and threw her arms up in despair on hearing of Manu's situation. She muttered something about divorce, and I carried on upstairs.

In the flat I pulled on a jersey and put the radio on. They were playing Mahler. I went onto my veranda, uncorked the brandy, and lay back in the hammock. The night was clear and cold, but I hardly felt the chill with the brandy racing through my bloodstream like a bush-fire. I stared at the stars and felt the emptiness flood over me.

21. How much death works

I awoke in the small hours with a dream of Nuria's lips on mine. The terrace door was banging against its frame, and with each thud I felt as if my lungs were being scraped out by an icy metal claw. I had fallen asleep with the half-empty bottle of brandy cradled in my arms, but surfacing into full consciousness, I could see it on the low table next to the hammock. A blanket was draped over my body, but again, I could not remember having fetched one from the bedroom. Manoeuvring stiffly out of the hammock, I shuffled indoors. My body was shivering, but my mind was ablaze. Crazy thoughts and images clamoured for brain-space, piling in after each other in a chaotic stream. The clock by my bedside stood at 3.30. Crossing the living room to my desk, still wrapped in the blanket, I opened an old notebook and started to write a few words, but my hand sprawled and slid across the page in the cold. I dropped the blanket and searched in the cupboard next to the bathroom, pulling out an electric fire that I had stored away in April. I set it down near the desk and took my old Olivetti typewriter from its case. Although I used a personal computer for my editorial work, I still reverted to the Olivetti from time to time. It was like a trusted friend. Feeding the paper and turning the scroll produced those comforting clicks that always suggested something akin to alchemy. I rubbed my hands and took a slug of brandy straight from the bottle, realising as I did so that the action indicated a sad state of aesthetic and moral bankruptcy. Shaking, I lit a Camel. I was down to the basic gestures now. The upturned bottle; the filling ashtray. I had to write something down, and the certainty with which I had brought myself to the task suggested that the words had already begun to filter through to consciousness, but once seated and ready, I forgot entirely what it was I had wanted to write.

No words came.

The room was quiet. Outside too, there was total silence.

I lit another cigarette, stared some more at the blank piece of paper, then got up and went to the kitchen to fetch a glass. I poured some brandy, took another drink.

My feet were cold. I went into the bedroom, opened a drawer and found a pair of thick woollen socks. Two socks as soft as rabbits. Sitting on the edge of the bed, I pulled them on and wriggled my toes. Everything about my body suddenly felt oddly distant. I could see the movement of my toes, for instance, but could not really feel them move. I put this down to the cold. But the cold seemed to be inside my body, rather than on the outside, coming in.

Back in the living space I put some music on the stereo, quietly. The old troubadour songs that Pontneuf had known about. The song *La Trystesse de la Dona Marie* was the first track. It pained me to hear it, and as the heartrending drone of the Galician pipes broke in on the serene lyric, my eyes filled. There was an almost unbearable nostalgia to the music that was compounded now by its association with my time at the Refuge, and by thoughts of Nuria. At the same time as experiencing a profound sadness, I realised that the music was merely feeding the wound. But what of it? I felt entitled to this moment of corrosive self-immersion. At the end of the song, I removed the disk from the player, went over to the typewriter, and ripped out the blank sheet of paper, crumpling it into a ball and tossing it in the waste basket. I returned to the bedroom, leaving the connecting door open. Lying on the bed, I gradually drifted off into a restless sleep.

When I awoke, it was midday. The physical dislocation that had set in the night before was not gone, but I took a shower and dressed anyway. I couldn't bring myself to shave as my hands were shaking too badly, and decided that I would attend to that later. Decided, in fact, that many things needed attending to later, including the state, for want of a better word, of my soul. What I needed, I determined, was some sudden and profound spiritual experience. That would do the trick. I laughed out loud, as I got into my jeans, standing on one leg and very nearly falling over, saved only by the proximity of a wall. No, on second thoughts, what I needed now was a drink. In another location. Somewhere with a view.

But first I needed coffee, and filled the small espresso pot. When it was done I poured half a cupful, stirred in sugar, then added a generous helping of Fundador. The *carajillo* breakfast gave me a physical jolt. I drank it quickly, pulled on a sweater, then, realising I was too warm, took it off again. I grabbed my leather jacket off the hook behind the door and went downstairs.

So began an afternoon of wandering in circles around the Gothic quarter. I dropped in on a disconsolate Igbar Zoff and we went to Santiago's bar in Neu de Sant Cugat, making a slight detour to stand outside the ex-convent, with me half-expecting the fire-eater to materialise on the steps, hand outstretched.

'What are we waiting here for?' asked Igbar, shuffling his feet in the cold. He was yellow-skinned and gaunt.

'An apparition, perhaps.'

'You haven't given up?'

'No.'

Igbar Zoff yawned.

'Maybe you should. Oh, I don't doubt the veracity of your tale, old chap. I just wonder at your tenacity in the act of obsessive return.'

'I see.'

'Do you?'

'No.'

'You're like a dog with a bone. Won't let go. But in a way I'm pleased for you, Lucas. At least you'll recognise your own doppelganger when you meet him. Damned if I will. I've been chasing him around for years now.'

'No one seeks out their doppelganger. It's the other way around. He looks for you.'

'Is that so? Things must be worse than I'd thought. I'm waiting for no one. Never have.'

'How about Sean?' I asked, without conviction.

'Sean cares only for himself. He's a cunt.'

'That's harsh.'

'Life, forgive the platitude, is harsh. The city of marvels is a brothel, after all. You get what your fantasy dictates.'

He looked up at me. The whites of his eyes were jaundiced and his gaze unfocussed.

'Who was it,' he asked, 'said, "something's boring me: I think it must be me," or similar?'

'Dylan Thomas?'

'Dylan bloody Thomas. That would follow. Another vitriolic dwarf. Except the something in my case isn't precisely me, nor is it anybody else. And besides, boredom isn't the word. It's to do with the opposite: losing the gift of spontaneous perception. Fatal for a painter, don't you think? I've become the kind of person who looks in mirrors and sees what isn't necessarily there.'

The bar was quiet: it was early for lunch. As we entered, Santiago lifted his head from his newspaper with what in anyone else would be called a scowl but might, for him, have passed for a smile, a black cigar trembling on his lip, and let out a grunt of acknowledgement. 'Oy,' he said to me, 'I thought you were dead,' and then, without waiting for a reply, re-immersed himself in his paper. I had not been back there since the incident with the fire-eater.

Igbar Zoff refused the offer of lunch, picking instead at a saucerful of tired looking anchovies, and barely perking up after a bottle of red. He was at that stage of drinking when the physical effect of alcohol is dulled, and the drink serves only to provide occasional, despairing insights into a chasm of despondency. He was intent on starting some new work, he said, as though trying to convince himself of this intention, rather than me. He planned a series of paintings describing a visual narrative of all the most run-down bodegas in the *barrio*. He had made this chronicling of low drinking dives the focus of his life work, like the brothels of Lautrec, Dégas and Picasso. But his talk of plans sounded weak, half-hearted, as though he were simply filling empty space, preoccupied with a wider, bleaker vision; perhaps the vision of his own death a year later.

I walked with Igbar back towards his flat, embraced him, and left him there, then continued up Carders, across Laietana, and over to the Ramblas. The evening was already drawing in. I must have spent longer with Igbar than I had thought. But I was in no hurry, settling instead into a kind of waiting game. Something, I was certain, was going to happen today. On the way down Ferran I bought a Havana cigar, and at the bottom of the street took a right and went to the Café de l'Opera on the Ramblas. Here was a place with a view, one that in the past had given me hours of pleasure, people-watching. There was a spare table in the front part of the café, so I sat and smoked and ordered a coffee and a brandy. The usual parade of dramatically weathered old queens, self-consciously artistic types, voluble Catalan theatre-goers, enthusiastic young Americans, and voyeurs (like myself) were attended in turn by the efficient and indifferent waiters. A parodic rendition of a vanished café society.

Before long I tired of the posing, the overloud declamations of a persistent and highly camp social observer at the next table, the laughter of the American students, and the taste of my cigar. I was sweating inside my shirt, and felt sticky and uncomfortable. So I paid and left, crossed the Ramblas, and sought out more modest, shadowy company in the cheap dives of the Barrio Chino. After all, as Igbar had reminded me, the city of marvels had something to offer for each occasion, every mood, did it not? The cold hit me in shivery gusts as I walked. I visited several bars that I knew, and some that I didn't, but never stayed for more than one drink.

I was impatient now, seeking something that I could not locate either in my imagination or my memory. The *Raval* held no interest for me, and I ignored the predictable invitations from the street-girls as I moved between bars. Then, tiring of the locale, and seeing the same faces in different drinking-holes once too often, I backtracked, and again walked over the Ramblas and up through the maze of alleys to take a drink at an Andalusian bar whose regular clientele consisted almost entirely of inebriate senior citizens, mostly women, one of whom was prone to burst into mournful song whenever the cash-register trilled. From there I ambled up to a bodega I knew between Palma de Sant Just and Avinyó, where I ordered a carafe of red wine and a portion of *patatas bravas*. I poked at the food, but couldn't bring myself to eat. The rough red wine went down easily enough, but had no effect. I ordered another carafe. A man wearing a cowboy hat, with a scar running from his ear to the corner of his lip, attempted to engage me in conversation. I heard him clearly enough, but felt no compulsion to acknowledge

313

him. On my failing to respond, he cursed me and turned away. I let him be.

Although not perceptibly drunk, that strange displacement from the physical world that I had begun to feel the night before had returned. If not an actual ghost, I was at the very least, a sleepwalker. So I slept as I walked, and I walked down to Plaça Reial, where both sleepwalkers and ghosts are invariably drawn. Creatures of the night were rousing themselves now, and as I entered the Square, I knew that I had come to the right place. As usual, a police van was parked at the far end, ready to weigh in on any overtly illegal activity and to collect the casualties of overdosing, or even of inhaling too sharply the rank air. There were benches around the circumference. I settled myself down on one of these, and lay on my back.

I don't know how long I had been lying there when I first noticed an excruciating pain in my side. With a great deal of effort, I tried to move, but it proved too much. I allowed myself a rest before trying again, and was about to close my eyes when the figure of a policeman moved between me and the nearest street lamp, casting a shadow across my face. Another cop stood behind him.

'You okay?'

I replied in the negative.

'What's the problem? Drugs?'

'No,' I said. 'I can't move.'

'Stand up please.' He obviously didn't believe me.

With a superhuman effort I swung my legs off the bench, and, leaning hard on its metal frame, attempted to push myself into a standing position. I was almost vertical when my knees buckled under me and I slid to the ground.

The first policeman leaned towards me and, with a firm hand under my armpit, heaved me up, while the second helped steady me from behind. I was now standing, with assistance, but remained very wobbly.

'Can you get me an ambulance?' I asked, and added redundantly, 'I think I'm ill.'

'Takes too long, an ambulance. You got insurance?'

'No.'

'Well then, come with us.'

The cop steered me towards a waiting car and helped me into the back seat. On the way to the hospital he tried asking me questions, while the other policeman drove. By now my teeth were chattering and my body shaking uncontrollably. I felt inside my jacket and fumbled for an identity card. He copied the name onto a notepad. Then I blacked out, and the next thing I knew I was in a brightly-lit hospital room, surrounded by medical staff dressed in green. I was gasping for air, and somebody placed an oxygen mask over my face. I was trolleyed down seemingly endless corridors and lifted into a bed with clean, crisp sheets. I dimly remember being told to keep the mask on my face, a nurse saying there was an elastic strap attached to the mask for this purpose. She lifted my hand behind my head to demonstrate this. Then I was left alone.

I knew that I was dying. Something that resided in my body was trying to lift itself upward, outward. Something weightless and ethereal. I had read about this in accounts of near-death experiences, but had never attached much significance to it. Now it was my sole reality. Whatever counted as me was trying to leave. It raised itself above the body and hovered there a while. My body retrieved it, not ready to relinquish this vagrant, fleeing element. Now that it was happening,

I was disappointed by my own lack of any sense of occasion, and while recognising that death had come before My Time, failed in any significant way to fight it. The body was willing to embrace death, and the mind did not respond so much as heave a sigh of resignation. I had not expected to face death in so unceremonious a manner. All I could register was sorrow.

That night I struggled with personal extinction. At times I managed to visualize Death, to make of him a person. He was not a cloaked Angel, nor a horned messenger from Hell: he appeared more as a weary, grey-faced tax-collector. He told me that my number was up, that it was nothing personal, but that I had thrown away my single chance at life and now my nemesis had come as a thing of little consequence. What else could I expect? I found this of little comfort, rather like being told that I had failed to attend school regularly, or been unpunctual at work, and must therefore be expelled, or sacked.

I imagined Death imparting these notices of dismissal in different guises. Death helping out by silently folding sheets in the hospital laundry; Death as caretaker of a park where children play, unaware of his custodial gaze; Death as the face reflected in the shop window when you pass by on a rainy day and do not recognise yourself. Death as a return to the warehouse of personal memory. And with that possibility, the images piled in. An onrush of faces, moments, fleeting instances dredged upward and into consciousness from the sludge of recall. Sitting in a puddle of warm sand and water on a Pembrokeshire beach, my mother in dark glasses, a fact that made me stare into those refracting lenses, questing after the eyes that lay behind them. A black spaniel dog; a white lighthouse at midday and a jade sea. Watching a boy in the schoolyard burning an ant with his magnifying glass; leaning on the railings of a Greek ferry as it entered an island harbour at nightfall. The passage of years filtered through random iconic moments: here the bent back of my Welsh *tad-cu*, there the thick, brilliantined black hair of my Spanish father, as he turned his dark eyes on me and told me that freedom must be wrung from the hands of the oppressors.

A spasm of shame grew inside me. I had died for nothing. I believed in nothing.

But Death stayed away; all that night and the following day and night I lay there, fighting for breath, sweating profusely, catching snatches of drug-induced slumber, monstrous nightmares, visions. I began to dream the same frenzied dreams around the clock, of pursuit, and of crawling through an oxygen-starved marshland. The air was so dense that even the strange creatures I encountered there were too lugubrious to do more than slaver and drool, though I was terrified of their jaws snapping at my heels as I heaved myself from puddle to puddle across this immense quagmire.

On the morning of the second full day I realised I was coughing up blood, struggled out of bed, wrenching free of a drip solution as I did so, and stumbled into the corridor. I stood there, leaning against the doorway and coughed some more blood onto the tiled floor. A nurse came towards me, looking worried, and urged me back to bed. I told her that I needed to pee, and she fetched a plastic bottle, re-connected me to the drip, and told me I was not to get out of bed again.

The following day a doctor came to see me, and I asked her what was wrong with me and if or when

I was going to die. She replied, matter-of-fact, that if I had been going to die, I would have done so by now, probably two nights earlier. The manner of her telling me this seemed to put into doubt whether she considered my survival of substantial benefit to humanity at large. Relenting slightly, she then told me that I had pneumonia, but that if I acted in accordance with her instructions, I would get better.

The room where I lay contained two beds, and for the first few days I was alone. After three days I was allowed to have a bath, in a huge white tub whose taps gushed a voluminous quantity of hot water, allowing a deep soak. I was given regulation pyjamas of the same pale blue that I had seen on Manu on my visit with the Baron. By this time I was able to go for half an hour or more without the oxygen, but if I made any rapid movements my breathing immediately became strained. On the fourth day I could sometimes manage a little more; the sweats had begun to die down, other than at night, and I began to eat the regular hospital meals. I was very hungry.

The days in hospital were long and passed slowly. I slept badly at night, still subject to vicious sweats and turbulent dreams, but I was able to catch up on sleep during the daytime. After several days' luxurious solitude, an elderly one-legged man was wheeled in from the operating theatre, and lifted onto the room's other bed. From where I sat in my bed I could read the name chalked on the small board at the top of his: Serafin Lopez Lopez. On his good leg the new incumbent lacked a big toe. Serafin Lopez Lopez said very little for the first twelve hours and then began to gurgle like an underground drain. He seemed to be on the way out of this life. His wife came in and sat beside him, looking profoundly miserable. There was also an obese young man whom I took to be a son, and a woman I assumed to be his daughter, who wore exaggerated shoulder pads and the same defiant, washed-out look as the son. I suspected they were waiting for the old man to die, and it crossed my mind that he might well do so at night, alone with me. But the poor fellow's clenched jaw seemed to indicate that he was in no way ready to give up without a fight.

Twice in the course of the day two nurses would come and scrub him down and on the first of these occasions I noticed that apart from missing a leg and the other big toe, he also had an enormous lump on the side of the neck. He urinated through a tube into a plastic bag. The two nurses manipulated him like a rag doll. He seemed accustomed to it all.

Later in the afternoon one of the nurses was fiddling with my neighbour's penis, trying to fix it up to his plastic tube with some kind of tape. He started rambling on in his unintelligible way. Who knows, perhaps she had given him an erection. In any case, the nurse wasn't remotely interested in his complaints. I began thinking about the consequences of human reproduction: the poor old broken man with one leg and his dick strapped up with sticky tape, the fat idiot son and vacuous daughter moping in the corridor outside the room along with the frightened, defeated wife. Feelings of compassion merged with a sense of revulsion. It was impossible to imagine them forty years ago, making plans, babies.

The highlight of my stay in hospital were the visits paid to me by Dr Fernandez, the physician who had waived my death sentence on the second day. I never learnt her first name. The next time she visited, she appeared at the side of the consultant, a courteous but overbearing Catalan named Larios, whose family, I was informed by one of the porters, had made their fortune in the famous brand of gin of that name. Larios was always trailed by a gaggle of students, to whom, after the fashion of senior consultants, he made sharp and laconic observations about the patients' conditions as though the owners of the bodies he discussed were not actually present.

Dr Fernandez however, fitted my ideal of the medical professional. Newly qualified, and with a stupefying seriousness, she examined me rigorously and intimately, usually ending with a reprimand of some kind. She was small and slim with a crop of dark brown curls and oversize glasses. Her open white coat and short skirt revealed the occasional glimpse of a tanned and athletic body. I began to fantasize about her, and from that point on knew that I was on the mend. Eugenia would probably have commented sardonically that I always wanted women who'd save me from myself, so why break a lifetime's habit when rescued from death's door?

The social life on the large ward outside my door was hectic, with patients receiving a steady flow of anxious and often tearful relatives throughout the day and evening. For this reason I was relieved to be kept in one of the small rooms off the main ward. In the evenings I sometimes sat in the lounge at the far end of the corridor. There was always football on the television, usually inaudible because of the loud conversations and analyses that were conducted over the commentary.

The ward also had its share of fatalities. One evening the man in bed 93 started convulsing and abruptly died. Minutes later, an elderly man with whom I had occasionally exchanged a greeting, came to my room, trembling with the excitement inspired by the bearing of Bad News.

'My neighbour in 93 died five minutes ago,' he wheezed. 'It was terrible, so quick.' He made the sign of the cross and exited quickly, proceeding to the next room on his self-ordained mission as the Messenger of Death.

Another night a man was brought in strapped to a trolley, screaming and cursing. He was put into bed 111, in a small room like my own, a little further down the corridor. He continued his ranting for two nights and a day, enraged, splenetic, as his body was forced through the horror of delirium tremens and withdrawal.

The day after this lunatic's sudden disappearance, when Serafin had been trolleyed off somewhere, and I had complained of a particularly acute pain in my liver, Dr Fernandez whacked me on the side with the flat of her hand and asked, 'Does that hurt?'

I winced with the pain, and groaned.

'Yes. Of course it does.'

She glared at mc through her spectacles.

'Have you been drinking?'

'No.'

There was, in fact, a bar in the basement of the hospital, used by staff as well as patients and their visitors. In theory, it would have been possible for me to drink there, but on the two occasions I visited the bar, I had merely taken a mineral water. Dr Fernandez made a clicking sound and looked at me suspiciously. I was, at that moment, suffering from an almost unbearable curiosity to explore what lay beneath the doctor's white coat.

'Why are you smiling?' she asked, unsmilingly.

'Because I'm happy. To be getting better. Under your care.'

Dr Fernandez frowned, then smiled in a sly manner.

'You know the man they brought in, the one who has been shouting the whole time?'

'You mean the beast of 111?'

'Precisely,' she answered, without flinching a facial muscle.

'What of him?' I asked. 'Has he pegged out?'

'No. He has been moved to psychiatric care. His liver is ruined, and his mind with it. She paused for maximum effect. That, Señor Lucas, is how you will be in a few years time if you do not heed my advice.'

She turned around and left, without awaiting a response.

While I waited to get better, eating quantities of fish, fruit and yogurt, I was also learning a kind of resignation with respect to the Cathar sect, beginning to view it as a strange learning experience with no clear-cut benefits, but with little harm caused either. While I was not prepared to take it to the extreme that Eugenia had suggested and regard it as a disposable fiction, I had, after all, graduated with my life intact, if not my love. But then the memory of the two weeks locked in the dark dungeon returned, and I could be left in no doubt that my captor's intentions were of the most sinister kind.

Lying in bed at night, once the acute phase of the pneumonia had passed, I stared at the window next to my bed, half-expecting to hear a tapping on the glass, and to see the face of the angel of Santa María del Mar beckoning me out onto the ledge: or else to see her suspended upside-down, bat-like, gesturing for me to follow her. I wondered whether the hospital was covered in any of the routes taken by the roof people, whether in fact they might have an encampment on top of this very building. As I grew stronger, the desire to drink began to leave me, though my craving for tobacco only increased, an addiction I attempted to satisfy in the television lounge, or else during walks in the foyer area of the hospital, and the bar. But smoking hurt my lungs, so I packed it in.

Finally, one Saturday morning, after a final valedictory lecture from Dr Fernandez, I was discharged. I had been in the hospital for eighteen days. I stepped out into the early winter sunshine, and caught a taxi home.

22. The art of ascent

During the course of my stay in hospital, I had resolved to do something about my mental inertia and my squandered finances. Both resolutions were addressed on my return to the flat in Santa Caterina. The mailbox contained a letter from my erstwhile employers, offering an extensive commission for some new translation work, along with payment for a piece of work I had long since given up on. Cheered by this, I climbed the stairs to the top floor, my breathing by no means back to normal. A change in lifestyle was in order: and if so, I reflected, as I entered the flat and surveyed the wreckage of my pre-hospital life, here was the place to start.

There were empty brandy bottles littered around the living space, ashtrays and saucers overflowing with dog-ends, and a sharp and distressing smell from the kitchen that indicated the decay of something that had once been alive. At that point my doorbell rang, and

I had to go down to the street door again, where I was greeted by the postwoman, who handed me a small registered package and asked me to sign for it.

The package was cube-shaped and wrapped in brown paper. The sender's address on the formal return slip was written in a neat black italic script and read *Fundació Joan Miró*. The name of the sender was Lluïsa Navarra. I knew nobody of this name, nor indeed anyone who worked at the Miró Foundation. I held the package apprehensively. Its alleged place of origin was, at best, something intended to intrigue: at worst a provocation of some kind. I again tested the package carefully in my hands. It was not heavy, though perhaps heavy enough to contain a small explosive device. But I did not suspect for a moment that this was the case. My stay in hospital had made me sensitive, I thought, to death's proximity. I was certain that whatever lay inside this package was not going to kill me.

I returned breathlessly to my apartment and placed the package on the kitchen table. The brown paper was tightly taped, and once removed, revealed a layer of bubble-wrap, equally tight. I cut through this, only to find a third layer of wrapping: tightly bound parcel tape. It was difficult to find a loose end, as though the tape were one continuous strip. I prised the tape away, half-expecting a further layer of wrapping. Instead I discovered a plain box, painted silver-grey. It appeared to be wooden, but I was not certain of this. In the centre of the lid was an exquisitely intricate, multi-coloured patch of embroidery, embedded in the painted wood. The embroidered design suggested a setting sun.

I lifted the lid, curiosity by now far exceeding apprehension. Peering inside I could make out two objects. I pulled the first one out. It was a sweet: an Italian chocolate to be precise, of a type called *Sospiri*. Sighs. My Italian stretched to that. I looked more closely at the label on the white wrapping. There was one other word, indicating, I supposed, the flavour of the sweet: *Mirto*. I had an idea of what this might mean, but before searching my library I reached inside the box for its second hidden treasure, and pulled out a plastic model of a bull: a tawny, lifelike child's toy, complete, I was pleased to observe, with *cojones* fully intact. I held the bull in the palm of my hand and looked at it, wondering what, out of so many possibilities, it was intended to mean.

Leaving the bull carefully on the table next to its box, I wandered into the living room and pulled the Italian dictionary from its place on the shelf. *Mirto* meant Myrtle, a plant sacred to the goddess Venus.

I returned to the kitchen. A plastic bull and a wrapped chocolate, whose content was blessed by the deity of love. A bull with balls: more, as I stared at its miniature painted eyes, a stubborn bull, stubbornness, along with patience, being the two most characteristic features of tauromachy. At the same time I remembered the Minotaur, half-man, half-bull; the guardian of the Cretan labyrinth, a creature outwitted by Theseus with the help of Ariadne's thread. Ariadne, the daughter of King Minos, who had elected to assist the Athenian youth, both of them fleeing the tyranny of her father and his labyrinthine palace.

I made myself a cup of tea and sat looking at the contents of my package: the embroidered, painted box, the sweet, the bull. I looked at the name of the sender, but could think of nothing that linked me to anyone of this name. I considered who might have sent me such

327

a gift, but there was only one real possibility: the provenance of the parcel, and above all, its contents, pointed to Nuria. Of this I was in no doubt at all. It was as if she had waited for this day before contacting me in an oblique and suggestive way, by means of a puzzle. But how could she have known that I would be at home just as the parcel was due to be delivered, unless she had in some way been surveying my movements all this time? She could hardly have engineered the postal delivery. The postwoman was genuine enough; I recognised her as our regular. And who was Lluisa Navarra?

My speculations led me nowhere, and my apartment was still in need of attention. I rolled up my sleeves, retrieved a long disused vacuum cleaner, a scrubbing brush and mop from the cupboard in the hallway, and piled everything disposable into plastic carrier bags. I then vacuumed everywhere, filled a bucket with hot water and detergent, and began to scrub. When I had finished in the living space and the bedroom, I began on the kitchen and bathroom. Last of all, I cleaned the veranda, again removing bottles and cigarette butts, before scrubbing and sluicing the whole area. I played Bach piano music on the stereo as I worked. When I had finished it was evening, and I was exhausted. I phoned for a taxi, put on my leather jacket and scarf, and rewarded myself with a meal in an upmarket vegetarian restaurant in Gràcia, washed down with a bottle of sparkling mineral water.

In the middle of the night I woke up suddenly, with a sharp pain in the chest, at precisely the moment that the conundrum of the package's sender revealed itself to me. 'Lluisa Navarra' was simply an anagram.

The following morning I phoned in at the editorial office where I had been offered work, and was told to collect the first manuscript at my convenience. The director there said that I had been missed.

I was re-joining the human race. I still felt as though a part of me was adrift, floating on an infinitely deep dark sea, and that no amount of attending to the details of my daily life would protect me for long against the next squall, let alone any impending hurricane. At times I craved alcohol with an excruciating intensity, but my fear of being unable to stop once I had started was more persistent than the craving. A drink might salvage some temporary sense of wellbeing, but would, without a doubt, lead me back into the quagmire.

I resisted sending a reply to the false name at the Miró Foundation: having begun several, I was unable to complete any of them. In any case, a letter would be unlikely to reach Nuria, since she had clearly invented the name and used that address to prevent my locating her. Short of hanging out at the Foundation on the off chance that she had taken up permanent residence in the lobby, I was going to have to let it go. If she was in Barcelona, I told myself, then we would meet when the time was right. Where finding Nuria was concerned, I could no more force the course of events than I could avoid experiencing a tremor of excitement whenever the phone rang, or when checking my mailbox each morning. Crossing the road I scanned faces, in the vain hope that I would see her standing out in a faceless crowd, but soon I began to see her everywhere. I had no more news of her, and was inclined to think of her package as a kind of valediction, a parting gift. I mollified myself with platitudes: that time heals all wounds; that attempting to moderate my emotional responses would

329

lead to a more peaceful life; even that the whole of the summer might just as well have been a dream, from which I could, if I was wise, learn something. None of this helped. I did all the right things: consumed pots of vitamin supplements, went to the gym, took long swims and steam baths, avoided tobacco and alcohol, and went to the cinema two or three times a week. One evening, after suffering an overwhelming desire to get drunk, I attended a meeting of Alcoholics Anonymous but found myself incapable of saying anything of any meaning to this group of earnest and well-intentioned strangers.

I read at night, since sleeping was a problem. I did not want to start taking prescribed medicines, so on Susie Serendipity's advice, took natural extract of valerian, ate oats and drank chamomile tea. None of these helped me sleep, but I began to relax a little. I had decided to read everything available about the Cathars. One book described everyday life in a Pyrenean Cathar village at the end of the thirteenth century, fifty years or so after Bernard Rocher's supposed departure from Mélissac. I pitched what I read against the version I had received from Pontneuf concerning our previous incarnations as Cathars. I was left wondering how much of his teaching he had contrived through studying the era in detail, and how much was his own invention. It would not have been difficult for him to assemble a particular version of events, but I needed to know what, precisely, he had invented. I began working my way through everything available from standard booksellers about the Cathars, and was considering a visit to the university in order to get a visitor's library card and pursue my reading further.

I discovered from his daughter (his wife would not speak to me) that Manu was serving a three-month sentence for the massacre at Plaça Sant Jaume. She gave me the visiting times, and when I went along to the prison, I found him less dejected than he had been during his long struggle with the City Council. He appeared to have accepted defeat gracefully, and was, he told me, enjoying a bit of peace and quiet. His wife had filed for a legal separation (divorce still being out of the question for a practising Catholic), which did not upset him in the least. He was considering a return to Córdoba, where he might find work on his cousin's farm. Yes, he informed me with a sigh, in answer to my question: his cousin farmed rabbits.

The days were cold and sunny and I made a couple of day trips out of town, setting out early to walk in the Collsacabra hills near Vic one day, and along the sea-front at Sitges another. It was on my return from Sitges that I saw the postcard lying on the floor just inside my doorway. This time I knew who'd brought it. Only the roof people would have gained access through the large roof patio, now bereft of Manu's hutches.

The postcard showed a picture of *La Pedrera*, Gaudí's famous building on the Passeig de Gràcia. Like all of Gaudí's work, it indicates an absolute rejection of the straight line. The photo was taken at night, from the roof terrace, which was itself a twisting labyrinth of pathways and ornate chimney stacks. I turned the card over in my hand. The message was in uniform upper case letters. In green ink, as before, was written a date and a time: December 24 - 23.00. Eleven o'clock on Christmas Eve.

Christmas Eve was the next day.

The use of the same green ink, the minimal content, and the meeting place suggested by the photo on the other side, all led me to believe that Nuria was the agent of this message, if not its author. No doubt, I was supposed to believe this. If the message was truly from her, and by following these instructions I would meet her again, I considered any risk worthwhile. I'd had enough of waiting: resolution was now due. I slept well that night, a sleep persistent with the memory of Nuria, and the delicious sense of waking with her body in a state of warm arousal next to mine.

It was another fine day. The sun hovered above the rooftops in the direction of the sea, and it was a joy to take my coffee onto the veranda, and to hear the bustle of the market below me. I showered and dressed, and immediately settled into my work, knowing that if I were to delay, I could easily spend the day in an agitated state of expectation for what the night might bring.

As it was, the hours passed easily enough. Before lunch I took a chance on her being in and phoned Eugenia. I wanted one person to know about my appointment in case I met with some misfortune. We arranged to meet at the restaurant in Gràcia, and I caught a taxi there from Laietana.

I brought Eugenia up to date on my life since my hospitalization, and showed her the postcard of La Pedrera.

'Are you certain you want to do this?' Eugenia asked, once we were settled at a table, eating a hot vegetable soup.

'Yes,' I replied. 'I have to.'

She nodded.

'Would you like me to come? Just to keep an eye on things? I could remain at twenty paces, lurk in the shadows.'

'Er, no thanks. I'll phone you tomorrow to confirm that I'm alive.'

'You don't have to go, you know. You could still let go of it all.'

I didn't answer. I had been waiting for some kind of a message, a sign, since arriving back in the city in August. I had first received the mysterious package, and now that I had this invitation (as I had convinced myself to think of it) there was no question of me not turning up.

'And another thing,' continued Eugenia, changing tack when she realised I was not going to respond to her challenge, 'why did you spend over two weeks in hospital without once phoning me, or letting me know what had happened? I tried to get in touch several times. I thought you might have disappeared again, or even died, the way you were heading. You should have called me. It's what friends are about.'

'I'm truly sorry. But I just needed time, completely unprejudiced by anyone else's opinions or views. Alone with the sick and the dying on that ward. It was an education for me. A special privilege almost, catching a glimpse of the dark corners of the soul. That first night. I was going to die, you know. I was convinced of it. I needed time out to reflect on everything.'

Eugenia shifted in her seat, smiled.

'I understand, Lucas. I think I do. You're forgiven.'

After our meal, and lingering over coffee, we went outside. It was getting dark now, and had turned cold. The streets, packed with Christmas shoppers, were in festive swing, but I felt apart from the whole performance of festivity; apart even from Eugenia. The sensations of warmth and intimacy with which I had woken that morning, on the heels of a benign dream whose details I could not recall, had stayed with me all day: I was convinced that, whatever else happened, I had to pursue this meeting or else spend the rest of my life regretting it.

I went home and had a rest. I lay on the bed for a long time listening to music and trying to capture an indistinct memory that I could not quite dredge up into consciousness.

Something stirred out on the veranda. A cat, maybe. At the same instant, I was gripped by a corresponding interior movement; a certainty of purpose about what I had to do, so long dormant that I had almost failed to recognise it. I had thought it was a poem. I hadn't written a poem for a year. I sat at my desk, in front of the old Olivetti, tapping on the desk with my fingers. Perhaps it wasn't a poem after all. Or if it was, perhaps the poem had fled screaming back to the unconscious broth from which it had emerged.

Slowly, my fingers picked out the keys one by one, using index and middle fingers only. I sat for a long time staring at the piece of paper, the two lines of words at the top of the page, a snail-track of story.

One evening in May as I was walking home, I witnessed a mugging, and did nothing to prevent it. I could see what was going to happen.

Shortly after ten I opened the silver-grey box, took out the myrtle candy, unwrapped it and popped it into my mouth. I then set out towards the Plaça Catalunya, and from there crossed to the Passeig de Gràcia. La Pedrera was only ten minutes' walk away, and I still had plenty of time, so I stopped off at the Café Torino for a coffee. The place was packed, and I stood at the bar in the smoke-filled room among customers wrapped in overcoats and scarves. When I left it was ten to eleven.

As I approached La Pedrera, I began to feel nervous. I stood at the corner of the building, where I had a view of both adjoining streets.

Somebody tapped me on the shoulder. I turned, and was confronted by the angel of Santa María del Mar. She smiled sweetly, and gestured for me to follow. I began to ask her where we were going, but remembered that she could not speak. We walked in silence.

We turned off Provença and entered a building. I knew from the address on his business card that this was where the Baron lived. From the hallway we followed a dark corridor that led beyond the stairwell. The angel took a huge key from the rucksack she was carrying, and unlocked a heavy wooden door that opened onto a small courtyard and a spiral stone stairway. We climbed until we reached what must have been the third storey of a town house, and stepped out onto another patio, overlooking an open expanse between taller apartment buildings. Where we stood was a private terrace, set with tubs of plants, railings and an overhead lattice for vines. Lounger chairs were stacked against the wall for winter and the house lay in darkness, shutters closed. On two sides the buildings rose above us for another three storeys. Opposite, through a gap in the juxtaposed houses, I could see the neon of a hotel sign and the lights on Montjuíc. Adjacent to our terrace, the west face of La Pedrera towered like a sandstone cliff.

My companion slid out of her rucksack, unzipped the top, and produced a grappling iron and a generous length of black nylon rope. I was sweating, and felt a sudden shortness of breath. But, whatever I had to do now, there was no turning back. I had implicitly accepted this assignation by arriving here.

The figure at my side was watching me inquisitively, her large dark eyes like some night-creature's. She was in her element, here on the rooftops. The element of flight. Then, after a calculated swing, she cast the iron high into the air, aiming for the upper parapets of La Pedrera. After a second or two she pulled hard on the rope. I was staring upward, alongside her, and saw the thing fall, plummeting through the air and crashing loudly onto the terrace a few paces in front of us. We waited there in the dark for some reaction, a response from one of the well-lit overlooking windows, but nothing happened. She picked up the instrument, which had unfolded on the ground like a giant insect, and shrugged.

Standing back a little more this time she swung the iron again, two, three times, and cast it high. Once more I heard a thud, and then a loud scratching sound from above us as the claws made purchase on stone. After a brief pause, the angel took my right hand and placed it firmly around the rope. She gestured, with a nod of her head, towards the roof. I followed her gaze upward again. When I next looked down, she was gone. Disappeared silently into the shadows.

So I was to do this alone.

I stood for a long time next to where the rope uncoiled on the terrace floor and stared up at the night sky stretched wide above me. Other than knowing that I had to ascend this rope, I had no idea what would happen next. But the absence of certainty, or even of understanding, no longer held any terror.

Gathering my strength, I placed one hand above the other, and pulled myself slowly upward. My feet clenched the rope below me as I moved into a rhythm; hoisting with the arms, then gripping with the feet. I made slow progress, trying to conserve my breath. I felt a pain shooting across my chest, and paused by the first set of windows. There were no lights on inside. I knew the building would not be occupied at night as it served as the administrative offices of a bank. I was more concerned that someone might spot me from one of the windows in an apartment opposite, and call the police. But I went slowly about my job and gradually reached the upper floor. Here there was a change in the architecture of the building: small attic windows now protruded from the bulging stonework. Looking down, a huge drop had opened up between me and the terrace below, amplified by the darkness in which I moved. I had only three or four metres to climb. If the grappling iron was going to dislodge itself, this would be the moment, while I was nearest to my goal, and furthest from the distant terrace. The angle of my ascent had been constant until now, but was more hazardous as I reached the top, the rope stretching at an obtuse angle. My body was soaked in sweat, the palms of my hands were sore, and my arms ached. I couldn't breathe. But I edged upwards, until I could make out the top of the parapet wall and security fence which marked out the perimeter of the building's undulating roof. Only a few more heaves on the rope were needed. As I reached the summit, I stretched one hand onto the parapet, then the other, and pulled myself onto the low wall, clambering over the fence and falling in a heap onto the walkway. With impeccable timing, the cathedral bells in the old city began to chime for midnight.

I stood up and looked for the grappling iron. It had been removed from the parapet, and was tied firmly to a nearby chimney-stack. There had been no danger of the rope slipping.

Nuria stood alone in the shadow by the stone chimney, dressed in a scuffed leather jacket, black leggings, and trainers. Her hair had been cut short.

Then she spoke, eyes dark, voice lucid.

'*Bienvenido a la Salida.*'

Welcome to the Exit. I looked around. I had never been on the roof of La Pedrera before. It was a labyrinth of marvels. The walkway of red tiles circled the roof, rising and falling in stages, and dividing in places to circumnavigate the large, sculptured chimney-stacks, some of them like tall human figures, or the statues of Easter Island. We were overlooking a deep inner courtyard far below, and all around us the lights of the city burned and flickered in an indigo mist. I had never seen Barcelona look so beautiful. I felt an intense and impenetrable happiness at being exactly there, precisely then.

Acknowledgements

While this is by no means an 'historical novel', it does contain certain correspondences with historical events. For those interested in reading further, *Montaillou* by Emmanuel Le Roy Ladurie, has never been improved upon in its portrayal of everyday life among the Cathars. Stephen O'Shea's *The Perfect Heresy* and René Weis's *The Yellow Cross* are highly readable accounts. Zoé Oldenbourg's *Massacre at Montségur* is a masterly study of the period. *The Cathars and Reincarnation* by Arthur Guirdham helped to spark the fuse, and *Càturs i Catarisme a Catalunya* by Anna Adroer i Tasis and Pere Català i Roca provided interesting local detail. Annabelle Mooney's *Rhetoric of Religious Cults* was a timely resource. I'm grateful to those friends and colleagues who read earlier drafts. Particular thanks are due to Gwen Davies, whose patient and skilful editorship spared the reader a much fatter book. Barcelona, city of marvels, is the real heroine of the story. Sadly, the old Santa Caterina market no longer exists, a recent victim of urban redevelopment.

diverse probing

profound **urban**

epic **comic**

rural savage

new

writing

www.parthianbooks.co.uk